FIGHTING MAC

Charon MC
Book 2

KHLOE WREN

Books by Khloe Wren

Charon MC:
Inking Eagle
Fighting Mac
Chasing Taz
Claiming Tiny
Saving Scout

Fire and Snow:
Guardian's Heart
Noble Guardian
Guardian's Shadow
Fierce Guardian
Necessary Alpha
Protective Instincts

Dragon Warriors:
Enchanting Eilagh
Binding Becky
Claiming Carina
Seducing Skye
Believing Binda

Jaguar Secrets:
Jaguar Secrets
FireStarter

Other Titles:
Fireworks
Tigers Are Forever
Bad Alpha Anthology
Scarred Perfection
Scandals: Zeck
Mirror Image Seduction
Deception

ISBN: 978-0-9876275-5-1

Cover Credits:
Model: Alfie Gordillo
Photographer: RLS Images
Digital Artist: Khloe Wren

Editing Credits:
Editor: Carolyn Depew of Write Right
Proofreader: Christine Halls

Acknowledgements

As always, I have to give a massive shout out to my wonderful husband. Who continues to put up with his insane author wife. And to my girls, these last few weeks have seen me locked away in my writing cave more often than not, yet they somehow still remember who I am!

I couldn't have written this book without several people who patiently answered all my many questions about Marine and MC life. Heath, Dawn, Erin, Diana and Shannon (I'm sure there were more and I'm sorry if I missed you by name) I can't thank you enough for all your help. Especially Heath. To Maggie, thank you for sharing all your nursing knowledge.

To Janelle, the inspiration behind Zara. Thank you for putting up with all my crazy questions and being patient with me. I hope you approve of how I represented Narcolepsy and Cataplexy.

To all my friends who helped me get back up each time I stumbled while writing this book. Becky McGraw, Eden Bradley and Tamsin Baker, you three especially.

To my editor, Carolyn, no matter what I throw at you, you always come through with a marvelous edit. I appreciate everything you do and thank you for another job well done.

Due to me rushing my poor beta team, only Andy and Tracie could step up this time, thank you both for dropping everything to help me get Fighting Mac just right.

xo

Khloe Wren

Biography

Khloe Wren grew up in the Adelaide Hills before her parents moved the family to country South Australia when she was a teen. A few years later, Khloe moved to Melbourne which was where she got her first taste of big city living.

After a few years living in the big city, she missed the fresh air and space of country living so returned to rural South Australia. Khloe currently lives in the Murraylands with her incredibly patient husband, two strong willed young daughters, an energetic dog and two curious cats.

As a child Khloe often had temporary tattoos all over her arms. When she got her first job at 19, she was at the local tattooist in the blink of an eye to get her first real tattoo. Khloe now has four, two taking up much of her back.

While Khloe doesn't ride a bike herself, she loves riding pillion behind her husband on the rare occasion they get to go out without their daughters.

Dedication

To Janelle,

if not for you, Zara would never have existed.

Author Note

The heroine of this book, Zara, suffers with the medical condition Narcolepsy.

Recently, they've classed Narcolepsy into two types. Type 1 has two major symptoms: day time sleeping and Cataplexy (sudden onset of muscle weakness that may be precipitated by excitement or emotion), while Type 2 doesn't have Cataplexy. Zara suffers from Type 1 Narcolepsy.

As with most medical conditions, no two cases of Narcolepsy are the same. Zara's symptoms are based heavily on a friend who has Type 1 Narcolepsy (with Cataplexy). I did that on purpose, as I wanted to make Zara as realistic as possible. Please keep in mind, however, that this story is a work of fiction and there was times where things get exaggerated from what is considered normal. Also, just because Zara reacts a certain way to a particular situation, it's not to say that every sufferer of this condition will react that way.

Charon:

Char·on \ˈsher-ən, ˈker-ən, -än\

In Greek mythology, the Charon is the ferryman who takes the dead across either the river Styx or Acheron, depending on whether the soul's destination is the Elysian Fields or Hades.

Chapter 1

Zara

Be careful what you wish for.

My mother used to tell me that regularly when I was growing up, but I'd never taken her seriously. Mind you, I was generally wishing for things like a pet pony and to make the cheerleading squad. I couldn't see how any harm could come from me getting what I wanted. Of course, I never got a pony or landed a spot on the squad, so I hadn't needed to worry about any consequences.

As a result, I stood at the coffee machine, filling a cup with frothy liquid for the fiftieth time today not thinking twice before wishing my life was more interesting. I'd had such big plans back in high school. I'd wanted to be a forensic medical examiner, to dissect dead bodies to figure out how the people had died. Puzzles had always caught my interest, and that seemed like the ultimate one. But then Mom got diagnosed with breast cancer in the summer before I was due to go off to college. Dad was forced to take on a second job to pay for everything, which meant he was too busy to care for her, so I'd shelved my dreams and stayed home and took on the responsibility. That's what you do, right? When the woman who raised you, whom you love with all your heart needs you, you do whatever you can. No matter the cost.

One day had flowed into the next, and even when Mom beat the disease and the doctors declared her cancer-free, I didn't leave town. I picked up a waitressing job and continued living at home, helping out around the house whenever I wasn't working.

Sixteen years later I was still waiting tables and making coffees. I was stuck in a rut. A very dull, boring, monotonous rut.

With a sigh, I loaded the current order onto a tray. *One double chocolate brownie and one large cafe latte coming right up.* I was returning from delivering the order to a customer sitting at one of the outside tables when I first heard the sound of an approaching motorcycle. The rumble was deep, and out of habit, I turned toward the road to see if I could spot the machine. The dark Harley Davidson was still a way up the road and I thought I caught the sight of more bikes coming up behind it. Just great. My throat went dry and I turned to hurry back inside. In Galveston, that many Harleys together could only mean one thing: the Iron Hammers MC. I avoided having anything to do with them at all costs.

I was reaching for the door when I caught sight of a large man covered in tattoos and wearing a leather vest rushing toward me. That vest meant he was one of them and he was about to run straight into me. Wanting to avoid that crash, I opened the door to rush in. But he was faster than I expected, and I only had one foot through the doorway when he reached me. With rough hands, he gripped my shoulders as though he was going to toss me aside. Hell, he certainly looked like he was strong enough to accomplish the task. I was twisting to try to free myself so I could get the hell away from him when the first crack ripped through the air.

Time seemed to slow down, mere seconds seeming to take forever to tick by. At the sound of that first gun shot, the cafe's customers went crazy, all rushing to flee. The man holding my shoulders shoved me inside. When my foot caught on the lip of the doorway, I stumbled and reached for the door frame to stabilize myself. The move left me able to see out to the street. Several bikes were now parked along the curb, each rider holding up a gun that was pointed in my direction.

"Oh fuck."

I tried to duck down, to get further inside where it would hopefully be safer, but only managed to get one shoulder free of his tight grip. I screamed when a series of loud bangs filled the air. Why the fuck were they shooting at me? Or were they shooting at the man behind me? If they were, I really needed to get the hell away from him ASAP. Pity he hadn't loosened his grip on my other shoulder.

"Motherfucker!"

The deep, growled curse came a split second before I was knocked to the ground. My fingers stung from being ripped from the door frame so abruptly, but I didn't have time to worry about it. My right shoulder slammed into the tiled floor as I landed heavily on my back with the man's body limp on top of me. Panic and adrenalin burst through my system, which made me panic for a whole new reason. *Dammit.* I'd remembered to take my medication this morning, but even so, with this much going on, I knew what was going to happen.

It had been three years since I'd been diagnosed with narcolepsy with cataplexy. I'd already learned the hard way that any sudden spike in emotion, especially an intense one, would set off my cataplexy and result in me being left completely paralyzed for anywhere from a few seconds to ten minutes. Having a man bleed to death on top of me—and he had to be bleeding out with the amount of warm liquid I could feel soaking into my shirt—definitely counted as an intense situation. And sure enough, before I could shove him off me, my body failed me and I slid into paralysis.

Even though my body is useless in a cataplexy attack, my ears work just fine. As do my nerves. I still feel and hear everything that happens when I'm down for the count, I just can't do anything about any of it. So when a minute or so after the shooting stopped, a few men approached, talking, I heard every word.

"Shit. Frank's gonna have your balls for this one, Sledge. No way this can be covered up."

"Fucking shut it, Tic. You know Frank will come through. And there's no one left here that can talk. All anyone will say is they heard bikes and gunshots. You know how citizens get. A little fucking noise and they run like scared little rabbits."

I heard some grunting, then the weight pinning me down was gone.

"Oh, fuck. You think she's dead?"

I held my breath, hoping they wouldn't check too closely. I hoped between my stillness and the amount of blood I was covered in they would assume I was gone. So long as they didn't look too hard, they wouldn't realize I didn't actually have any holes in me. Pain shot up my leg when one of the bastards kicked my calf. *Asshole.*

"Yeah, she's gone. Pity. Pretty little thing."

"Quit thinking with your fucking cock. Grab his cut and empty his pockets, then we'll get the fuck outta here. Fucking Satan's Cowboys think they can come deal in our territory like they own it."

Oh, shit. This wasn't good, not at all. I'd heard that name before. Satan's Cowboys were another MC, a nasty one from up in northern Texas. I hoped this wasn't the start of a biker turf war. That would mean a lot more shootings like this one. How many had they killed today? Innocents simply going about their day. I tried to think back to how many customers had been sitting outside. How many would have run fast enough to get away?

"Chuck? Any survivors?"

"Not an issue, Prez. Everyone living fled. Just bodies here now. But we need to get moving. LEO are less than five minutes away. You need to get on to Frank, man. He knows we need longer than this to finish up a job."

Who, or what was the LEO?

"Yeah, I'll pull him aside later. You got everything, Tic?

"Yep. Let's roll."

The thunderous sound of the Harleys all taking off at once filled the air, then nothing but silence. In the void of noise, I focused on staying calm. I knew if I fought the attack, it would do nothing but extend the time it took me to get through it and now the bad guys had gone, I needed to wake the fuck up and get out of here.

When I could finally move again, my upper body jerked up off the floor. Opening my eyes, I gasped at the destruction around me. How many bullets had they put into the place? Glass and wood lay scattered everywhere, and there were bodies. Bile rose up my throat and I slapped a palm over my mouth when I saw the man I'd served just minutes ago, lying lifeless on the ground near me.

"Fuck. Fuck. Fuck!"

My head bobbed once, twice, then I crumbled back to the floor, unable to move. I wanted to scream. This stupid, fucking disease was such a pain the in ass. How the hell was I going to get away from here if every time I opened my damn eyes, I got overwhelmed at the carnage around me and passed out?

Sirens filled the air and accepting defeat, I stayed on the ground with my eyes closed and waited for them to arrive. I'd let the paramedics get me out of the building. I couldn't afford the bills that went with them taking me to hospital, but if they could get me out of the building, I'd be able to pull myself together. Hopefully. I didn't need any more visuals of the carnage lying around me. I already had enough to give me nightmares. In fact, I was one-hundred percent positive I'd be having nightmares about this day for months, maybe even years.

Mac

With my arms crossed over my chest, I stood next to Eagle and surveyed the room.

"What do you think?"

"You did good. Place looks great."

Eagle wasn't just a fellow Charon. Along with Taz, the three of us had served together in the USMC. Then, when we all retired nearly three years back, we decided to buy ourselves Harleys and tour the country. You know, fully enjoy the freedom of not having to fucking follow orders every moment of the day. Then, a little over a year ago the three of us were approached by our former CO about taking on an undercover job for the FBI. The job had sounded pretty easy. Get in tight with the Charon MC and report back anything we might hear about illegal activities. So far we'd only given the feds one piece of information, and the fuckers had leaked it. Not only did we nearly get our asses burned, Eagle nearly lost his woman.

The experience had left a nasty taste in our mouths, that's for sure, making it so none of us were overly keen on helping out the feds with anything again. Especially since all three of us were pretty happy living up the MC life. I was sure they'd come check on us sooner or later, but for now we were all simply ignoring our handler in the hopes he'd give up and go away. I doubted it would work, but hey, it was worth a shot, right?

It hadn't taken long to get in with the Charons. The three of us rode in a public poker run they sponsored, chatted to the guys, and in no time the three of us were prospects. The ease with which we were accepted wasn't really a surprise—there's not too many MCs that would turn down three decorated Marines. I knew we had to be a prospect before we could be full club members, but it had still sucked. At least with our skills we weren't given the really shitty jobs. Scout had us mainly doing security and technical work. But we were still kept in the dark about most club business—another thing that nearly cost Eagle his woman. Thankfully, that all changed about a month ago when we'd finally fucking earned our top rockers. Taz and I were enjoying our increased freedom, and the fact that we were actually included and told shit now. While Eagle, the lucky fucker, had managed to convince his woman Silk, the niece of the club's VP, into being his old lady already. He'd also managed to knock the woman up.

"How's Silk doing? Still sick?"

"Yeah, she's still throwing up and moody as fuck. Pregnancy sucks, man. Hopefully it'll pass soon. No way can I handle her being like this for nine fucking months."

I knew shit about pregnancy so couldn't comment, but it was clear to me why the man had spent so much time helping me here with my project. After I got my top rocker, I asked the club if I could start running some self-defense for women classes out of the club gym. Scout, the club president, had called a vote and I was given permission to go with it. However, the club's gym was an old school fight-club type thing, so to do what I wanted to, the place needed a massive overhaul. Modernizing the place, making it female-friendly, and more inviting to the younger crowd was the goal.

All the renovations were now finished and the new gym looked fucking fantastic. I'd led a crew of about a dozen men over the past couple of weeks to get the job done. In that time we'd torn down walls, put new ones up and painted the entire place, inside and out. The club had put up the money to get several new pieces of equipment, and we'd set up a small locker room for the men and a separate one for the ladies. Now, the place looked as good as any city gym I'd ever seen. Excluding the backroom, that is. We'd left that basically untouched for the old-timers and macho idiots who didn't want women anywhere near their 'space'. There was even a separate entrance back there for the precious fucking snowflakes.

Today was the first day we'd opened to the public. Chip, the man who'd been running the gym for the last who knew how many years, had agreed with me, when I suggested we open the general gym area this week and hold off starting classes until next week. That gave us time to get names down for the first classes. As much as I was happy to teach the sessions, I didn't want to be wasting my time in an empty fucking room. It also gave us time to hopefully find a female instructor for fitness classes. I was good with self-defense and martial arts shit, but bouncing around to music was not ever going to be something I was prepared to do.

"I'm sure when you're holding your kid in your arms at the end, you'll think it's all worth it."

"Yeah, I'm sure I will. But until then…"

As Eagle spoke, Scout strolled up and stood with us, looking completely out of fucking place with his leather cut, black t-shirt, jeans and biker boots.

"You did good, brother."

I couldn't help but smile at the man. Even weeks after patching in, I still got a buzz out of being called brother by the prez. Only patched-in members got that honor, and after spending nearly a year prospecting, it felt good to be included with all the other full club brothers.

"Thanks, Prez. The boys all worked their asses off and got shit done fast. I wasn't sure we'd be able to pull it off so quickly, but I'm fucking glad we have."

Well, I was half glad, half pissed off, actually. This renovation had taken all my time and energy for the past three weeks. I'd spent a week with Chip planning everything out before we started the actual physical work that took the rest of the time. But now that was done, I was back to having too much free time on my hands. If I wasn't busy, I started to think, to remember. And there wasn't any fucking point in it. The past was done. Nothing could be changed about the choices I'd made so recklessly.

Yep, absolutely nothing would bring back Beatrice. And nothing could change what I did to gain vengeance for my sister's murder. Somehow, sweet innocent Bee had gotten mixed up with a gangbanger. Neither our folks nor I even realized she'd had a serious boyfriend. It wasn't until her body was lying cold on a morgue table, covered in bruises and wounds that we knew exactly how much we'd let her down. I still couldn't figure out how she'd managed to keep it all from us. Still wished she'd told me about him sooner, so I could have dealt with the prick. Before it cost my sister her life. *Fucking bastard.*

I didn't regret that I'd killed him. No way. But I did regret how I went about it. I'd known how much power that gang of his had in our area of L.A., had known my only way to win over them was with someone more powerful. There had only been one option, really. The mob.

"You okay there?"

I shook my head to clear the images of blood and gore and focused back on Scout.

"Yeah, I'm good. Just drifted off there for a moment. I need to eat. Skipped lunch."

Wasn't sure going with the whole low-blood-sugar angle would work, but I sure as shit wasn't talking about what was really going on in my head. Especially here.

Eagle slapped me on the back. "I'll go to that little cafe up the street and grab you something. Back soon."

"Thanks, man."

Eagle strolled out the door and I could feel Scout frowning at me.

"For the record, I don't believe you. Being hungry doesn't make your skin go that odd shade of gray, brother. But I'm not gonna push you. Just know, if you ever need to talk shit through, my door's always open."

If I hadn't opened up about my past to Eagle and Taz, who'd literally been to war with me, I wasn't going to start spilling my past to Scout any time soon. Still, I appreciated the offer.

"Thanks. This shit isn't something that needs to be talked through. It's just past crap that pops back up every now and then. Honestly, I'm solid." I needed to get Scout off this line of thinking, fast. I was feeling a little too raw with the images fresh in my mind to keep my guard up for long. "You find a VCR player yet?"

A little over a month ago, just before we got patched in, shit hit the fan in a big way when Silk was snatched by the L.A. mob. Turned out her father, John, who'd died on the plane that hit the south tower in the 9/11 attacks, had been keeping ledgers of crimes committed by several groups. The L.A. mob was one of the organizations he'd focused on. Through a reporter, the mob had learned Silk's father's bag had missed the flight and was still at the L.A. airport, so they'd needed Silk to get it for them. Only thing was, when she went to get the bag, it wasn't just one damn book, but six of the fuckers.

John hadn't been happy to just rip off and dig up dirt on one organization. Nope. Bastard went after six that we knew about: L.A. mob, N.Y. mob, Charon MC, Iron Hammers MC, Ice Riders MC and Satan's Cowboys MC. In order to keep Silk safe, the club gave the L.A. boys their book and the N.Y. mob one, but had copied the thing first, of course—you know? Just in case. Although, in the weeks since we'd killed three of Sabella's goons and given him the bodies and the ledger, we hadn't seen any sign of them, so hopefully that was all done with. I was extra grateful that I'd not ever met Antonio Sabella in my younger years. Things could have really blown up if I'd been recognized. Eagle and Taz thought my connection with the mob was through distant relatives, and I wanted it to stay that way. Didn't need anyone knowing how closely I was really linked with them.

But all that shit only dealt with two of the ledgers, and we still had to deal with the others. Especially the one on the Iron Hammers MC. They were a club based down in Galveston and our closest rivals, constantly pulling shit trying to take over Charon territory. John's book on them led us to a safety deposit box that contained photos and VHS videos. The photos were of some seriously fucked-up shit. Teenage girls being held down and drugged up, or raped. Scout was trying to locate a VHS player to watch the videos, but personally, I didn't think he was trying too hard. We all knew those videos would be more of what the photos showed, and no one wanted to see that shit if they didn't have to.

"Nah, haven't found one local that I can borrow. I could buy one off the net but honestly, I'm starting to wonder if we should even bother. We all know what shit they'll contain. The photos were hard enough to fucking look at, but videos? That shit would turn even my stomach. I like my porn to have consenting adults in it, fuck you very much."

I huffed a laugh. "Yeah, no one in their right fucking mind would volunteer to see that shit. So, any ideas on what we're going to do about it?"

Scout ran a hand over his head and adjusted his ever-present bandana. The club president was an old-school biker, complete with bushy beard and bandana wrapped around his skull. He truly did stand out like a sore fucking thumb here in the gym.

"Still trying to come up with something that won't end with a bunch of our brothers lying dead in the street. Although after yesterday, we may have an ally against them."

That got my attention and I turned away from watching the few people working out in the gym to face him.

"What happened?"

I'd been so buried in getting this place up and going, I hadn't been keeping much of an eye on the news, or anything else for that matter. Scout rolled his eyes at me before he turned toward the back of the room.

"Let's head into the office. Chip and the others can hold things down out here for a while."

The need for complete privacy had me even more curious. I led the way back to the office and shut the door behind us as fast as I could.

"What the hell happened?"

I was starting to really regret not keeping an ear to the ground while I'd been working. Obviously I'd missed something major.

"Fucking shoot out. That's what happened. Clearly you've had your head up your ass, brother. Down in Galveston, late morning yesterday, half the fucking Iron Hammer boys pumped a cafe full of lead."

I slumped down into the chair behind the desk.

"Fuckin' hell. How many dead? Any word on why?"

"The why was a Satan's Cowboy who'd been dealing on their turf. And there's seven dead."

"They leave anyone alive?"

"Well, when the shots started up, there were people running all over the damn place. They were actually fucking lucky only a few got caught in the bullet shower. Naturally, no one saw a fucking thing. Except for one woman. A chick by the name of Claire Flynn. She ended up under the dead Cowboy. Guess he saved her by landing on her and taking the shots."

I looked up and caught Scout's gaze. "That woman's gonna be in a shit-ton of trouble if the Iron Hammers get hold of her. Where is she now?"

His face looked grave, as though he was imagining the same nightmare I was. That fucked-up club would use her hard, then kill her slowly.

"I spoke with Donald this morning. She disappeared after she was questioned. Crazy girl tried to do the right thing and report what she heard the Iron Hammers saying after the bullets stopped flying. She even gave fucking road names."

Donald was an older police officer here in Bridgewater and, from what I'd picked up, he often helped the club out.

"What's the bet the Iron Hammers have at least one member of the force down there on the books and they stepped in to help clean up the fucking problem?"

"That was my guess too, but Donald said the wrong people are up in arms about her disappearing for that to be the case. And she literally ran off from the scene on foot. Alone. From what she told them before she ran, the cops were forced to bring in their Prez, VP and SAA. But with her missing and unable to make a formal statement, they can't make any charges stick. Especially since the club's inside man, or men, will be doing all they can to get the fuckers back on the street."

I rubbed a palm over my rough jaw, my need to protect this unknown woman rising up.

"You got a description of her? Any way to track her down?"

"I wish. All we have is her name, Claire Flynn. Donald said the only photo they have is her license and that's not only out of date, but shit quality. He said he'd get us a copy of it, but don't hold your breath that it'll do us any good. He did tell me she's got strawberry blonde hair and hazel eyes. I've got Keys looking into it too. He should be able to find something. If she knows anything about club politics, she'll head this way. But the fact she was stupid enough to give that fucking statement in the first place would lead me to believe she doesn't know shit and just ran off like a scared rabbit."

I hated to see a woman in trouble, and wished like fuck she was heading our way so we could keep her safe. But there wasn't anything we could do about it unless she showed herself, especially if we didn't even know what the woman looked like.

"Aside from the girl, you thinking the Satan's Cowboys will want to help us take the Iron Hammers down now?"

Scout shrugged. "Not sure. I'm going to stand back and wait for a bit. See if they retaliate for the deaths. If we get lucky, we won't have to lift a damn finger to get the job done."

I sat back in my chair to think over what might happen. This could start a fucking war between those two clubs. Would that provide us the in to get close enough to find out if the Iron Hammers were still abusing women? And if the Satan's Cowboys did take out the Iron Hammers, what would that mean for the Charons? Or for any women the Iron Hammers were holding? The Satan's Cowboys were a one-percenter club with a rough reputation. I had no idea how they'd treat a woman. Especially ones that were downtrodden after suffering years of abuse.

Sadly, there wasn't fuck-all any of us could do about it. And I knew it. Because even though the Charon MC was growing in numbers, we had nothing on those two bigger MCs. It sucked, but our options really were limited at this point in time.

Chapter 2

Zara

What a shitty, fucking day. And it was barely half-way through.

I'm not sure what possessed me to tell the police what I'd overheard after the shooting. Well, that's a lie. I knew full well why. I'd still been recovering mentally from the damn cataplexy attack. It always took me a while to get my bearings straight after an episode, and this young cop, Tom, caught me while I'd still been reeling. Bastard had taken advantage of it too, and now I was in more trouble than I knew how to handle.

While I was speaking with Tom, an older officer approached, looking angry, and as he'd gotten closer I'd seen his name tag read Frank Clarke. My blood had run cold as my throat closed up. The bikers had mentioned the name Frank more than once. I knew I couldn't afford to panic. If I did that, I'd go down again, and then who knew what would happen to me.

Without uttering another word, I'd shaken my head before turning and fleeing. I'd vaguely heard Tom call out after me but a deeper voice growled something and he hadn't spoken again.

I'd been so fucking stupid! Everyone in this town knew not to speak out against the Iron Hammers. Now I was jogging along the footpath up to my house and wondering how long I had before someone would come gunning for me. I'm sure I made quite a sight, covered in blood and running like my life depended on it. *Because it did.*

Thankfully, my little condo wasn't far from the cafe. I charged in through the front door and within seconds had my bloody clothes off and in the bin. After giving my arms and face a quick scrub, I got dressed in jeans and a t-shirt before I pulled out my suitcase and began tossing random stuff in it. Clothes, toiletries, and the cash I'd been stashing under the mattress. It all went in, then I zipped it up and heaved it out to my car. When I went back to lock up everything, my neighbor and friend, Gemma, was standing on my front sidewalk looking worried.

"What the hell happened, Claire?"

"I can't talk now, Gem. I gotta run. The Hammers shot up the cafe, and I had an attack. The fucking cops started questioning me before I could get my mind straight, so I talked about the shit I'd heard. I'm in so much fucking trouble. I gotta go, and you need to get home before anyone sees you with me."

The color had drained from her face as I'd spoken, but she hadn't moved.

"Do you know where you're going to go?"

I shrugged. "No idea. But it won't take them long to find out where I live. I have to get moving."

I turned back toward my car, tossing my handbag into the front passenger seat before moving around to the driver's side.

"Go north-east, get to Bridgewater. The club there, the Charon MC? They hate the Iron Hammers. Enough that the Iron Hammers won't dare step foot in their territory. You'll be as safe as you can be there."

"Thank you, but please, go back inside. Hell, go out somewhere and pretend you never saw me today. I don't want you harmed because of me."

I'd hate for one of my very few friends to be hurt because I was a fucking idiot. She nodded once. "Good luck, and you know my number if you need anything."

Then, with a wince, she turned and jogged back toward her own unit. After one last glance at my home, I got in, started up my car and drove out of my driveway. Hopefully it wasn't for the last time.

Tears pricked my eyes at the thought I might never see Gemma, my home or the things in it again, but it was better than being dead. I hadn't been living in my condo very long, but it was still mine and I hated being forced to leave it. After my parents had been shot down in my childhood home three years ago, I couldn't keep living there. I'd used the money from their estate to buy my little home. It was small, but I didn't need a ton of space. Taking a deep breath, I drove north, making sure to keep just under the speed limit. I didn't want to do anything that would attract the attention of the police.

I stopped at a gas station to fill up and after paying, I went to the ATM and drained my savings account. I didn't want to be traced by having to use my card to pay for something later. Speaking of needing to be untraceable, I also grabbed myself a new phone.

Following road signs, which were thankfully regular enough I didn't have to stop and sort out my new phone to use an online map, I was driving into Bridgewater a little over an hour later. But now what? I had no plan at all, other than to get out of Galveston.

I drove around the town for a while, trying to get a feel for the place. It was small, not even half the size of Galveston, but it felt friendly. The streets were clean of trash and graffiti, and every store I passed looked like it had been recently painted. Seeing a sweet little cafe, I found a parking space and walked back to it. As I reached the entrance, a shiver ran over me and a flash of what happened this morning filled my vision. Pushing down the memory before it could affect me, I walked through the door and into the warm interior. November in Texas wasn't freezing like further north was this time of year, but it was still cold enough I appreciated not having to stand out in it.

Making my way up to the counter, I ordered a sandwich and a coffee. After I paid—in cash—the older woman behind the counter gave me an order number and I moved off. I spent a couple minutes looking over a bulletin board of notices before I found a table in a corner. I couldn't help the sigh that escaped me as I sat. I'd made it to Bridgewater in one piece and if Gemma was to be believed, I'd be safe here. Maybe if I never went into a police station to finalize my statement, the Iron Hammers would forget all about me in time and I could return to my home? *And pigs might fly.*

Regardless, I needed to get myself settled here for at least a little while. Unfortunately, there hadn't been any great inspiration posted on the board for what the hell I was going to do, though. No rooms for rent or jobs listed. Closing my eyes, I rubbed my temples with my fingertips. I had about fifteen hundred dollars cash. That wasn't going to last me long. I needed to find work.

The thunderous sound of Harleys coming closer had me freezing in my seat. Not again! Had the Iron Hammers followed me after all?

"Are you all right, sugar?"

My gaze flicked over to the woman who'd waited on me, now standing beside me with my order in her hands. Her name badge read "Marie". She was older, old enough to be my mother, and had a motherly aura about her that drew me in. I'd always been close to my mom, and these past three years had been so hard to bear without her support. There wasn't a day that went by that I didn't feel the loss of my parents. Especially since it had been their sudden deaths that had triggered my narcolepsy.

The whole mess had been totally avoidable. The police had labeled the murders a robbery gone wrong. After all my mother's medical bills, they didn't have much and I guess the bastard who broke in took offense to them not having more shit for him to steal. So he'd shot them both dead before he'd left. I'd been out at a movie with a girlfriend and returned to see the killer pulling out of our driveway. Having no idea why he'd been there, I rushed inside to see what had happened. Never in my wildest nightmares did I imagine that I would find what I did. Both my parents, lying dead in pools of blood. Yeah, I had more than one reason to hate the sound of Harleys. It had been an Iron Hammer prospect that had pulled the trigger that night.

I cleared my throat. "Ah, yeah. I just get a little tense around the sound of Harleys. Really, I'm fine."

The lady chuckled and relaxed. "Clearly, you're not from around here then, sugar. That's just a few of the Charon MC boys. The local club here in Bridgewater. So long as you're doing nothing to harm anyone, you have nothing to fear from those men. Quite the opposite. So, you visiting or moving to the area?"

I looked her in the eye to try to figure out if I should trust this woman, at least a little. As much as her motherly vibe was drawing me in, I was nervous to trust it. After the morning I'd had, I was so tense I felt like I would shatter completely at any moment, which wasn't good for my cataplexy. Ultimately, I figured I didn't have anything to lose by giving Marie a little information.

"Well, actually, I just arrived in town, looking to get a fresh start here in Bridgewater. I don't suppose you know of any work available?"

"Well, sugar, that all depends on what you're willing to do to earn your bread."

"I've worked as a waitress, barista and cleaner. I can cook and prepare basic stuff. Honestly, at this point I'll take whatever I can get."

"Got any references on you?"

That made me wince. I didn't even know if my boss had survived the attack, but even if he had, he wouldn't be giving a reference to a worker that ran off without giving any notice. "Sorry, I, ah, I had to leave in a hurry and didn't think to grab them on my way out."

That earned me a raised eyebrow from the older woman but she didn't say anything for a few moments.

"You got trouble following you?"

Fuck. How was I going to answer that one? Before I could form a viable lie, the Harleys pulled up in front of the shop. My gaze jerked toward the window, but before I completely lost it and had another attack, I saw the words Charon MC on each of the vests the men were wearing and breathed easier. I was okay. It wasn't the Iron Hammers, but the local club. The club which both Gemma, and now Marie, had told me would keep me safe. I wasn't sure I'd ever fully believe a MC could equal safety, but it looked like I would at least need to learn to live with them around me.

"Relax and enjoy your sandwich, sugar, and I'll be back over to chat some more after."

I had no idea what the hell I'd tell her about the trouble when she returned, but pushed the thought aside as I lifted my sandwich to take a bite. Damn, but I really was hungry. In no time I had my sandwich eaten, then I sat sipping my coffee as I watched the four bikers flirt with Marie. I was surprised to see them hand over money for their orders. I figured all MCs were like the Iron Hammers and thought they didn't need to pay for anything, if they could get away with it.

As Marie got busy behind the coffee machine, the four men all wandered over and sat at a table only two away from mine. I couldn't stop my heart rate from picking up when one of them glanced my way and gave me a wink and a flash of a grin before he turned back to his friends. He had his hair really short on the sides and only a little longer on the top. His arms were covered in tattoos—even his hands had ink on them, along with his neck, but his face had looked friendly when he'd winked at me and now he was smiling and laughing with the other men. *Just like a normal man.* The other three looked more serious. One was an older man with a big, bushy beard that was mostly gray with a little dark brown threaded through it. He had a blue bandana around his forehead that he adjusted often, as though it was a subconscious action. The other two had their backs to me so I had no idea what they looked like, aside from their broad shoulders and clearly muscled bodies.

I was still staring at them in wonder at how non-threatening they seemed to be, when Marie returned.

"They certainly are easy on the eyes, aren't they?"

Heat raced over my cheeks as I glanced away from them and toward her.

"I wasn't really looking at them—more staring off into space."

She laughed at that, loudly enough the tattooed biker looked my way again.

"Oh, sugar. No need to make excuses. Trust me, we all look our fill. Now, about work. I own this place and could use an extra worker. You came in after the lunch rush today, so you didn't see how busy it gets. But my last girl up and disappeared on me a few days ago, and I've been too busy since to look at replacing her."

That brought my full attention from the bikers to her. I almost couldn't believe what I'd heard. Seriously? The first place I asked had work that lined up with my skills?

"For real?"

With a chuckle she slid into the seat beside me. "For real. What's your name, sugar?"

"Zara."

Technically it was my middle name. But using Claire seemed too risky. I wasn't sure how far, or fast word would spread about me running off this morning. However, it seemed better to play it safe when I could. When it came to paperwork, I'd just tell Marie I'd always gone by my middle name.

"Pretty. Well, how about you come on back here at closing time and I'll let you know what I need from you. We'll get all the paperwork sorted then too, and I'll show you how to work the few machines I have here."

Yeah, as much as I knew how to make coffee, every machine was a little different. "That sounds wonderful."

Marie left to serve more customers and I sat motionless. I was a little in shock at my luck. Looked like coming to Bridgewater really was a good idea. I looked around the cafe with new interest. It was clean and tidy, and homey. The last place I worked at had tried to look like a Starbucks, without actually being one. This place was its own identity. And the coffee was amazing. Marie clearly believed in serving quality products.

I had a strong feeling I could be happy working here.

Now, I just hoped that hotel I'd seen a few blocks away had a weekly rental rate that wouldn't kill my finances.

Mac

I parked my ride with the other bikes out the front of the club's bar, Styx – named after one of the two rivers Greek mythology states the Charon ferried souls across.

Some days I wondered if the MC didn't take the whole Greek Charon thing way too far. They'd called the gym Acheron. I mean, seriously? Who names a fucking gym after the river of pain? I had to chuckle, since Styx was the river of hatred. Hardly made sense for a bar, either. They should have named it after the Greek god of excess or some shit if they wanted to keep it relevant.

Still mentally debating Greek mythology, and trying to remember the name of the Greek god of excess, I made my way inside. I hadn't been here many times. Normally I just hung out at the clubhouse. The place had a bar and good company, even had women available if I had an itch that needed to be scratched. But Taz had convinced me we needed a variety of scenery now that we were patched in. Which really meant Taz had done all the club whores too many times and wanted someone new to fuck. At some point, the man was going to have to deal with whatever the fuck it was that he was trying to bury under pussy and tattoos, but considering I wasn't ready to air my own shit, I wasn't going to start hassling my brother about his baggage.

I returned the gesture, when the prospect manning the door gave me a chin lift as I passed him. I entered with a smile, so fucking glad I didn't have to do those shit prospect jobs anymore.

Having a top rocker was a sweet, sweet thing.

"Hey, Mac!"

Nodding at Taz, I made my way over to where he stood at the bar. Within moments, I had my favorite beer in hand and turned my back to lean against the bar so I could watch the crowd. Thursday nights were busy, but not crazy like a Saturday.

"Hey, Taz, do you know what the name of the Greek god of excess is?

Taz jerked back from the bar to glare at me. "What the fuck do you want to know that shit for? And that's what Google is for, mate."

Not feeling like explaining myself, I ignored his question as I slipped my phone out of my pocket and started looking it up.

"So, whatcha been up to?"

In response to my question, the big Aussie shrugged a shoulder as he turned back to the bar to take a swig of his own brew. "Not much today. Been out at the range for most of it."

The club wanted to buy the local gun range, but the current owner, Gus, wasn't willing to sell out to an MC. What he was happy to do was let a decorated USMC sniper in to practice. So, Taz had been given the task of softening up the old man so he'd hopefully sell to the club at some point. I actually wondered if it wouldn't be a better idea to have Taz buy it, with the club funding him. Maybe that was what Scout was planning. I made a mental note to suggest it to Scout at church next week, just in case the man hadn't already considered it.

Finally Google loaded and gave me what I wanted. "Ha! Got it. Dionysus. Huh, guess that answers that, then."

"Dion-who? And what the fuck does that answer?"

Taz was looking at me like I'd lost my fucking mind.

"I was thinking about how stupid it was that the bar was named after the river of hatred. Figured it would make more sense to use the Greek god of excess, but his name is Dionysus. Barely say that shit sober, can you imagine trying to say it when you're wasted?"

Taz just shook his head at me. "You're fucked up, mate. And not in the good way. You need to get laid, or at least have your dick sucked. Plenty of willing ladies to choose from. What do you say? Shall we go find ourselves a little somethin'?"

With a smirk at Taz's enthusiasm, I shrugged a shoulder. I wasn't in the mood to deal with some bitch who just wanted to be with a Charon. Most of them whined way too much to make it worth the release. Especially the ones who wanted to be an old lady and thought they were such a good lay, all they had to do was get a brother in bed to get the title. Nope. I wouldn't be picking up a barfly tonight. If I wanted some relief, I'd get it from one of the whores who knew the score back at the clubhouse.

"Maybe later. I've been working my ass off all fucking day and want to relax for a bit."

"So, how's the first week at the gym going?"

"Really good. Had a few of the old boys bitching on Monday when they first came in, but we showed them their back room and they settled the fuck down. Damn glad we decided to keep the entrance back there open so they don't have to come through the main gym area."

Taz wriggled his eyebrows at me with a smirk. "Any hot sheilas come in?"

"Sheilas?"

Having been hanging around with Taz for over a decade, I knew exactly what he meant. But it was always fun to tease him.

He rolled his eyes. "You know what I mean. Women, asshole. Any good looking women come in?"

Lifting my beer I took a slow drink, mainly so I could watch him squirm as he got increasingly frustrated with me.

"Of course we've had women come into the gym. That was the whole fucking point of cleaning the place up, remember?"

"Yeah, but I'm asking about good-looking ones."

I shrugged. "There's been a few pretty ones come in. Why you asking? Lost interest in all the ones at the clubhouse already?"

Taz drained his beer, suddenly looking more serious than I'd seen him in a long while. I frowned at him. What the fuck?

"Hey, I'm not trying to bust your balls here, man. If you want to come work out at the gym and troll for a girl, you know you're welcome to. You certainly won't be the only one."

He ordered another drink before turning back to me. "Nah, mate. You're right. Best to just stick to the willing and wet at the clubhouse."

Interesting. So he hadn't dragged me out here to find something new to fuck after all. I'd never seen Taz look more broken than he did in that moment and I wished like hell I knew how to help him. Before I could think of anything to say, Keg came over and joined us.

"Hey, Taz, you tell Mac about that new piece of ass working for Marie yet?"

I winced at the tension that continued to radiate off Taz. Clearly he could use a few minutes to get his head on straight.

"How the fuck did you get named Keg, anyway? What? You set a record for drinking one or something?"

A wide grin split the young man's face. "Nah. When I first approached Scout about prospecting in, he shut me down. So I started turning up with a keg whenever I could afford to. Six months later, he gave me my prospect cut and started calling me Keg."

Now, that made me laugh. Some of the stories behind road names were fucking hilarious.

"How about you? What the fuck is Mac supposed to mean? You take on a truck and win or something?"

"Short for MacGyver. You know? The old TV show? I'm handy with my knife and can, pretty much, make anything out of anything. Got given the name at boot camp."

"Huh. Might have to test that someday. Could be fun. What about you, Taz? Fun story behind your name?"

Taz had drained his new beer and his shoulders had dropped to a more relaxed-looking posture. I hoped like hell whatever had gotten under his skin earlier was out now.

"Nah, mate. No story. The boys in boot camp thought it was funny to call me Tassie Devil because I'm Aussie. I'm not from Tasmania, but the guys didn't give a shit about that and the name stuck."

I grinned. "I heard it was more to do with the fact that when he loses his temper, he destroys shit. Just like that cartoon character, the Tasmanian Devil."

He flipped me the bird, but was laughing. "Yeah, I wasn't real good at controlling my temper back in the early days. The USMC doesn't waste time in forcing you to get that shit under control, though."

I wasn't so sure he had complete control of it. He'd just gotten real good at hiding it. On deployment he'd used humor, stateside he seemed to have mixed it up with sex and ink.

"So, Keg, tell me about this new girl Marie's got working for her."

"She's no girl, my man. That one is all woman and soft curves."

That caught my attention. Marie's Cafe was only about a block away from the gym, so I'd been going there for food nearly every day while we were doing renovations. I hadn't been in there this week, though. Now we had the public working out in the gym, I couldn't just wander off whenever I felt like it.

In fact, a lot of the Charons were regulars at Marie's because she had the best damn coffee in town. Normally Marie hired teenagers. Of course, that was also why she was often run off her feet, because those young girls would just take off with no notice. I was glad to hear she'd finally hired someone older, who hopefully had some kind of work ethic in her.

"A real woman, huh? Might have to go check her out tomorrow." I gave Keg a smirk. "Not like you'd know what to do with a real woman, Keg."

Keg wasn't quite at Taz's manwhore level, but he wasn't far off.

"Hey, just because I take advantage of the easy and willing at the clubhouse, that are all young and dumb, doesn't mean I don't want something more. I mean, not yet, I'm still having way too much fun with the variety right now, but one day I want to settle down with a good old lady and have me a couple kids, you know?"

Raising an eyebrow, I glanced over at the man. He was maybe twenty-two years old. So fucking naive and innocent. At his age I'd already been to the Middle East more than once on deployment, had killed men. How different my life could have been...

Chapter 3

Zara

It was exactly one week after I first walked into Marie's Cafe when I first laid eyes on him. I'd been wiping down a table when he strolled through the front door wearing nothing but running shoes, gym shorts and a tank. I'm pretty sure I drooled. I mean, who wouldn't? He was over six feet tall, with ink-covered broad shoulders and a jawline that begged to be nibbled on. My attention dropped to his biceps when they flexed as he closed the door behind him. I'd always had a thing for well-defined, muscular arms, and his were divine.

He glanced around the room and when his gaze caught mine, one side of his mouth kicked up in a little smile. Heat raced over my cheeks as I jerked my focus down to the table that, despite being spotless, I was still wiping. *Fuck!* He'd caught me ogling him. I hoped Marie hadn't seen. That woman would tease me for days over it.

I kept him in the corner of my vision as I moved onto another table. He strolled up to the counter with a swagger that was filled with confidence. He must work at the gym down the street, with what he was wearing. Marie greeted him with a smile and within minutes he was moving toward me. My heart skipped a beat.

"Hi. You must be the new girl everyone is talking about. What's your name, darlin'?"

My face heated again and I suddenly felt like I was a fifteen-year-old girl stumbling to talk to my first crush.

"Ah, hi. I'm Cl—Zara." I winced. I was so nervous, I nearly said Claire. I couldn't risk that. In the week I'd been here, I hadn't gotten the impression anyone had clued in to my real identity. Thankfully, Marie hadn't recognized the name when we did all the paperwork that first day, either.

Before he could say another word, I rushed off toward the counter. I knew full well I was being a coward but honestly, I didn't care. The man was causing all sorts of havoc inside my mind and body, and I didn't need that right now. I needed to keep a nice, low profile that didn't attract any attention. Maybe after a couple of years I could spread my wings some, and date a man or something. Once the Iron Hammers had forgotten all about me.

"Oh, girl, looks like you gained another fan in that one."

I gave Marie a puzzled look. "What do you mean?"

"Mac. He's watching every move you make. Which is funny as hell, after the way you blushed and ran off on him just now."

I rolled my eyes. Of course she'd seen it. "I'm a new face, that's all. A lot of men have introduced themselves to me this week—women, too."

Marie smirked at me. "That, they have. A few of those men have even looked about as hungry as Mac there does. Been great for business." She winked at me when I glared at her. "Here, take his order to him. Maybe try to talk to the man. You could do worse than that one."

With a frown, I took in Marie's now carefully blank expression. "Why are you pushing me so hard at a man?"

"Oh, sugar. So many reasons. Mainly because you look like you could use your world being rocked. And a man built like that? He'd most definitely rock your world. And if you hook up with a local, you'll hang around and keep working for me."

Shaking my head, I took the tray that Marie had sat a coffee and piece of pie on. Looks like I was going to have to put my big girl panties on, and try to sound like a functioning adult. It shouldn't be too hard. After all, I was a thirty-two-year-old woman. It wasn't like I was in high school anymore.

With a deep breath, I turned and headed back toward Mac. He was sitting with his back to the wall, and his ice-blue eyes followed my every step. My skin prickled as I reached his side.

"Here you go."

I carefully set the coffee mug and plate of pie in front of him, before adding the wrapped cutlery beside it.

"Thanks, Zara. I don't suppose you're due for a break any time soon? It's not much fun to eat alone."

Before I could respond, the cafe door opened, and three big men dressed in Charon MC vests strolled in, including the one who'd winked at me on my first day. My whole body froze as fear raced through my system when they headed straight for me. Did they know who I was? Were they going to hand me over to the Iron Hammers?

"Hey, Zara, you okay? You've gone pale all the sudden."

I tried to smile, to pretend like everything was okay but couldn't quite pull it off. When the men got to us, they all pulled out seats to join Mac, all the while giving me odd looks. I took a deep breath, and tried again to plaster on a smile.

"No problem. Just got a little dizzy there for a moment. Looks like you're all set to not eat alone now, so I'll leave you be."

I turned tail and barely resisted the urge to sprint back to the counter, where I found Marie laughing openly at me. *Bitch.*

"It's not funny."

"Oh, sugar. It truly is. And if you want, you can take five to sit with him. We've got some time before the lunch crowd starts coming in."

I glared at her as I went over to the coffee machine to give it a wipe-down it didn't really need. But it got me away from the counter before Mac's buddies came up to order. I didn't care how many people told me the Charon MC was good, I couldn't afford to risk them being wrong. What if the Charons had some secret deal with the Iron Hammers? And if they discovered who I was, they'd hand me over to keep the other club out of their town. Anything was possible with a club that could get away with shooting up a cafe in broad daylight.

Marie took pity on me and took the bikers their orders, saving me from having to act like they didn't scare the piss out of me. She'd seen on my first day how I didn't like Harleys or their riders and for the most part, she allowed me to get away with not interacting with any bikers that came in. When she came back to the counter, I frowned at her.

"Hey, Marie, if you knew Mac was a Charon, why'd you send me over with his order?"

Marie moved to stand right by me. "Because, Zara, you need to get over your fear of them if you wanna make a life here in Bridgewater. I figured with Mac not wearing his cut you might feel relaxed enough to chat with him. Realize that underneath it all, they're just men."

"A cut? What the hell is that?"

She chuckled at me again. "The leather vest they wear. It has their club logo and name on the back, and their name and other stuff on the front. They call that their cut." She patted her palm on my shoulder. "Don't worry, sugar. Even if you do keep trying to avoid them, you'll soon pick up on how they speak."

The woman had this glint in her eye that had me a little concerned, but before I could quiz her any further, Mac came up to us, ending that particular conversation.

"Hey, Marie. I forgot to ask you earlier—can I put this up on the notice board?"

"Well now, that all depends on what it's for."

"It's for the gym. For the self-defense for women class we're starting next week."

When Marie took the piece of paper from Mac to read it over, Mac turned his gaze on me.

"You should come, Zara. It'll help boost your self-confidence, knowing you can take care of yourself."

Oh, sure. Going to hang out in a gym with a bunch of bikers was going to help me feel safe.

"Maybe one day."

I didn't want to say no and have him and Marie keep at me until I changed my mind.

"I'd love to see you there, and I'm serious about it being a great confidence builder."

I turned back to the coffee machine, busying myself until Mac stepped away toward the notice board.

"It might be a good idea, sugar. I don't know what you're running from, but I know it's something that makes you panic whenever you see anything even remotely club-related. Learning a few moves couldn't hurt."

"I'll think about it, okay?"

My hand trembled when I lifted it a moment later to pull down a mug to fill. Dammit. I hadn't realized Marie had seen through me. Of course, I probably should have. She had that whole motherly-vibe thing going on, which included seeing shit she wasn't supposed to. And it wasn't like I hadn't been as obvious as hell, freezing up whenever I saw or heard anything to do with a Harley.

I needed to be more careful.

Mac

Zara intrigued me. She'd been all sweet blushes and stammered words until my club brothers came in. The moment Taz, Eagle and Arrow had entered the place, she'd nearly passed out, before scampering away. Guess she didn't like bikers for some reason. I had no idea why, but I suddenly needed to find out.

I found myself watching her as she worked. She was a pretty little thing. Wide, hazel eyes, pale skin with a few freckles. She'd pulled her long, reddish-blonde hair back into a braid that hung down her back. I couldn't help but wonder how it'd look loose, spread over her bare tits as she rode me.

That thought had me hard as a fucking rock. *Dammit.* I shifted my legs under the table, making sure my lower half stayed out of sight. Not like my gym shorts were gonna hide the fact my cock was hard as steel. I picked up my cup and took another mouthful of coffee, enjoying the bitter brew. Marie certainly knew what made a good cup of java.

It didn't take long for my thoughts to wander back to Zara. I couldn't help but smirk at how much of a little coward she'd been a short while ago, hiding behind the coffee machine so she wouldn't have to serve my brothers when they went up to order. Funny thing was, for everyone else she'd been open and friendly. The fact she was even all smiles for the male customers had me thinking her issue was with the club, not with men in general. What the hell could have happened? The Charon MC never hurt women, at least not that I knew about.

"Are you even listening, Mac? Or am I just talking for the fucking hell of it?"

I turned my attention from the little waitress to Arrow, the club treasurer. "Sorry, man. What did you say?"

"I was saying how you were spot-on with the gym renovation. It won't take long at all to cover the costs of doing up the fucking joint, then we'll be making bank. But you don't give a shit, do you?"

I raised an eyebrow at him. "Of course I fucking give a shit. I'd be pretty pissed if we'd done all that work at my suggestion, only for it to fall flat and not benefit the club."

I'll be even more pissed if the classes don't take off. That was the real reason I'd offered to take on the remodel. My gaze caught on Zara again. She'd been watching us, but jerked around when I caught her. She could really use a class or two—dozen. If she knew she could take care of herself, she wouldn't have to act like a scared rabbit.

"Yeah, but you care *more* about the hot piece of ass over there. The one that scurried away like a mouse when we came in. Did we cock block you, bro?"

The smirk on the man's face indicated he didn't give a shit if he had.

"Yeah, I was totally planning on bending her over the table and taking her before you bastards came in and ruined things." I gave him an eye roll. "This ain't the clubhouse. I'm curious about her. There's something going on with her that I can't figure out, that's all."

Arrow continued to smirk as he nudged Taz. "Your habits are rubbing off on your buddy, brother."

Taz barked out a laugh. "Nah, mate. Mac's just sitting there trying to hide his fucking hard-on. If I were him, I'd have her out back, already helping me relieve the issue."

I highly doubted that. Sure, Taz buried himself in random sex regularly, but never outside the clubhouse. No way would he touch a woman like Zara unless he intended to keep her. And I couldn't see Taz settling down with one woman any time soon.

Arrow shook his head with a chuckle. "Yeah, doubt Marie would like either one of you acting out that suggestion." His expression turned serious as he focused in on me. "You planning on going after her? Probably should have Keys check her out if you are. Because, brother, that woman doesn't look like the kind you fuck and throw away. That, right there, is old lady material."

I nearly choked on my final mouthful of coffee.

"How would you know that? She's like any other girl."

Fuck, that was such a lie. I already knew she was special. Arrow shook his head. "Nope, she ain't. You can see it in her eyes. True, she avoids us best she can, but when she's forced to serve us? She holds strong, chin up and does her job. I've looked into that girl's eyes. She ain't no shallow bitch that'll suck your cock in the parking lot just because you're wearing colors. Nope, that one there is a full-on Miss Independent. Crack that shell of hers and you better wanna keep what you find inside for a long time."

I sat back, stunned.

"Guess I know how you got your name."

Bastard actually winked at me. "I shoot straight. Won't blow smoke up your ass. I'll catch you boys later." With that, the man stood, and with a rap of his knuckles on the table, strolled out.

Taz let out a low whistle. "Well, there you go. So, Mac, you looking to settle down like Eagle here? She's certainly pretty. Just need to work out what the fuck's up with her and bikers. Any ideas?"

I relaxed into my seat. I was good with all my Charon brothers, but I'd known Eagle and Taz for over a decade. Our bond was stronger, and they knew nearly everything about me. Neither of them knew about my sister. But that was about the only thing I'd kept from them.

"No fucking clue. But watch her, she doesn't have an issue talking to male customers, and she was fine with me until you assholes walked in wearing your cuts. It's a biker thing, not a man thing. And how the fuck should I know if I want to claim the damn woman? Only met her today and we've barely spoken more than a handful of words, so all you fucking cupids need to settle the fuck down, okay?"

Taz raised his palms in surrender. "Whoa, mate. Settle down, it was just a question." He cleared his throat and glanced around the cafe before he leaned in and spoke again. "Speaking of questions—I've got Mr. Smith on my case about this shooting. Wants to know anything we can dig up."

Mr. Smith was the very original, very fake name of our FBI handler. The handler who'd somehow allowed the L.A. mob to discover the information we'd given him about them a month or so back. Since then all three of us were wary about telling the feds anything.

"Did he tell you anything?"

"That they had an eyewitness finger the Iron Hammers for the Galveston shooting, and that she's disappeared."

Eagle leaned in. "Why the hell are the feds even on this case?"

Taz shrugged a shoulder. "The way Mr. Smith tells it, the fact one of the bodies left behind was a Satan's Cowboy is enough to have the feds in the mix."

I sat back and folded my arms over my chest. "I don't like it. Them being involved this early on in the case stinks to me."

Eagle nodded. "Wouldn't surprise me if the Cowboys had an inside guy, or guys, with the feds. Especially after the way the bastards let slip to the mob what we gave them. We don't have anything to give them on this one yet, but we need to decide what we're going to do if that changes."

I nodded. "With both the feds and Scout suspecting the witness will head this way, there's a good chance she'll end up here sooner or later. Did Mr. Smith give you details on the witness? Scout only had the name Claire Flynn and the fact she's strawberry-blonde, whatever the hell color that is, with hazel eyes."

Taz shook his head. "Bastard didn't even give me a name. When I asked, he told me I must be confused, because it's us that gives him information, not the other way around. Bastard."

I clenched and stretched out my fingers a few times, thinking. "I don't want to give them anything. They've already proven they're fucking dirty, and if the club finds out we're ratting them out? We'll end up like Runt."

Runt had been a spy sent into the Charons by the Iron Hammers. Poor bastard got pinned with the blame for giving the feds the shit we did. I didn't feel too guilty over it though, because the little shit had been funneling all sorts of information he shouldn't have to the Hammers.

"I'm with you, brother. I don't want to give the feds another word of information. But I don't think we can just go radio silence on them and they'll go away."

I ran a hand over the back of my neck. "I know. But that's a problem for another day. Like Eagle pointed out, at this stage, we don't have shit to tell them about it, anyway."

I checked my watch. "Fuck. I gotta run. I should have already been back at the gym. I'll talk to you two later."

Chapter 4

Zara

I'd just finished wiping down the last table when Marie spoke up.

"That class down at the gym starts tonight. You gonna be there?"

I stood up straight and stretched out my back. The day hadn't been too bad, but I was still looking forward to a nice, hot shower when I got back to my motel room.

"I wasn't planning on it."

"I know why you're scared, sugar. But you need those boys on your side."

The blood rushed from my face and I threw out a hand to grab at the closest table. She knew? How'd she find out? Oh fuck, I needed to leave, right now.

As panic flooded me, I couldn't fight it off. I crumpled into a heap on the floor.

"Damn it, I didn't mean to set off your cataplexy, Zara."

I heard her shuffling around, and from the noise I guessed she was pulling the blinds down over the front windows. Then her strong, warm hands were on me, moving me to a more comfortable position. My head ended up in her lap and she stroked my hair.

"You told me you can still hear everything when this happens, so I'm going to keep talking. I overheard a couple of cops chatting yesterday about the shooting. They mentioned how no one had seen the witness since she ran off. They mentioned your name, sugar. I know it's you. I won't tell anyone. You should know that about me by now. But you need to let the Charons know who you are. They'll protect you against those pieces of shit Iron Hammers, but they can't if they don't know. Mac clearly has you in his sights and as an old lady, you can be guaranteed that the club will move heaven and earth to keep your ass safe." Her voice dropped to a whisper, "Because, sugar, you really don't want to fall into the hands of those assholes. You've no idea what they'd do to you."

With a gasp, I jerked free of the attack and sat up. Part of me wanted to stay where I was. Marie stroking my hair gently had felt so nice.

"No biker is safe, Marie. What if they barter me over to them to keep them out of Bridgewater?"

She shook her head. "They would never give that club anything, let alone a woman. Especially one that had caught the eye of one of their own."

I was torn about asking. Did I really want to know? But in the end my curiosity won out.

"How do you know what they'd do? The Iron Hammers. You sound like you know more than just rumors."

The older woman's eyes glossed over with tears. "I grew up in Galveston. When I was eighteen, one of my friends got us an invite to a party at the Iron Hammers clubhouse. We were so excited. We'd be able to drink—have fun with no parents anywhere near us. The two of us went into that hellhole and we only just made it out. They held us down and injected drugs into us. Then they tossed us into a tiny room. There were other girls in there already. The men would come in and force more drugs into the ones coming around, other men came in to fuck whoever caught their eye. My friend and I pretended to be drugged-out, unconscious to avoid getting shot up again. Fuck. I've never been so scared in all my life, Zara. Early the next morning, when all the men had passed out from their fun and games, we managed to sneak out.

"Just like you, Zara, we both came here. I wasn't as sneaky as you, though. Scout, the president of the

Charons MC, found us soon after we arrived in town. He took us in, let us stay in his home until we recovered enough to function. The club helped me set up this place. The Charons are good men, sweetheart. They're not going to hand you over."

Tears ran down my face for Marie and her friend.

"Did you tell Scout about the other women? Get him to go help the others?"

"It's not that simple. The Charons were a lot smaller than the Iron Hammers and they didn't have the manpower to go in and take them down. Hell, they still don't. And, well, we didn't tell Scout everything. We were young, scared and embarrassed about what had happened. All Scout knew was that we'd had drugs and were scared shitless of the Iron Hammers. We didn't confess about the other stuff. We'd thought if we had, and the Charons went charging in, they'd probably be slaughtered and the Iron Hammers would take us back."

Pulling my knees up against my chest, I wiped my eyes against my knees.

"I don't know what to think, or do. I'm so fucking scared, Marie."

She shuffled over to sit beside me before she pulled me in for a hug. "You need to talk to Mac. Tell him who you are. And go to that damn class. Learning how to hand a man his ass when he steps out of line is a handy skill for any woman to have."

I nodded against her shoulder. "I'll think about it."

"Well, don't think for too long, sugar. From what the cops were saying, the Iron Hammers have quite the hard-on for you and everyone knows Bridgewater is the place you go to hide from them. They won't take long to come to town."

I didn't respond, just stayed pressed against Marie, soaking in the comfort as I thought through my options. Which was a joke really. I didn't have any fucking options. Either risk someone else figuring out who I was that would hand me over, or go to the Charons for protection. I had to wonder about what the price tag attached to that protection would be.

Mac

The first self-defense class was about to start and I was more than happy with the turnout. I grinned with excitement. The dozen or so women included all sorts. There were a couple of giggling high schoolers, who I suspected were only here to try to catch a Charon, rather than learn any skills. A few were clearly young mothers, who had that tired, but happy look about them. There were even a couple of ladies that had to be in their fifties. This was good. I hoped that in time word would spread, and we'd be able to do separate classes for each age group.

The door opened right at starting time and my heart began to race. She'd come. I'd given up hope she would. But Zara was here, standing in the doorway chewing her lip and looking beyond adorable... and scared.

"Your girl came after all."

I nodded at Chip's words. "Looks like."

"Go grab her. She can fill out the paperwork afterward. We need to get started."

With a nod, I strode over to Zara.

"Glad you made it. We're about to start, so I'll sit down with you after and go over the paperwork, okay?"

"Um, sure."

As I led her over to where we'd set up, I just knew she was going to do a runner on me after class. The question was, did I try to stop her, or let her go? Not like I didn't know where to find her tomorrow. I decided I'd keep an eye on her and see how it went. Maybe she'd settle down by the time we finished class and she'd stick around.

Joining Chip at the front of the room, I got everyone's attention, introduced the pair of us, and started my first self-defense for women class. I'd planned this first lesson to be very basic. To start with, I ran through several different maneuvers with Chip as my crash-test dummy. The women all got into it, cheering and laughing every time I dropped Chip. I was going to owe him a bottle of Jack for all the times he let me put him on the mat.

For the last part of the class we did a couple of demonstrations. One was to show them exactly how to get free from having your arm pinned up behind your back, and the other was how to handle someone coming at you with a knife. Once we demonstrated, we put the ladies in pairs, gave each pair a toy knife to use, and had them practice both situations. Chip and I moved around the room, helping out each pair as we went. I was pleased with how everyone was doing. Even the giggling schoolgirls had settled down and got with the program.

Time flew and before I knew it, the hour was up. I called time and ended the class, telling them I'd see them all next week. My chest swelled a little at how every woman was smiling on her way out of the door. I hoped like hell these classes would save at least one of these ladies from being a victim at some point in the future.

Zara was the last to leave, surprising me by not trying to sneak out. She shocked me even more when she strolled straight up to me, chin raised.

"If you don't mind, could I take that paperwork with me? I'll give it to you next time you're in the cafe."

I cocked my head at her, certain she was up to something.

"It's not exactly protocol. For insurance purposes we need you to fill out and sign a single page form. It won't take long. I can help you now and it'll be done in a couple of minutes."

She winced and pulled her lower lip into her mouth to chew on it. The sight had my dick twitching, which wasn't ideal when I was wearing loose gym shorts.

"That's fine, darlin'. Here's the form, one of us will be in to Marie's in a few days to collect it, okay?"

She turned to smile at Chip as he handed her the form as he'd spoken to her.

"Thanks. That'll be great."

And with that, she scurried out the door and into the night. I stood glaring as Chip went over and locked the door behind her.

"What the fuck, Chip?"

"Settle down. That girl is as about as skittish as they get. You want to frighten her off? She'll never step foot in here again if you're not careful."

We both headed to the locker room to change out of our gym clothes.

"How was I supposed to be any more careful than I was? It's a legality that we actually need that form signed, asshole. And if she's trying to hide something that she'd have to put on it. I want to know what."

Chip rolled his eyes at me. "I'm sure you want to know all sorts of things about that girl, and the fucking form ain't gonna tell you shit about most of them. Go see her at Marie's tomorrow. Go just before closing and see if she'll sit with you for a while."

"It won't be that easy, and you know it. She's sneaky when she wants to be. You watch, next week's class will be here before I get anywhere near her, or her form."

With a smirk, Chip headed out. I silently followed, flipping off the lights and locking the side door as I went. We both knew I was right. I hadn't even kissed this chick and she was driving me nuts.

Jumping on my bike, I didn't go straight back to the clubhouse. I needed to clear my head so made my way out of town for a ride. There was something about having the wind in my face and the feel of my Harley beneath me that helped soothe me. Always had.

Chapter 5

Zara

"You've been dodging that man all week. What happened?"

I was helping Marie close up after Mac finally left. He'd come in every day near closing since I went to the gym last Thursday, and waited for me. Each time I avoided him until he gave up and left.

"I went to his class like you wanted. But I can't go back. They want me to fill out paperwork. They'll recognize my name."

I turned to face Marie when I felt her glare heat up my back.

"We went over this. You want them to know who you are, remember? Would you like me to call Scout? Explain to him what's going on."

My eyes widened and the blood drained from my face. "You can't do that!"

"Okay, calm down. It was just a suggestion. I wouldn't do it without your permission, sugar. You know that."

I shook my head to clear it. "I'm not ready to trust them. That shooting wasn't my first run in with asshole bikers. It's not easy to get over a lifetime of hatred for them."

Her face softened and I winced. Of course, she knew exactly what I was talking about. After what happened to her and her friend, I was kind of surprised she'd even serve a biker.

"Not all clubs are the same, Zara. But I can see that even if I tell you until I'm blue in the face, you still won't take my word for it, so I'll leave it be. But you think about it. Not many men would do what Mac has done this past week. To keep coming back in every day to see you, only for you to shut him down every time. There's another class tonight. Maybe you should go chat with him." I started to speak but she held her palm up. "Not another word. I won't bring it up again, I promise."

We finished up closing in silence. I mean, what could either of us say? We both knew the facts. And I knew I was being a coward. I walked out to my car and got in. I probably should have gotten rid of it, since it was registered to me, but I couldn't afford to buy a new one, and this one was paid for. Besides, I didn't drive around much, only between the motel and work, so hopefully no one who was looking for me saw my car.

With a sigh, I cranked the engine and headed out of the parking lot. This constantly looking over my shoulder and worrying about getting caught was wearing me out. I wasn't sure how much longer I could live like this. When I was at work, I was occupied and mostly okay, but once I got back to my motel room, my narcolepsy was worse than ever. I'd upped my meds but I was still so fucking tired all the time.

I was nearly at the motel when I saw him. A lone black Harley coming toward me on the road. It passed without slowing down, but when I looked in my rear view mirror I saw his back. The familiar large hammer on his vest chilled my blood. *Fuck.* They were here in town. Did they know I was here for sure? Did he recognize my car? I kept an eye on him until he turned down a side street. Was he turning around to follow me?

Before I could talk myself out of it, I turned toward the gym. Mac just became the lesser of the evils I could risk trusting. Tiredness tried to pull me down and I began to do what I'd done a hundred times before, when I've needed to fight off my Narcolepsy. I started to alternatively slap and pinch my thigh to keep myself awake. I had to hit or pinch hard enough to trigger some adrenaline into my system. It wasn't the first time I'd had to do it. My thighs were often covered in bruises from it, but it was better than falling asleep at the wheel and crashing.

I made it to the gym's parking lot but couldn't find the energy to get out of my car. I needed to sleep desperately. Fuck, I hoped I was going to be safe in my car here, because there wasn't anything I could do to stop what was about to happen. I hit the door locks and tilted my seat back. Then, within seconds I was out.

Mac

I was about to change out of my street clothes when my phone rang. Seeing it was Keys calling, I answered right away. With a class due to start in half an hour, I knew the man would be watching the CCTVs that monitored the outside of the gym, paranoid bastard that he was.

"Hey, brother. What's up?"

"Shit's going down in your parking lot, brother. Get moving, and not alone. I'll tell you more after you start moving."

Pulling the phone away from my mouth, I bolted out of the locker room and glanced around. I'd never been more thankful to see Taz not far away.

"Yo! Taz. Need you now. Move out." The man was instantly on alert and came jogging over.

"What's up?"

"Trouble in the parking lot."

Without another word, he followed as I lifted the phone back up.

"Make it quick, Keys."

"Looks like your girl, Zara, pulled up about ten minutes ago. She's still in her cage and some scumbag is trying to break into her ride."

The MC was worse than a fucking high school for gossip. I'd barely spoken to the girl and the club had us paired off already. And how the fuck did Keys know what her car looked like? Something to worry about later. If Zara was in trouble, whoever was after her was about to learn why Marines have the reputation they do.

"Recognize him?"

"Not from the CCTV feed. Little shit's wearing a black hoodie. Original all the way, this fucker. Arrow's on his way over with a cage to bring him back here, but he's not gonna arrive in time to save your girl."

"Gotcha. Call you back after."

I'd thought all the cameras Keys insisted on installing around the gym had been overkill, but now I was grateful for them—along with the fact that Keys was paranoid enough to be watching the damn things tonight.

"Zara's out there in her car with some fucker trying to break into it. No idea what condition she's in. I'll handle Zara, you keep the bastard detained until Arrow arrives with a cage."

Taz was all business when he gave me a quick "Yes, sir."

We both slipped out the side door and silently made our way over to Zara's little, faded blue hatchback, sticking to the shadows. That thing was as old as the hills. No way would someone be trying to steal it, especially when there was a woman inside the damn thing. As we got closer I could see Zara was either sleeping or unconscious. Her seat was tilted back, so I was hoping she was sleeping. I couldn't see any blood on her, but that didn't mean she was unharmed. Especially considering she'd parked her car at an angle over two spaces.

The bastard had his back to us and wasn't paying any attention to his surroundings. *So fucking stupid.* And a mistake that made it clear this guy had no training. Taz moved in from his left, as I moved in from his right, getting the idiot's attention.

"What the fuck do you think you're doing?"

With a curse, the bastard turned to sprint away, but Taz was there waiting for him and with a hand wrapped around his throat, threw the fucker roughly down to the ground before he knew what hit him. Knowing Taz could handle the bastard with his eyes closed, I turned my focus to Zara. What the fuck was wrong with her? I grabbed my Leatherman off my belt, extra glad I hadn't changed into my gym gear before Keys called, and got to work on the lock.

A few excruciating seconds later I had the door open and reached in for her.

"Zara?"

She moaned softly and raised a hand to her face. Relief washed through me. Whatever the fuck had happened, it hadn't killed her.

"She alive?"

"Yeah, she's waking up now. I'm going to take her inside, make sure she's not hurt. You okay to wait for Arrow? He shouldn't—"

I stopped talking when the man in question came through the parking lot in one of the club's vans. One with blacked-out back windows.

"You go with him, Taz. Keep me updated on what happens."

"How about I stay here with you, and watch your back? That way Arrow can talk to me and you can focus on your girl?"

I winced. *Fuck.* Every so often I forgot it was more than just me, Eagle and Taz now. That I could, in fact, trust my MC brothers as much as my Marine ones.

"Of course. Shit. I'm not thinking straight."

I watched as Taz hauled the guy off the ground, then tossed him against the side of the van. Arrow wrapped some duct tape around his wrists and ankles, then Taz threw the guy in the back.

"Let me know what he has to say, yeah?"

"Of course, brother. Let me know what happened with her. We'll make sure he pays."

I left Taz and Arrow to their conversation and turned back to Zara. She was rubbing a palm over the back of her neck as she adjusted her seat so she was sitting up normally.

"C'mon, Zara. Let me take you inside."

She frowned up at me, looking dazed. Slowly, so she knew what I was intending to do, I slid an arm behind her back, and the other one under her knees before lifting her against me. Damn, but she was light. I needed to see to it that she ate more. I mentally shook my head. I was thinking crazy. This was the woman who'd avoided me like I had the plague all week. Like she'd let me care for her like that?

Leaving Taz to deal with locking up her car, I strode back to the gym's side entrance. One of the prospects that had been working out stood there, ready to open the door for me.

"Thanks, man. Can you go open the office door for me?"

He rushed off to do my bidding and I followed behind him, wanting to get Zara away from public exposure as soon as possible.

Once in the office, I kicked the door shut before I sat down on the couch with her on my lap. She was still not fully awake. Nor had she made a sound, other than that first groan. I gently ran my fingers through her hair, brushing over her skull to check for bumps, thinking she might have hit her head on something earlier and have a concussion.

A shiver went through her and a smile tugged at my lips as she snuggled against me. It was only a precious few moments before she pulled back, but it was enough to have my whole being in tune with her. And my cock as hard as a rock. I forced my brain to focus. She might be injured. I ran my gaze over her again, still not seeing any obvious injuries. In the next few seconds, she seemed to wake up fully and slipped from my lap to stand.

"Where am I? What happened?"

She started to pace nervously, chewing her thumb nail as she moved.

"You're safe, Zara. Everything's okay. You're in the office at the gym."

Dropping her hand away from her mouth, she turned to look me in the eye. The uncertainty and fear in her gaze had me twitching to pull her back onto my lap. I was so screwed. I'd barely spoken to this girl and she had me in knots.

"How did I get here from my car? I was in my car..."

Pushing aside all my shit, I focused back on the issue at hand. "You were passed out in your car and some bastard was trying to break into it. We stopped him, then I brought you in here because I thought you might be hurt. Are you injured in some way? Maybe hit your head earlier? Do you know why you passed out?"

My temper flared as she lifted a palm to wave off my questions as though they were nothing, then she came and sat beside me. "I have narcolepsy, so I often fall asleep without much warning. I wasn't hurt."

I jerked a little in shock. Holy shit! That was the last thing I expected her to say.

"I've never dealt with someone who has that condition, so I've got no idea what you need. You have to tell me what I should do for you. Medicine? Hospital?"

She shook her head with a small chuckle. "No hospital, and if I take meds now I'll be wide awake for the next eight hours. Don't worry, I'll be fine. I could use a drink of water though, if you have it? And where's my handbag?"

"Water and your bag. Right. I'll go round those up for you." I gave her knee a quick squeeze as I rose and headed out of the office to grab her a bottle from the fridge in the front. As I moved, I focused on calming my heart rate down. Zara was fine. Nothing had happened to her. She'd just had a narcolepsy episode, or was it called, an attack? Who the fuck cared. All that mattered was that she was okay now.

I was nearly back to the office when Taz came out through the door with a frown on his face and his phone to his ear. I went to brush past, but Taz grabbed my arm and shook his head.

"Just let me give Zara this. I'll be right back."

Wondering what the fuck was going on, I quickly handed Zara the bottle. She was already looking better, getting a little color back in her cheeks. She was nursing her handbag, which I'd forgotten she'd asked for. Good thing Taz had guessed she'd want it.

"I just need to have a quick chat with Taz. I won't be long."

With a nod and a quiet thank you, she took the water and I left her alone again. Taz pocketed his phone as I approached.

"That little punk was chasing a bounty from the Iron Hammers. Don't suppose you ever got your girl to fill out that paperwork, huh?"

With my hands on my hips I frowned at one of my best friends. "Well, no. I didn't. Not yet. But what the fuck has that got to do with this?"

Taz took a few steps away from the office, indicating I follow. Of course I did. I wanted to know what the hell was going on, and Zara was as safe as she could be inside that office. No one would dare go in there without checking with either Chip or me first.

"Zara is her middle name, mate. Wanna guess what her first and last ones are?"

I sucked in a breath, everything suddenly making sense. Why she wouldn't go near a biker, why she wouldn't fill out paperwork for me. I ran a palm over my freshly shaven skull.

"Fuck me. She's that witness, isn't she? Claire Flynn."

Chapter 6

Zara

I winced as I overheard Taz speak to Mac about my would-be attacker. I'd been right, the Iron Hammers had found me. I gave myself only a few minutes to feel more like myself, more stable on my feet. Then, when Mac still hadn't returned, I took that as a bad sign for my future. Was he out there planning with someone to hand me over and get the money?

Tears burned my eyes. I'd come here to talk to him about helping me, but now I couldn't be sure what he'd do. Not with a bounty now up for grabs. How much had those bastards put on my head? Would it be enough to tempt Mac to hand me over?

I had to leave. Get out of here and run. I'd been saving for a rental deposit, so I had money stashed back in my motel room. I'd go grab that, then just drive. I had no idea where, but maybe if I got out of Texas, I'd be okay.

With a deep breath, I grabbed the keys out of my bag before I slung it over my shoulder. I crept over to the door and slowly opened it enough to look out. Mac's back was toward me and Taz was facing him, but fortunately, Mac's body was large enough to block the other man's line of sight to me.

As quietly as I could, I slipped out of the office, then through the side door. Once I was outside, I sprinted to my car and got in. Jamming the key into the ignition, I was all set to go. Except the damn thing wouldn't start. *Fuck!* I tried turning the key again and again, but it refused to even turn over. My eyes burned as I let my head fall forward against the top of the steering wheel. What the fuck was I supposed to do now?

I rolled my face to the side when I heard the building's door open, wincing when Mac stepped out into the sun. My heart sped up at how good he looked as he walked with powerful steps toward me. He was in jeans and a black wife-beater with his leather vest over it, and looked good enough to lick. I was so screwed.

He opened the door before he leaned his arms against the car roof to put his face down closer to mine. My gaze was stuck on the way the ink on his arms looked as his muscles flexed and moved.

"You shouldn't be out here on your own, Zara. Or do you prefer Claire?"

Forcing myself to stop ogling the man, I winced as I spoke. "Zara. I prefer Zara."

What else could I say? I couldn't tell him I was afraid he'd sell me out, or that I was so fucking confused and scared I didn't know what to do anymore.

Taz came up and stood next to Mac. "Scout said to take her to the clubhouse. Safest place for her at this point."

"You going to be a good girl and follow me? Or do I need to drive us there?"

"I can't follow you. It won't start."

"Yeah, that was me. Pop the hood and I'll fix it."

Mac chuckled at Taz admitting he'd disabled my car somehow. I was both pissed off that he'd done it, and impressed he'd anticipated me running. Although, I guess that wouldn't be so hard to figure out. The one thing they knew about me for sure was that when I'd been put in a corner in Galveston, I'd ran.

"I'll follow."

I nearly groaned. Even I could hear the defeat in my voice.

"If you change your mind and take off, I will find you."

I closed my eyes and took a deep breath. "Yeah, I figured that out already."

With a nod he strode off, leaving me with Taz. Before he could say anything, I popped the hood and he lifted it up but didn't do anything. I was about to ask why when the loud rumble of a Harley starting up filled the air. I rolled my eyes when Taz leaned down and fiddled with something in the engine. Of course he'd waited for Mac to be ready before he fixed my car.

My heart sank. I had no way of escaping these two, and once I was at the clubhouse I wouldn't be escaping there, either. Not until someone permitted me to leave. I blinked back tears as I shut my door and turned the key to start my car. Taz dropped the hood and I slowly backed out before I followed Mac down the road.

I tried to stay positive, to remember what Marie had said about the club being protective, especially of women. But I couldn't be sure if they would be swayed by the bounty now on my head. How much had the Iron Hammers decided I was worth?

After following Mac through a set of huge, open gates, I jerked to a stop as my heart started to race for an entirely different reason than earlier. Of course, I should have expected the dozen or so Harleys parked in a neat row in front of an older, but well-maintained, multi-story brick building.

"Please don't let this be a mistake."

I had no clue where to leave my car, so I stayed where I was until Mac parked his bike and pointed me over to the opposite side of the yard. When I saw two other vehicles already parked, I lined my car up with them before I got out. I still wasn't sold on this being a good idea. By now I was sure everyone in that building knew I had a bounty on my head. They probably knew how much, too, which was more than I did. I moved to the back of my car and leaned against the familiar metal and folded my arms over my chest.

There was a young guy, barely legal, just outside the front door, who gave me a smirk but didn't move or say anything. Not that I'd have heard him from where I was. The land this place was on was huge, probably double the size of the small park that had been opposite the house where I grew up.

Mac, making his way over, caught my attention. No doubt about it, the man knew how to swagger just right. I wiped my hand over my mouth to make sure I hadn't drooled as he got closer.

"No one will hurt you, bunny. You're safe here."

I frowned. He'd never called me anything other than my name before. Was bunny some kind of pet name or a joke? What was he playing at? Suddenly it was all too much to process and I figured I'd just be honest with the man.

"I don't understand any of this. And I'm scared."

His expression softened as he moved in closer, near enough I could feel the heat from his body against mine. He cupped my face in his large palms. His hands were warm and rough, and they felt so good I struggled to contain my moan.

"I know you're scared. You've got good reason to be. But not of what's in there. When you ran, you came here to Bridgewater. Why?"

I nuzzled a little against his skin. I couldn't help it. "Because my neighbor told me the Charon MC hates the Iron Hammer MC, and that the Iron Hammers don't come near Bridgewater."

"Exactly. So, why are you scared now?"

I squeezed my eyes closed. "Because money changes people. I didn't realize until I overheard you talking before how badly they wanted me."

"Look at me, Zara." He stayed silent, just gently holding my face, until with a sigh, I relented and opened my eyes. His ice-blue gaze was hard and intense and I couldn't look away. "No amount of money is worth a human life. Especially yours. I promise I'll protect you. The whole club will."

I opened my mouth to argue that he couldn't make that promise but he cut me off by covering mine with his. Instantly, my world turned upside down. I moaned as his lips caressed mine, gently testing his welcome. Needing more of his heat, I ran my fingers up his chest, over every bulge of muscle. When I wrapped my arms around his neck, he broke the kiss to lift me away from the car and up against him. My legs went around his waist automatically, which put his very healthy erection right between my thighs.

"Fuck, baby. I need more of you."

I couldn't remember a time when I'd felt as protected and content as I did with him holding me with one hand under my ass, and the other around my upper back. I leaned in, face upturned, to meet his next kiss. When he ran the tip of his tongue over my lower lip, I answered by opening my mouth.

Apparently that was like waving a red flag in front of him. With a growl, he crushed me tighter against him as he deepened the kiss. Thoughts swirled together and I could do nothing but enjoy the ride as he devoured my mouth. Arousal spiraled through me, growing hotter until I started to grind myself against his erection.

"Get a room!"

Those three words were like a bucket of ice water. What was I doing? Heat rushed over my face and I shoved against Mac.

"Oh, shit. Mac, put me down. I can't believe we just did that."

With a chuckle, he loosened his grip enough I could put my feet back on the ground, but he didn't let me go.

"Don't be embarrassed, bunny. I guarantee you things a lot more heated than our kiss have happened in this parking lot."

I shook my head. "I'm not that sorta girl."

"Yeah, I caught that when it took me over a week to get you to say more than hi to me."

A fresh flush of heat rushed over my cheeks and I turned my face away from him, hoping he wouldn't see it. He ran his knuckles gently down my cheek and along my jaw before he trailed his fingers down until he had my hand in his.

"C'mon, let's get inside. We'll chat with Scout, then I'll get you settled for the night."

I wanted to ask where he thought I was going to be sleeping, but before I worked up the nerve, he had me across the yard and was opening the door. Deep male voices and laughter filtered out into the night, making me nervous all over again. *Please let this not be a mistake.*

Mac

Fuck, but Zara was adorable when she was flustered. And kissing her had been sexy as sin. I couldn't wait till I had her all to myself later tonight. Because if that woman was staying at the clubhouse, she was going to be sleeping with me in my fucking bed.

I pulled her through the door behind me, then tucked her in against my side so I could wrap my arm around her. Being just after dinner time on a Thursday, the place wasn't too busy yet, but considering how on edge Zara was, I didn't want to risk her trying to bolt out the door.

"Good, you're here. Follow me."

Scout's gruff voice had her stiffening against me, so I ran my palm up and down her arm as I guided her over to the hallway and down to Scout's office. He waited for us to pass him before he followed us in and shut the door. I sat on the couch and pulled Zara down next to me as Scout settled behind his desk.

"So, ah, I'm not sure what the fuck to call you. Zara? Claire?"

I'd called Zara bunny earlier because she'd been so shy and hard to corner, and she was really living up to that right now. She looked down and licked her lips before taking a deep breath and answering Scout's simple, harmless question as though he'd asked her for some kind of national secret she was guarding.

"Um, I think I'm going to stick with Zara for now."

"Right. So, Zara, clearly you're the little waitress the Iron Hammers have such a hard-on for. Care to fill me in on why?"

I did my best not to grin with pride as her shoulders straightened before she lifted her chin and stared the club president square in the eyes. Arrow had been right about her having some serious inner strength, when she wasn't hiding it away. I needed to help her use it more often. As cute as she was all meek and shy, it wasn't the real her.

"I'm quite sure you know precisely why they want me."

Scout frowned at her, clearly not impressed with her answer.

"I've only heard whispers, darlin'. How about you give me the facts?"

With a huff, she stood in a rush and started pacing, chewing her thumbnail for a moment, like she had back at the gym, before she dropped her hand and started talking.

"Two and a half weeks ago, I was at work, waiting tables, when the Iron Hammers shot the place up. I'd been coming back inside from delivering an order when a big biker came at me. I think he must have been running from the Iron Hammers already. Anyhow, when the bullets started flying, he got shot and that pushed him into me. I went down with him covering me."

Scout held up a palm. "Why did you stay down and not try to get out from under him?"

When she started clenching then stretching out her fingers, I wanted to pull her into my lap so badly. I ground my jaw to keep myself from reaching for her. I knew if I did that Scout would kick me out of the room. And she'd be pissed at me for the move, too.

"Well, the guy was fucking huge and weighed a ton. But that didn't really matter. I have cataplexy. When I experience intense situations, or emotions, my muscles fail and I go down. Strangely enough, being shot at was enough to trigger an attack."

Fucking hell, the poor girl. So not only did she suffer narcolepsy, she had this cataplexy illness on top of it? I rubbed a hand over my shaven scalp, kind of wishing I had some hair to tug on to vent some of my frustration as she continued to speak.

"When I have one of these attacks, I can't move at all. Can't even blink. But I can hear and I can feel. When the shooters came into the cafe they rolled the guy off me, and since I was covered in blood and didn't move when they kicked me, they assumed I was dead. They talked—"

"Who? What names did you hear?"

Scout was now sitting forward in his seat, completely focused on what Zara was saying. I was listening too, but for the most part I was trying to resist the urge to grab her and run. She was still pacing and looking so heartbreakingly fragile. Clearly the burst of sass she'd given Scout before had been all she had in her for now.

"Um, Sledge spoke with Chuck and Tic. They mentioned the name Frank, that he wouldn't be happy. I couldn't figure out why until I saw him later. Frank turned out to be a cop."

"About that—why'd you talk to the cops? I assume you grew up in Galveston, so you know not to do that shit."

I winced when she slapped herself on the thigh. Hard.

"It's the cataplexy. I was still coming out of it and my mind was hazy. A young cop decided to take advantage and started questioning me. Trust me, if I'd been in my right mind, I never would have said a word."

Now she was pinching herself as she paced. Every few seconds she'd either pinch or slap her thigh. And she wasn't messing around. I was sure she was leaving bruises.

"Zara? What the fuck are you doing? That's gotta be painful."

She glanced over at me with wide eyes. "Ah, I'm keeping myself awake. I've had a stressful afternoon and I didn't get enough sleep earlier in the car."

Scout stood and came around the desk toward her. "Is that part of that cataplexy thing?"

She shook her head, "No, this is a narcolepsy thing."

"Fuck me. Mac, get her out of here. Come back once you get her settled."

Zara stumbled as Scout growled his words and I jumped to get to her before she went down. She leaned heavily against me when I wrapped an arm around her, so I scooped her up against my chest before she tried to hurt herself again.

"Grab the door for me?"

Scout didn't look happy, but the man opened the door and let me pass. I headed directly for the stairs and by the time I reached the top, she'd passed out against me. This woman was going to keep me on my toes, that's for fucking sure.

I grabbed a passing prospect to unlock and open my door for me, then I was laying her on my bed. I closed and locked the door before I turned back to her. Fuck me, this wasn't quite what I had in mind when I'd said I wanted her sleeping in my bed tonight. I roughly scrubbed both palms over my head before I moved to her. I carefully took her shoes and socks off, before standing back up. Should I take her pants off? She'd be more comfortable, and I really wanted to check her thighs for injury. I was fairly certain she'd be pissed at me in the morning for it, but she needed a good sleep more than I needed her not to yell at me.

Carefully, I undid the button and zipper, then rolled them down her legs. I tried not to jostle her too much, but I had to move her around a fair bit to get her pants down. I didn't look at the flesh I revealed until I had the material off and on the floor. Then I moved my gaze to her thighs.

"Fucking hell."

The whispered curse slipped free as I very gently traced a fingertip over the black and blue of her thigh. Clearly she hurt herself like that often. Shaking my head to clear the image, I pulled the covers over her and tucked her in. Before I forced myself to leave her be, I pressed a light kiss to her temple.

"I'll be back soon, bunny. The door will be locked. You're safe here."

I had no idea if she could hear me, or if this sleep was due to narcolepsy or cataplexy. Either way, I felt better saying the words.

When I got back down to the ground level, I found Scout in the main room nursing a drink. Whiskey, by the looks of it.

"She all right?"

"Not real sure. She's comfortable and asleep, that's all I can tell you."

"You claiming her, then?"

I eyed off his drink. "Let me grab one of those for myself, then I'll answer that."

It didn't take long for the prospect manning the bar to hand over my own poison, then I headed back over to the table where Scout was sitting. I took a healthy swallow before I answered Scout's question.

"I want her, like I've never wanted a woman before. Not sure I'm ready to commit to making her my old lady just yet, though."

He gave me a nod. "Don't want to rush into that shit. But this girl is in need of some serious protecting. You up for that?"

"Yeah. As fucked up as it sounds, that makes her even more appealing to me."

In that moment I was tempted to tell Scout about my sister. He'd understand, he wouldn't judge me for the call I made to avenge her. Maybe.

I threw back the rest of my drink.

"You know what? I don't like the idea of her up there alone. Mind if we discuss the rest of this shit in the morning?"

He gave me a knowing look and a nod. "Sure, brother. It can wait. Especially since we now have her locked down here for the night."

I didn't say another word, just got up and headed back to my room where my woman was sleeping in my fucking bed. Pity sleep was all either of us were going to be doing tonight by the looks of things.

Totally not what I'd had in mind earlier when I'd vowed she'd be in my bed tonight.

Chapter 7

Zara

In the past three years, I'd woken up to find myself in all sorts of odd places. But this had to be the first time I woke up warm and comfortable in a strange bed with a thick, masculine arm resting over my stomach. I was lying on my back so I could easily trail my gaze from those callused, work-roughened fingers, up a lightly haired forearm to a beautifully colored-in bicep. Mac had tattoos from his elbow to up over his shoulder. My fingers twitched with my need to trace the patterns, but I was pretty sure that would wake him up and ruin my chance to really look at him.

He was lying on his side, so I couldn't see much of his chest, but the bit I could see showed solid, defined pecs lightly dusted with hair. I quietly sighed when my gaze ran over his perfect six pack. When I noticed the track pants covering his lower half, a smile pulled at my lips. Mac was such a gentleman. *A biker gentleman.* Not only had he worn pants to bed, but he'd also slept on top of the covers. I flicked my gaze up to his face, soft in sleep. His jaw had at least a few days' worth of stubble on it, while his scalp only had a tiny amount. I guessed he must shave his head every day, while his face only saw a razor once or maybe twice a week. The look worked for him. Roughly sexy, and all man. I loved how he'd left his chest hair natural too. So many men waxed themselves smooth. But men weren't meant to be like that, they were meant to be rough around the edges. At least, in my opinion they were.

Another sigh escaped me and his arm tightened, pulling me closer to him.

"Like what you see, bunny?"

Busted. Somehow in the quiet of the morning, I didn't feel embarrassed at being caught. And if he was awake, I could give in to touching him. I rolled to my side and began to run a fingertip over the swirls in his tattoos. His upper arms were silky smooth and rippled under my touch.

"Why have you started calling me bunny?"

"Because you get all timid, are incredibly hard to corner, but when you do get cornered, then you run like a rabbit. You didn't answer my question."

"Yeah, I like what I see." I ran my palm down his arm before moving to touch his ribs. There was a jagged scar across them. "How'd you get that? It looks nasty."

"I was in the Marines for sixteen years. I've got a lot more than that one scar."

I nodded against the pillow. I bet he did. It made sense he'd been in the military. The smooth quiet way he moved, the way he saw everything. Speaking of work...

"What time is it?"

He rolled away from me to glance over his shoulder before he rolled back.

"Still early, just past five. You always wake up this early?"

I shrugged a shoulder. "I don't really have a normal when it comes to sleep. You?"

"Not normally awake this early anymore, but I can't sleep when I have a beautiful woman eating me up with her gaze."

I chuckled. "Such a charmer."

"Hmm."

He moved over me, rolling me onto my back so he covered my body with his. Even with the bedding between us, he felt good on top of me. I palmed his cheeks and drew him down closer, and he didn't need any more encouragement. He took my mouth with his, branding me with a powerful kiss. When I started moaning, he moved from my mouth to my jaw where he nipped and kissed up to my ear.

"I need more of you."

"Please."

I knew this was crazy and probably a mistake, but he made me feel alive. It had been so long since I'd been with a man. I'd been too busy caring for Mom, then too busy trying to learn how to live with my conditions for a relationship, and the odd one-night stand I'd managed to fit in never did much for me. I desperately wanted to feel something, anything.

A gasp tore from me when he moved fast as lightning to stand next to the bed. He tossed the covers off me and pulled me from the mattress until I stood in front of him.

"You took my pants off last night?"

"They didn't look comfortable to sleep in, so yeah, I took 'em off."

His hands slid over my hips and up my ribs, taking my shirt with them. He didn't stop until the material was over my head and off.

He groaned a masculine, gravelly sound. "You are so fucking sexy, bunny."

I felt sexy with him staring at me like he was, with so much heat in his gaze. I was very glad I put on my matching lacy black bra and panties yesterday. I moved forward until I was pressed against Mac's hard, hot body.

At five feet five, I wasn't a short woman, but compared to Mac's six feet three, I felt like I was.

He delved his fingers into my hair, holding me still when I nipped along his collarbone. I ran my palms down his sides, loving how his muscles rippled under my touch. I hooked my thumbs into the waistband of his track pants and lowered them an inch, teasing him. Moving my mouth, I kissed and nipped my way down his chest, and he loosened his hold as I moved. A groan vibrated his torso as I left a trail of wet kisses down his center.

Once I landed on my knees, I ran my nose up the side of his very impressive erection. Damn, the man was huge everywhere. His grip tightened in my hair and forced me to look at him.

"You do this, you know where we're gonna end up, don't you? If you don't want me to fuck you, this, right here, is your last chance to stop."

A tremor ran through my body and heat rushed from my core, further dampening my panties.

"I'm sure, babe."

He continued to keep my face turned to his, his hot, blue irises locked onto mine, even as I pulled his pants down, shoving them, and helping take them all the way off as he lifted each foot. His thick, hard erection sprung free, the head tapping against my cheek. I licked my lips, desperate for a taste of him, but unable to reach him until he loosened his hold on my hair.

With a growl, he took one hand from my hair and gripped his dick. With the other, he guided my movements, completely controlling me.

"Open that pretty little mouth wide, bunny."

I rested my palms on his thighs as he fed his dick into my mouth. I ran my tongue around the head, groaning when his taste exploded over my senses. He pushed deeper in, his whole body tensing the more of him I took. I was surprised at how turned on I was getting, being controlled like this. It was hot, thrilling... then suddenly it was too much. He was too big and I couldn't breathe. He pulled back instantly, before I could truly panic.

"Fuck, that's good. Again. Breathe through your nose, take me a little further. I wanna feel your throat around me."

My throat? I'd never liked giving head before, I'd certainly never even attempted to deep throat anyone. I'd gone down on a couple of boys in high school but it wasn't something I'd enjoyed. *Or known how to do.* With Mac guiding me, controlling it, and filling me with him, it was fucking perfect. He pressed into my mouth again, and like he instructed, I focused on breathing through my nose. The head of his dick touched something that made me gag and again, he instantly pulled out a little.

My eyes watered but they were still locked onto his gaze. Flames burned behind his eyes. He was loving this. Hell, I was loving this. I couldn't quite believe that I was, but this was totally getting me hotter than I'd ever been before. My body shook with arousal and my eyes continued to water as he kept thrusting deep into my mouth.

Mac

Holy fucking shit! Zara had the hottest damn mouth I'd ever been in. I thought kissing her was sexy as fuck, but watching her swallow my cock put that shit to shame. She'd stopped gagging on me and was deep throating me like a fucking pro on each stroke. Her eyes were wet but she didn't take her focus off mine for a moment. The green in her hazel irises had grown stronger, the color so unusual and beautiful.

On my next thrust in, the little tease swallowed and that was it. I was barely holding off, but I was not coming down her throat this first time. I pulled her all the way off me and grinned when she moaned and frowned up at me.

"Next time I'll let you push me over the edge with that wicked mouth of yours." I ran my thumb over her lower lip. "You'd swallow me down, wouldn't you, Zara? You'd fucking take everything I gave you, right?" She snuck her tongue out and licked at my thumb as she continued to gaze up at me, looking all sweet and innocent. She wouldn't be either of those things for long. Not if I had any say in the matter.

Keeping my hand tight in her red-blonde hair, I gripped her elbow with the other and helped her to stand. As soon as she was on her feet, I pulled one half of her bra down, so one of her tits was pushed up for my view. Her nipple was already rock-hard as I tweaked it and gave it a tug.

"Take off your bra, I need you naked."

I lowered my mouth to kiss and suck at her neck as she reached behind her back and unclipped the black lace. I moved lower, until I could get one of those hard nipples deep in my mouth. As I tongued and suckled her, I kneaded the other breast and tweaked her nipple with my fingers. My other hand smoothed down her belly and over her panties. Fuck me, she was soaked. The material was wet to the touch.

I ripped myself away and quickly lifted her, tossing her back on the bed. Before she could catch her breath, I had her panties off. With a palm on each thigh, I spread her wide for me. Glistening. Her pussy was smooth and wet and she was squirming on my bed.

Mine. All fucking mine.

"My turn, bunny. I need to get a good, long taste of you."

I crawled onto the bed and lowered myself down until I could put my mouth on her. The first lick had me moaning in bliss. I moved my palms under her ass to hold her up for me to get deeper into her. Then I set about making a meal out of my woman. She tasted like heaven, and smelled like jasmine and sunshine. The first time I thrust my tongue in deep she shrieked. When I looked up at her, her head was thrown back, her tits thrust up and her hands were fisted in the bedding. *Fucking perfect.*

Watching her closely, I worked her body until she was on the edge. I kept her there for a minute, loving the rosy blush that spread over her chest and face as she panted and thrashed her head against the sheets. When I was sure she was about to start cursing me, I thrust two fingers into her deeply to rub over her g-spot as I suckled on her clit. She blew apart with a scream an instant later. With a palm on each hip, I kept her thrashing body pinned to the mattress as I lapped up every bit of cream she gave me.

Now this was the perfect way to wake up in the morning. I crawled up over her body, planning on grabbing a condom and sliding in deep when I noticed she wasn't moving. Like, not even twitching. Her eyes were closed and she lay dead still. What the fuck? Frowning, I pressed fingers against her throat, relief washing through me at her pulse that was still pounding from the orgasm. What she'd said to Scout earlier ran through my mind *"When I experience intense situations, or emotions, my muscles fail and I go down."* Was this a cataplexy attack?

"Zara? Can you hear me? C'mon, wake up for me, babe."

I stroked my fingers over her face, learning every dip and rise of her features, as I lay beside her, wondering what the hell I should be doing for her. About thirty seconds later, she stirred, moaning and rubbing her thighs together as she rolled toward me.

"Fuck, Zara. That scared the shit out of me. Are you all right? I didn't hurt you, did I?"

She rubbed her face against my chest. "Take it as a compliment. You're so good, you left me paralyzed."

I chuckled, despite myself. "That's not funny."

"Sure it is. Well, it is if you still want me. If that totally ruined the mood and your desire to sleep with me, then no, it's not funny."

"Sleep with you? We did that already. What I want now is to slide my cock deep in that sweet pussy of yours and fuck you hard."

She blushed and ducked her head back against my chest, making me smile.

"C'mon, bunny. You swear all the time, you trying to tell me you're not comfortable with some dirty talk?"

She shrugged. "I don't mind when you do it."

"Yeah, well, I'm gonna need you to do it too. So, how about you have another go at telling me what you want me to do to you now you're back in the land of the living?"

I rolled her onto her back and moved to cover her body with mine once more, sliding my still rock-hard cock over her slick, bare mound.

"I want." She paused to lick her lips and swallow. "I want you to fuck me."

I grinned. That wasn't good enough and she knew it. "Yeah, I caught that. But with what and where? Be specific, bunny. Dirty talk is supposed to be dirty and hot. And detailed. It's also very fucking sexy."

That blush of hers reddened her cheeks and her gaze flickered away from mine. Then her chest rose and fell with a deep breath before she focused her gaze back on mine. I raised an eyebrow at her.

"I-want-you-to-slide-your-cock-into-my-pussy-and-f uck-me."

Laughing, I leaned down to kiss her lips. She'd rushed the words out so fast, I barely caught them. But I had a feeling it was as good as I was going to get for the moment. I stretched over to grab a condom out of the drawer of my nightstand, then moved to kneel between her thighs.

"I can see we're gonna have to practice a lot to get you comfortable with saying what you want from me."

I opened the foil square and rolled the latex over my cock, slowing down when she started biting her lip as she watched me. Everything this woman did was a turn-on. Pressing a hand against the mattress beside her shoulder, I leaned over her. I gave each of her nipples a lick and tug before I moved to take her mouth again. Her hands gripped my shoulders, and when I started to press into her, she dug her fingers in deep. Deep enough to leave her marks on me, I was sure.

Her pussy was slick and tight. *So fucking perfect.* She whimpered and tensed up as I gently thrust into her. I paused to eat at her mouth until she relaxed enough that I could get all the way inside her. When her heat surrounded the full length of my cock, I rested my forehead against hers with a groan.

"So fucking good, bunny."

"Uh huh."

She tried to grind up against me and I took the hint. I lifted up, putting my weight on that one arm so I could torment her tits with the other, while I thrust deep into her pussy. After a minute, it wasn't enough. I needed to get deeper inside her. Pulling out, I flipped her over and lifted her on all fours. She whimpered and shuddered, but before she could voice her displeasure, I thrust back in to her all the way to the hilt. Fuck, that felt good. Better than good. Gripping her hips, I started pounding into her as I watched my cock slide in and out of her.

Chapter 8

Zara

With every thrust, Mac sent my arousal spiraling higher and higher. My elbows started to shake from the effort of holding myself up so I let them collapse. With my head down, Mac hit a whole new bunch of nerves that had me screaming into the pillow. Damn, but this man could fuck like some sort of fertility god.

Then he leaned over my back, wrapping one hand around a breast while the other zeroed in on my clit, which he started to torture as he picked up speed.

"Come for me, Zara. Take me with you."

I didn't stand a chance trying to resist him. Completely over-stimulated, I climaxed like I never had before. My vision blurred as I jerked and thrashed beneath Mac. My foggy mind registered his arms holding me tightly to him as his cock jerked within me when he, too, came hard. My entire body went limp but Mac didn't let me collapse beneath him. Keeping me tucked in against him, he gently rolled to the side, before he loosened his hold and slid from my body. I mentally winced as he did. I hadn't had sex in a long time, and I'd never been taken like he just took me. I was definitely going to be sore today.

Mac's weight lifted from the bed and his footfalls got further distant. An ache started in my chest. Would he really walk away from me now he'd had me? Was I just a notch in his bedpost? My eyes stung with tears just as his hand stroked up my thigh, lifting it up. A warm, wet cloth wiped between my legs and over my upper thighs. Relief poured through me. He hadn't abandoned me, but had gone to get something to clean me up with. *My gentleman-biker.*

When he finished, he tossed the cloth somewhere, then spooned up behind me, pillowing my head on one of his strong biceps. He kissed my shoulder as he ran his fingers lightly over my skin, over my breasts and ribs, down my arm, over my hip. When I could, I turned my face to press a kiss against his arm, running my tongue over his ink.

That got me a growl and a tap on the ass. "Keep that up, I'll be inside you again, and I'm not sure we got time for another round before you need to be at work. What time do you normally start? Or do you want to call in sick and stay in bed with me all day?"

I shuffled over onto my back so I could see his face. He was so beautiful. I palmed his cheek before I ran my short nails through the scruff on his jaw.

"I can't just take a day off to screw around. Marie's had enough waitresses pull that shit with her. Plus, she's been pushing me at you hard for weeks now. She'll be pissed if I don't tell her first that I finally lost the fight."

He leaned down and gave my mouth a quick peck. "You fought well, but we all knew I was going to win you over in the end."

I shook my head on a chuckle. "Well, after this morning, I suspect you fought well enough that I'm now ruined for all other men."

This expression of clear male pride crossed his face. "Good to hear it. You don't ever need to be even thinking about another man again. You're mine and I'll always take care of you."

I glanced over his shoulder at the clock beside the bed.

"Shit! I've got to get moving." I rolled away from Mac and sat on the end of the bed. I searched for my clothes and found them spread around the floor, each item now a wrinkled mess. "Especially since I now need to go back to my place and get changed."

"Sorry about that. I wasn't thinking about your clothes when I took them off you. I'll follow you on my bike, then escort you to Marie's. Until we figure out how to deal with the Iron Hammers, I don't want you going anywhere alone. Okay?"

"Sure."

I wasn't sure what that meant for my living arrangements, but I really needed to get moving so I'd have to worry about that later. My panties were too damp to be comfortable, so I didn't bother with them. My pants felt strange with nothing on underneath and by the groan Mac made, he'd noticed my lack of underwear. After picking up my shirt and bra, I turned to drop them on the bed and stopped still. Mac was standing with his back to me and was pulling jeans up over his bare ass. But it wasn't that he was going commando like me that caught my attention, it was the huge-ass tattoo across his back. The Charon insignia spanned nearly the full width. It wasn't a bad-looking design, as far as MC logos went. A funky looking skull in the center, with a bat wing on one side and a feathered wing on the other. There was a crossbones made out of pistons behind the skull, too. All inked in black and greys, it was quite the statement.

"Keep staring and you'll never get to work."

"Ah, yeah. That's some tattoo."

He drew a tight black t-shirt over his head before reaching for his vest—no, his cut—and putting that on over the top. I turned away and rushed to get my bra and shirt on. I needed to stop ogling him and get my head on straight.

Grabbing my handbag, I ducked into the bathroom that was attached to his room and after using the facilities, did my best to finger comb out my hair. Hopefully it was too early for anyone to be up and around to see me anyway. I took my meds, then went back out to Mac.

"Ready to go?"

"As ready as I can be."

My heart melted a little when he took my hand in the hallway and didn't let go until we were by my car. He gave me a deep kiss, before pulling away with a groan.

"Don't try to lose me, bunny. No more running away from me, okay?"

I rolled my eyes. "Yeah, because running has worked out so well for me so far."

The Iron Hammers had still found me, and he'd well and truly caught me. Yeah, I wasn't going to be trying to run away again anytime soon.

Mac pulled me against him and held me tightly. I rubbed my face against his chest, inhaling his scent deeply.

"How about I just make it so you'll never need to run again?"

That made me chuckle. "No one can promise that. C'mon, I'm already going to be late."

Ten minutes later I pulled up outside the motel and stayed put as I watched Mac ride up behind me. Damn, but he looked hot on that large blue bike of his. Shaking myself free from my daydream, I hopped out and headed up the stairs to my room, certain in the knowledge he'd follow me. I'd just slid the old-school key into the lock when Mac came up behind me, radiating rage.

"Are you fucking kidding me?"

I winced at his volume as I opened the door. Dragging the damn man inside, I closed it before he could utter another word.

"I'm trying to *not* attract attention, remember?"

I hissed the words at him just as his gaze ran over the room and his expression turned even more thunderous.

"You're not staying here."

I frowned, "Why not? I've been here for weeks. I've nearly got enough saved to find something more permanent. It wasn't like I've got a heap of options open to me, Mac."

He spun and prowled towards me, the look on his face making me back up until I hit a wall. He kept coming until he stood a breath away from me, forcing me to look up in order for us to maintain eye contact.

"Now you have another option. While you work today, I'll move all your shit over to the clubhouse. I'd prefer you stay in my room with me, but if you don't want that, you can have your own room."

My mouth dropped open as it took me a moment to formulate a response to his demand. "So because I let you control me in bed once, you think you can tell me where I'm going to live?"

With a growl he dropped his head and nipped at my lower lip before I could turn away.

"I didn't hear you complaining about my demands this morning. And considering I'm currently trying to keep you alive, you shouldn't be complaining now. Clearly, the Iron Hammers haven't found you yet, because if they had, they'd have you. It'd take them half a second to break down that door and grab you. I'm actually surprised it hasn't happened yet. You're under my protection now, Zara. I take that shit seriously. I take your safety seriously. So, be a good girl, and let me move you to the clubhouse. Stay there until we deal with this Iron Hammer threat, at least."

He was too close. Between his big body and his scent filling my head and lungs, he surrounded me. He did have a good point about this place being easy to break into. I knew it. So why the fuck was I arguing?

"I want to pack my own things."

"Fine. But you're doing it now. So, you better call Marie and let her know you're gonna be late, because I'm not waiting till tonight to move you out of this fucking rat-trap."

I swallowed and licked my lips when he didn't move away.

"I can't call if you don't back off me."

"Fucking hell. How you tempt me, woman."

Before I could ask what the hell that meant, his palms cupped my face and his mouth was on mine, his tongue and lips devouring me. Whimpering under the onslaught, I gripped his shoulders and gave in to him. Again.

I could see a theme starting here with this man.

Mac

Turned out Zara didn't need long to pack. Stupidly, I'd assumed she was like all women and had a heap of shit. But of course, she didn't. The woman had been forced to leave her home in a rush, and she'd been lucky to manage to fill the suitcase she had, really. I wondered again what her place in Galveston looked like. Would she want to move back there once all this shit with the Iron Hammers died down? I hoped she didn't. I liked living here in

Bridgewater, liked being part of the Charon MC. I was also getting really attached to Zara.

I hoped like hell I wouldn't have to choose between the club and her. Whatever the fuck I had with Zara was so new, I was sure at this point I'd choose the club. But I'd be fucking miserable without her. I already knew that much.

I pulled Zara's little car into the clubhouse yard and got out to the sounds of laughter.

"Gee, Mac, how the fuck did you even fit in that thing?"

I flipped off the prospect who was on guard duty, but didn't say anything. Hell, I'm sure I would have laughed at me too. You know? If it wasn't me that had just been crammed into the matchbox Zara called her car. I popped the trunk and grabbed her suitcase, before I headed inside.

"Seriously though, Scout asked you to meet him in church as soon as you got in."

"Sure. I'll just chuck this up in my room then I'll be there."

I took the stairs two at a time, and dumped Zara's stuff inside my room before turning to head back down.

"You moving her in already?"

I glanced over at Arrow as he joined me in the hallway. "At least for now."

He nodded. "No denying the clubhouse is the safest place for her, considering who's after her. But you remember what I said about her being a keeper?"

"I remember. How about we focus on dealing with the bastards after her first, then you can over-analyze my personal life all you like, okay?"

"Sure, brother."

Bastard smirked at me as he led the way down the stairs. I followed him back to the meeting room, where it looked like most of the club was waiting. Scout gave me a chin lift and indicated I go to him.

"Where are we at?"

"She was staying at that piece of shit motel out on the eastern edge of town. So I got her to pack her things and they're now in my room upstairs. I've got her car here, and I intend to leave it here. I've left my bike at Marie's and planned on getting a lift back there when it's time for her to knock off so I can bring her back here on it. I don't want her being able to run if something spooks her."

Scout silently adjusted his bandana for a minute.

"I already put a couple prospects on Marie's. I figured your girl would want to go to work today. I know for certain Marie wants her to keep coming in." He grinned with a chuckle. "She called me this morning to tell me she expects the best worker she's had in years to not be prevented from doing her job."

I didn't know what the fuck was between Scout and Marie, but clearly there was some history there. "Sounds like Marie. I did try to get Zara to take the day off but she flat out refused."

"She ain't as timid as she appears, is she?"

"She's got claws that's for sure. But underneath it all, I think she's mainly just a woman scared out of her fucking mind, doing what she can to survive. You got any ideas on how we can fix this shit? And how much did they put on her?"

"We've got some ideas, but I'm only saying this shit once. So take a seat, I think everyone who's in town is here now."

I moved away to sit in my usual spot, next to Eagle and Taz.

"Heard you had a good morning, mate."

"Shut the fuck up."

That made him laugh loud enough to attract attention from about half the room, so I shoved him hard enough he fell off his seat.

"Okay, enough fucking around. We got serious shit to discuss."

Scout's loud voice silenced the room, thankfully that included Taz. Bastard still smirked at me as he righted his seat before he sat back in it.

"By now, you've all heard about the shooting last month down in Galveston. But in case you've had your head up your ass or something, here's the basics—a Satan's Cowboy was dealing on Iron Hammers turf. Iron Hammers found him at a cafe and shot the place up, killing the Cowboy and six others."

"Did anyone ever find that witness?"

I wasn't sure who called out the question, but Scout looked straight at me as he responded. "Yeah, turns out she was under our noses the whole time. The new girl down at Marie's Cafe, Zara, is the witness." A few whistles and smartass remarks filled the room. "Yeah, you all can cut that shit out right fucking now. Mac's claimed her and as of this morning, she's staying here with him. Now, the reason I've called you all in, is we need to figure out what the fuck we're going to do with her. The Iron Hammers have a real hard-on for her, so much so, that they've put a bounty on her. Mac and Taz stopped a fucker from taking her yesterday. He wasn't part of their club, but a hang-around who wanted the money and the glory. He was kind enough to tell us it's worth ten grand and a top rocker to bring her back to them alive. So expect an influx of money-hungry biker wannabes roaming our streets."

Fuck me. Ten grand? That was enough money to bring some serious heat to town.

"What'd she do that they want her so bad? I don't get it. I mean, she just about hides under the counter whenever we go into Marie's."

"Mac? You want to answer that one? Not sure how much Zara wants everyone to know."

Yeah, neither did I. Would she lose her shit if I told the whole club about her illnesses? Probably.

"Ah, okay. Zara has a medical condition, and it made her mind a little fuzzy after the attack was over. A young cop took advantage, asked her questions she shouldn't have answered, but did. She knew she fucked up as soon as she spoke, it's why she ran off and disappeared. She has no fucking intention of making her statement official. I'm certain of it. And considering she was shot at by an MC, it kinda makes sense the girl gets a bit nervous around bikers, doesn't it?"

Nitro, the club's Sergeant at Arms, stood up and came around to lean back against the table. "So, we have Zara with us. And both the Iron Hammers and the police are after her. Zara confirmed who their inside guy is, so I don't recommend she goes to the cops to clear this up. Her running off made it clear she didn't want to make an official statement. Clearly, we ain't handing her over to the Iron Hammers. So that leaves us with two options. We try to buy her freedom with that ledger John left of their shit, or we approach the Satan's Cowboys about helping us out on this one. You know, following the whole 'enemy of my enemy is my friend' bullshit."

I glanced over at Eagle and Taz. There was a third option. We could involve the FBI. But my gut was telling me no, so when both Eagle and Taz gave me a slight shake of their heads, I dropped the idea. We could always go to them later, if things got desperate.

I spoke up over the low chatter that had started up. "I don't think even revealing we have that book is a good idea. Not until we know what we're going to do with it. We need to find out if they're still doing that shit, and if they are, it needs to be stopped. This is separate, and honestly? Handing over that thing ain't gonna stop those bastards from coming after Zara. She's been quiet for a month. They know she's not going to finalize that statement she made. They're after her for a different reason. Did that fucker who came after her say anything else?"

That brought Bulldog into the conversation. "That was my thinking. They want her for something else. The fact they've not only put money on her head, but want her alive? It's not adding up. I'm fresh out of ideas on figuring out what that is though, because that fucker you caught didn't know shit."

Scout spoke up again. "I've had a bit to do with the Cowboy's current VP, Maverick, over the years. I can reach out, see if he can tell me what they're planning. I'll try to do it without disclosing we have Zara, but I can't lie to them. If I do and they find out, we're done."

Couldn't argue with that. Satan's Cowboys were the biggest MC in Texas, and they wore their one-percenter patches with pride. Piss them off, it wasn't going to end well for you.

"That doesn't add up either. Why haven't they gone after the Iron Hammers yet?"

Scout turned to me as I'd spoken. "My first guess? The fucker that was dealing down there wasn't doing it with club permission. That, and the Cowboys ain't stupid. They go down there guns blazing with a second shootout within a month, they'll have all sorts of law enforcement coming down hard on all their chapters. No club is going to bring that kind of heat down on themselves without a damn good reason. Right. Let's call this shit. Everyone in favor of me checking in with the Cowboys' VP?"

Everyone's hands went up and Scout brought down the hammer.

"Done. I'll call you all in when I know something. Before you all run off, we'll be having a barbecue tonight, let Zara meet everyone."

"We'll get the old ladies onto it, Prez."

That was Keys. His old lady, Donna was tough as nails and funny as hell. I figured she had to be both those things to put up with the old geek and all his toys long-term. I stayed seated as the room started to empty. I rolled my shoulders, then stood. I hated this shit—not knowing what the fuck was really going on, which meant I had no chance of getting on top of any of it. I fully knew how Eagle felt when the mob came gunning for Silk now. Fucking stressful shit. At least the barbecue would be some fun. A damn good excuse to have Zara real close for a few hours before I took her back to bed. That left me grinning. I needed to buy her something suitable to wear.

"Eagle, you bring a cage?"

"Yeah, Silk's not getting on a bike till after this baby is born. Why?"

"Give me a lift to Marie's?"

He slapped me on the back with a chuckle. "Sure, man." He shook his head. "Pussy whipped already. Man, at least I pretended to fight it for a while."

Maybe I should just walk to Marie's.

"That's because you're an idiot. Why the fuck would I fight having a hot chick in my bed?"

Bastard just laughed harder as he left the room and grabbed his phone from the lockers.

Whatever. I needed to go have a quick look in Zara's suitcase before we left so I didn't have time to try to figure out what the fuck Eagle found so funny.

Chapter 9

Zara

Marie had been smirking at me all damn day. It hadn't taken me long to pack up my few things so I'd only been about an hour late. It had, thankfully, been late enough that the cafe was starting to fill with customers, so Marie hadn't had time to grill me for gossip. But I'd known she would. It was in her gaze every time she smirked at me.

And now the day was winding down, she had time. *Awesome.*

"So, you went and spoke to Mac like I suggested? Must have gone well considering we now have Charons guarding the shop all day."

"Not like you think. And we have what, now?"

She nodded at the front window and I glanced over to see two young guys wearing cuts leaning against their bikes across the road.

"I spoke with Scout this morning. He said we'd have prospects out front for a while."

I walked to the back of the shop, grateful there were no customers at the moment.

"This is all so crazy. And it's happening way too fast."

Marie stopped cleaning and stared at me for a moment. "What happened yesterday after you left here?"

"I wasn't going to go to the gym. I'd planned on doing what I always do. Go back to my motel room and stay there. But on my way I saw an Iron Hammer riding toward me. Even though he drove straight past me, I still freaked out. Panicked that they'd found me. I drove straight to the gym, but my narcolepsy decided to kick in and by the time I got to the parking lot, I had to lock the doors and sleep for a bit." I paused to lick my lips before continuing. "I woke up in the gym's office with Mac fussing over me. Some thug had tried to break into my car."

Marie came over to me and rested her palm on my upper arm. "Was it one of the Iron Hammers?"

"I don't know. He at least knows them. They've put a bounty on my head, Marie. I don't know how much. I overheard Taz talking to Mac about it, so I tried to sneak out on them. I, ah, I was going to run again."

My cheeks heated with shame.

"Oh, sugar, ain't no one in that club that'll turn you over for money. And you know after what I told you, I'd certainly never do it to you. You don't need to keep running, Zara."

"Yeah, I'm hearing that a lot." I took a deep breath before I continued. "I made it out to my car, but Taz had done something so it wouldn't start. Mac came out and basically said the same as you. That I'm safe with him, with the club. Then Taz announced Scout wanted me at the clubhouse, so off we went. I told Scout and Mac both about what happened."

Marie was back to smirking. "And then, I'm guessing, you spent the night with Mac? He followed you this morning to make sure you were safe, and when he saw the shithole you were staying in, he went caveman on you?"

That had me chuckling as heat raced over my face again. "Yeah, something like that."

The door swung open and I jerked at Mac's deep voice.

"Everything okay?"

"Well, good afternoon to you to, Mac. Everything is just peachy. You come to take your girl?"

"Sorry, Marie. Didn't mean to be rude. You heard about tonight yet?"

"Tonight?"

"Yeah, Scout's ordered a barbecue tonight, to welcome Zara."

Marie's whole body stiffened a moment before a wide smile broke out across her face. "Oh, I wouldn't miss that for the world."

"Um, why is that exactly?"

I felt like I was missing something here. Marie didn't seem like the biker barbecue kind of woman to me.

"Watching you with that many drunk bikers around you? Gonna be more entertaining than anything on television."

I opened my mouth to respond when Mac plastered himself against my back and wrapped an arm around my waist, pulling me tight back against him. "Thankfully, Zara has promised me she won't run off again. But just in case her inner rabbit gets any ideas, I intend to stay very close to her all night."

He nipped my ear before he nuzzled my neck, melting me and short-circuiting any brain function I may have had prior to him touching me. Marie gave me a knowing look, complete with raised eyebrow and smirk.

"Well, Mac. Now you've rendered my best worker completely useless, you might as well take her away. Let Scout know I'll be over later in the evening."

He released his hold on me as he spoke. "Thanks, Marie. C'mon bunny, go grab your bag. You're about to get your first ride on my Harley."

Like a bucket of cold water, that one sentence washed all the arousal out of my body.

"Oh, no. I'm not riding on a bike. I've got my car."

I turned to face him when he didn't respond.

"You did bring my car back, right?"

"Your matchbox is back at the clubhouse. I barely fit in that little thing. It's a short ride from here to the clubhouse, only a few minutes. You'll be fine. I can't fucking wait to have you sitting behind me with your arms wrapped around me as we thunder down the road."

Okay, so that part sounded all right. Well, it sounded hot as hell, actually. But still, it was a bike. A loud, noisy, dangerous bike.

"What if we wreck?"

"Sweetheart, you're more likely to wreck in that little matchbox of yours than we are on my bike. I've been riding since I was a teenager, and never wrecked yet. C'mon, be brave. I know you can."

Marie, the traitor, had gone and gotten my bag. She handed it to me, and, with a shove, pushed me toward Mac. "Go on, sugar. You'll love it. Nothing quite like the feel of the wind on your face while you're wrapped around a warm, hard body on the back of a Harley."

Mac didn't give me a chance to respond. He gave Marie a wink, then scooped me up against his chest and strode out of the cafe.

"We'll see you later, Marie!"

Once outside, Mac sent a nod to the prospects and they hopped on their Harleys and took off.

"You like getting your way, don't you?"

"Sure do. You can blame the USMC. As a Gunnery Sergeant, I got to tell lots of other big, tough Marines what to do and they had to follow orders."

I ran a finger under the edge of the neck of his t-shirt, stroking over his warm skin.

"I have a feeling you were all take-charge before you got anywhere near the USMC, babe."

He shrugged before setting me on my feet next to his bike. "You're probably right."

After giving me a quick kiss, he turned to the Harley and opened one of the side bag thingies. I winced. Marie had a point about needing to learn the biker lingo.

"What do you call that?"

He glanced up at me with a quizzical look. "Call what?"

"Mac, I don't know shit about what you MC guys call everything. I'm about to be thrown in with a whole bunch of you and I'd like to not make a complete ass of myself. So, I'm asking what you call that bag thing."

He gave me a sweet smile. "It's a saddle bag, bunny." He pulled out a helmet and came over to me where he placed it on my head. He sat on the bike's seat and pulled me closer to him, so I was nestled between his thighs. "Chin up." I did as instructed and he did up the strap for me. "You'll pick up a lot by just listening in tonight. If you don't understand anything, just ask me quietly. Or one of the other old ladies."

I screwed up my nose. "Old ladies? That's not very nice."

He grinned. "Yeah, it took me a little bit to get used to calling them that, too. An old lady is a biker's wife. Although not all bikers marry their old ladies, the meaning is the same. It's a serious commitment for a brother to offer his property patch to his woman."

"Property patch? You're not making this sound better here, Mac."

He actually laughed at me, so I gave his chest a light slap. Damn man.

"Settle down, Zara. You'll see tonight some of the women will be wearing cuts—vests—that say 'Property of', then the name of their old man. It's a respect thing. It doesn't mean the woman is like a piece of furniture her man owns, it's more like she's the most precious thing in his world and he'll do anything for her. The patch shows everyone else who'll come after them if they're dumb enough to fuck with her."

I ran my palm down the various patches on the front of Mac's cut. What would it be like for him to claim me like that? To be the most important thing in his world?

"You're thinking way too hard, bunny."

Then his lips were on mine and his hands were on my ass, squeezing and stroking me as his kiss erased all my thoughts. Again. When he broke the kiss I was breathing heavily and wanted more.

"You can have more, once we get back to the clubhouse. We've been out in the open for too long already." He gently guided me back as he stood from his bike. After he easily swung his leg over the seat, he patted the leather behind him. "On you get. Put your feet on the pegs, here." He pointed out the little metal pegs. I put a hand on his shoulder and climbed on to sit behind him. "When we go around a corner, I'll lean into it. I need you to go with me. Don't look so scared, bunny. Keep your body pressed against my back, with your arms around me and you'll naturally follow my movements."

With a nod, I did as he'd instructed and cuddled in close. With my nose pressed against his cut, my senses were filled with the scent of leather and man. *Hmmm.* And my hands were against his tight, ribbed abs. Yeah, Marie was right. This did feel damn good.

I tensed when the Harley started. Damn thing was loud! And it throbbed between my thighs. I hadn't expected that. It wasn't a bad feeling, actually. Mac went slowly until we were on the road, then he opened it up and took off. With a squeal, I tightened my grip. From the shaking I felt through his stomach, I guessed he was laughing at me. But I didn't give a shit. I was too worried about falling off the fucking back of the bike.

Damn men.

Mac

I took the long way home to give Zara more time to get used to the feel of being on a bike. After about five minutes, she stopped digging her nails into my stomach like she was trying to claw out my liver, which was a nice improvement. I couldn't hold back the grin when, by the time we pulled into the clubhouse yard, she was wriggling against me. Looked like my girl liked the feel of a motorcycle between her thighs after all. Which was a good thing. A very good thing.

I pulled up in line with the other bikes then peeled her hands off my waist so I could help her climb off. I dismounted and snatched her to me. Holding her face so it was tilted up to mine, I slammed my lips down over hers and took her mouth until we were both panting.

"Fuck, I love having you on the back of my bike, babe. You liked it too, didn't you? I felt how you were squirming against me. That sweet pussy of yours is all hot and wet for me right now, isn't it?"

Her cheeks pinkened at my words. *So sweet and innocent.* I wanted to lean her over the seat and take her now. But she wasn't that kinda girl, and I didn't want the prospects on guard duty to see her come apart. That was for my eyes only. I tugged at the strap on her helmet, undoing it quickly before taking it from her head. I got mine off in record time, and flipped open the saddlebag to store them away. Before I did, I grabbed the shopping bags from my little field trip earlier.

I saw her open her mouth to ask about it, but I just shook my head, took her hand and headed inside. A few of the guys tried to catch us as we passed through the main downstairs room, but I had other plans. When we were finally inside my room, I tossed the shopping bags on her suitcase, then had her up against the door in a heartbeat.

"That was rude. You didn't even say hi to any of your friends."

I nuzzled my face into her neck, and when she tilted her head to give me more room, I kissed the soft skin of her throat. "My brothers understand I have other priorities at the moment."

"Apparently."

Her voice was hoarse with arousal and it made my cock throb with need. Her palms slid up my body, underneath my shirt. She seemed fascinated with all the dips and swells of my abs and pecs, which suited me just fine because I loved having her touch me. I shrugged out of my cut and pulled the shirt over my head. Before she could return to her stroking, I started in on her clothes, not stopping until she was naked in front of me.

"Damn, you're sexy as fuck, bunny."

I lifted her against the wall so her tits were at face level. When she wrapped her legs around my waist and I felt her wet pussy against my stomach, I shuddered with a groan. I buried my face between her tits, nuzzling a moment before turning to take a nipple in my mouth. I sucked, licked and bit at first one, then the other. I kept at her until she'd coated my abs with her cream.

When the feel of her grinding against me got too much, I lifted her away from the wall and strode to the bed, where I dropped her on the mattress. That earned me one of her adorable little squeals. I grinned at her as I toed off my boots and stripped out of my jeans. I had one knee on the bed when she twisted over and scrambled to the other side. Thinking she was planning on running, I grabbed for her ankle. I caught her just as she reached for the nightstand. Fuck me, the girl was going for a condom. She was as hot for me as I was for her. Good to know.

The moment the drawer shut, I pulled her across the mattress, so she was back in front of me, one leg on either side. I stared at the feast in front of me. From her bright hazel eyes, her lush tits now marked up from my whiskers and mouth, to her flat belly and smooth pussy. Slowly, like she knew I was on the edge, she sat up and put the foil square to her mouth, tearing it open with her teeth. Damn, even that was sexy as fuck when she did it. She took the rubber out and reached for me. I shuddered as she gave my cock a couple strokes before she pressed the latex to the tip and rolled it down the length.

Looked like she wanted to take some of the control this round. That was fine by me. I could give her that. *Maybe.* I leaned forward, forcing her to lie down beneath me.

"You wanna ride me, bunny? Because I can't lie—watching you take your pleasure is gonna be hot as hell. Your tits will bounce and they'll thrust out when you throw your head back. Not sure I'll be able to last long, but it'll be worth it."

Her eyes closed for a second before she blinked open to reveal her irises had gone that strange green color again. Oh yeah, she liked that idea. A whole lot.

"You want it, you gotta ask me for it, bunny. Use all those dirty words I know you have in there somewhere."

My sexy bunny reached down and stroked my cock again, and as good as that felt, I stopped her. Pulling both hands up above her head, I pinned them to the bed. "Words, babe. I need you to tell me all the dirty, filthy things you want me to do—or that you want to do to me."

She huffed out a breath and glared at me, but I just ground the underside of my cock over her mound as I smiled down at her.

"Fine! I want to ride your cock. I want your hands on my breasts while I ride you until you come inside me. Is that filthy enough?"

"It's a start."

Releasing her hands, I rolled us both over so she was straddling me. She gasped at the fast movement, then pressed her soft palms against my pecs to lift herself up. Her double Ds were all natural and swayed with each breath, way too much temptation for me to resist. I wrapped a palm around each one, and lifting my head and shoulders, I drew one up so I could suckle on her nipple. I pinched at the other one while I tormented the first with my mouth and it wasn't long before she was sliding her slick pussy up and down my cock, coating it with her cream. Releasing her nipple I moved my mouth up an inch and sucked hard, making certain she'd be left with my mark on her for at least a couple of days. I made sure to keep it low enough her work shirts shouldn't show it, but the outfit I bought for her to wear tonight was a different story.

"Mac!"

I laid back down and stared up at the beautiful woman above me. "Ride me, bunny. Take my cock inside that sweet, wet pussy of yours."

Clearly a little nervous, she wrapped a hand around my cock. I was a big man, and her fingers felt small on me. She gave me a couple of strokes before she braced herself with a palm against my shoulder and lifted up so she could press my head against her opening. Little tease held me there, taunting me with her opening.

"Enough."

With a growl, I gripped her hips and pulled her down, impaling myself deep within her. With a gasp she leaned back, her red-blonde hair trailing down her back. The shit was long enough that the tips tickled my thighs as she moved her hips up and down my shaft. I helped her set the rhythm with my hands on her hips. Slow and deep, we moved together.

"Play with your tits for me, bunny. Show me what you like."

Her movement faltered, but my hands on her hips, never quit working her up and down on my cock. Slowly, she lifted her palms to her chest where she cupped each one, as though her hands were a bra.

"I didn't say cover 'em up, Zara. Play with them. Squeeze, tug, roll your nipples. Show me what you like."

"I like you doing all that."

"But I have your clit to play with, so you need to occupy those pretty tits of yours."

I moved my hand so my thumb was over the top of her slit, and as soon as she began to squeeze her tits, I pressed down, rubbing in small circles that had her body shuddering. The hotter she got, the braver she got. Soon she was tugging at her nipples and rolling them between her fingers. When she pulled on both at the same time, stretching them out, I couldn't take any more.

With a growl, I rolled us over, hitched one of her legs high up on my waist and started to pound into her. With the first thrust, she quit playing and, with a gasp, threw her hands out to take fistfuls of bedding. Her head thrashed as she tilted her hips at me with every thrust. When my balls drew up ready to blow, I slid my hand between us and pinched and flicked at her clit.

"C'mon, bunny. Come apart for me. I'm not going over without you going first."

One more flick and she tightened down on me with a scream. Her channel rippled and clenched around my dick and that was it. I buried my face against her neck as, calling her name, I jerked and filled her up with my come. Fuck, I wish she was fully mine. That I didn't need to wear a fucking condom because she'd want to have my seed inside her, would want my kid growing inside her belly. Twisting my head, I left another bite mark on her shoulder. Knowing she would be out of it for a couple minutes, I took my time easing from her body. I feathered kisses over her face and toyed with her nipples and tits some more. Both her tight little points were rosy red now and I was certain they'd be sensitive as hell for at least the next day. I was gonna have fun teasing them every chance I got. She'd feel every little brush against them. Hmmm. Tonight was gonna be so much fun.

"You are so fucking sexy, Zara. I'm not ever gonna get my fill of you."

I was tempted to say so much more. She looked like she was sleeping peacefully, but she'd proven she heard what was said when she was out with cataplexy. I needed to keep my growing feelings inside for now. She'd run for sure if she knew how much I wanted her to be wearing my fucking property patch already.

Chapter 10

Zara

Mac was sucking me in under his spell. The way he caressed and kissed me until I came back out of my attack had my heart melting. The ache in his voice when he'd said he'd never get enough had warmth spreading throughout my body—and for once it wasn't from embarrassment.

When I could move, I trailed my fingers up his arm, loving the feel of his muscles twitching and flexing beneath my touch.

"Welcome back, bunny. C'mon, time for a shower, then we need to get downstairs. Probably considered rude to miss your own party."

"Since when is it my party?"

"It always was, bunny. Scout wanted you to meet everyone, get you familiar with the club since you're now living here."

He dragged me with him out of bed and over to the bathroom. Unfortunately, or maybe it was fortunate, the shower stall was only big enough for one, so we washed up separately. Even though he couldn't be the one to clean me up, he stood watching me with his hot, intense stare the entire time. It was enough to make me start squirming all over again. Needing a moment away from his hot stare, I toweled off as fast as I could, and went back into the bedroom. I went over to my suitcase sitting just inside the door, and pulled it out far enough I could lie it down to open it. I had the zip half undone when Mac came out of the bathroom. My mouth went dry at the sight he made. With only a towel wrapped around his lean waist, and water droplets clinging to every inch of exposed skin, I wanted nothing more than to lick the moisture off him.

I forced my eyes closed as I took a deep breath.

"Whatever idea just flashed through your mind, I want to know about."

"No, you really don't. Not if you want to go downstairs anytime soon."

When I reopened my eyes, he immediately held my gaze captive for a few moments. "Fair enough. You can keep it for later, then. I bought you some clothes for tonight. I thought you'd want to fit in."

I smiled. "You didn't have to do that. But it's very sweet of you."

My first clue he was up to something was the lopsided smirk he wore as he headed to the shopping bags he'd brought in earlier.

"Come here and I'll show you what I got you. Might even help you put it on, if you'll let me."

I rolled my eyes. "I can dress myself, Mac. I think you've proven well enough I don't mind you controlling me in bed, but out of it is a different story. And now I'm kind of worried about what the hell you bought me. I did bring clothes. I own jeans and stuff. Just because all you've seen me in is work or gym clothes, doesn't mean that's the limit of my wardrobe."

Despite my tough words, I went to him. Curiosity at what he'd bought quickly won out over my show of independence. First thing out of the bag was a beautiful emerald lacy bra, together with a matching thong. My lips stretched up into a grin. I didn't normally wear thongs, but this set was gorgeous. I reached out to run a finger over the lacy cup.

"How did you know what size to buy?"

"I took a little peek in your suitcase this morning. I wanted to surprise you."

Before I realized what he was doing, he jerked the towel off my body. "Mac!"

"What? I've seen it all, touched it all, and I intend to do all that and more later. Lift your foot..."

He snapped off the tag and held the thong out for me to step into like a child. But for some stupid reason I lifted my foot and then the other. The lace was amazingly soft, and it felt luxurious as Mac slid it up my legs. He settled the underwear over my hips and then cupped my ass and squeezed it.

"Hmm, I was right. That color is perfect on your pale skin with your reddish-blonde hair."

"It's strawberry blonde, not really red."

He quirked his brow at me as he pulled the tag off the bra.

"That quick temper of yours spells redhead to me, bunny."

With a growl I snatched the bra and clipped it on before Mac could do it. Damn infuriating man.

"Just show me what you want me to wear already."

I almost sighed in relief at the shirt he pulled out next. A tight shirt with a low V neckline, in a similar green to the underwear.

"I can see you picked a theme and stuck with it."

He shrugged, looking completely confident. Again, I took it from his hands and pulled it over my head before he could get any ideas about helping. The next thing out of the bag had me frowning.

"Oh, hell no."

It was a skirt. A fucking incredibly short one.

"Oh, c'mon, Zara. You'll rock this thing. And just think of how easy it will be for me to get to you to ease that ache you get around me."

Ah, it all made sense now. "So, the real reason you bought me a new outfit was because you wanted to guarantee you'd have easy access to my—to my—um…"

"Your pussy. Say it, Zara." He stood and cupped that very body part in his palm. "This, right here, is the sweetest pussy I've ever had and yes, I want to have easy access to it. Maybe later, after the kids have all disappeared, I can sit with you out the back by the fire pit, unzip my pants, flip up your skirt, and fuck you nice and slow by the firelight. No one will see a thing out there. And I guarantee we won't be the only ones doing it."

My mouth fell open. "Oh my—you're actually serious, aren't you?"

"Hell yeah, I am. C'mon, just wear the skirt. If, after half an hour you still feel uncomfortable wearing it, you can come up here and change into jeans. How about that?"

I ran my gaze over him, then the skirt. It wasn't like I didn't like how my legs looked. And it was his club, he'd know what I'd need to wear to fit in.

"Okay. Half an hour."

I held out my hand for the skirt and he did his thing with pulling off the tag and handed it over. I slipped it up my thighs and buttoned the front closure up. Then I turned to head back into the bathroom to look in the mirror.

"Holy shit, Mac! What the fuck did you do?"

Poking out the top of the shirt edge was a huge fucking love-bite. He came up behind me and wrapped his arms around my waist.

"I was simply marking what's mine, just in case I'm not by your side for a minute and some other fucker thinks you're available."

He pushed the shirt down off one shoulder and revealed another one.

"What the fuck? You part vampire or something?"

"Nah, bunny. Just a little possessive of my property." He gave my ass a tap as he moved away. "We need to get moving."

I watched in the mirror as he strode over to a wardrobe where he dropped the towel, before pulling out a clean pair of jeans. Damn, but that man had a very fine ass. Shaking my head, I dashed over to my suitcase to grab my toiletries bag, then headed back to the bathroom. I kept my makeup light and brushed out my hair, not bothering to put it up. Between my boobs out and proud and all the leg I was showing, I didn't think I needed to do anything else to attract attention.

When I was done I turned around and stopped dead in my tracks.

"Oh my—"

Mac had added a belt with a large Harley Davidson buckle and his cut. No shirt for my man, and it left me speechless. He prowled over to me and I tilted my head up for his kiss. Wanting it. Needing it. I pressed my palms against his tummy, then slid them up under the leather until they rested against his solid pectorals, the hair there tickling my skin.

He took my mouth, slamming his lips over mine. Owning me, branding me with his kiss. Then he pulled back with a groan.

"Okay baby, time to go. I didn't get you new shoes. Had no fucking clue where to even start on that one."

With a chuckle, wondering if he did try but couldn't find any green ones, I headed over and grabbed a pair of black sandals with a nice, solid wedge heel. Mac had mentioned something about a fire pit in the yard and I didn't want to be falling on my ass, so wedges it was.

With one last, quick kiss, Mac took my hand in his and led me downstairs. My nerves increased with every step. How many people would be here? How many knew who I was?

After clearing the bottom step, I froze up. All those questions were short-circuiting my mind. Mac kept walking a few steps, but stopped when my hand slipped from his.

"Zara? What's wrong, sweetheart?"

I looked past him out to the bar area, at the throng of people. Mostly men—make that mostly tall, heavily muscled men.

"Do they all know who I am?" *What I'm worth?*

He came back to me, pulling me against him as he wrapped his strong arms around me.

"Relax, bunny. Club business isn't discussed with everyone. Only patched in members know what's going on with you. You've seen a few prospects. They're the ones without a top rocker on the back of their cuts, and they don't know anything official. They would have heard shit on the street, of course. But they won't know for sure you're that girl. As far as the women, some of the brothers might have told their old ladies, but most won't have a clue. The club whores definitely won't know, but they won't go near you anyway."

I rested my forehead against his shoulder.

"I'm gonna need a drink. A strong one."

That had Mac barking out a laugh. "Sure, bunny. Let's go get you that drink."

Mac

Still chuckling over my girl's bout of nerves, I dragged her over to the bar, intent on getting her that drink before I took her to find the old ladies.

"Mac! You got a sec?"

I glanced over to Scout and by the serious, hard look in his gaze, I knew it was important.

"Sure, Prez." I turned to Zara and pressed a kiss to her temple. "Go to the bar and grab yourself whatever you want, then stay there. I won't be long."

She pulled her lower lip between her teeth as her gaze bounced around the room.

"Bunny, I'm not going to leave the room, okay? Just going to have a chat with Scout over there. I'll have my eyes on you the whole time."

She gave me a tentative smile. "Okay."

I gave her a light tap on the ass as she stepped away from me. She glared over her shoulder at me before walking the rest of the way across the room with a bit more confidence. Yep, that's the trick to my little rabbit. Just had to piss her off a little and she found her backbone.

"You finished mooning over your girl yet?"

"Yeah, yeah."

I followed Scout over to a corner where I could still see Zara, but far enough away from everyone we wouldn't be overheard unless someone could lip-read.

"What's up Prez?"

"We'll be having church a little later. Got a small group of Satan's Cowboys joining us this evening."

I winced. "Not exactly the welcome I wanted for Zara. She's promised not to run again, but I didn't want to test her that fucking much on the first night she's meeting the club."

"Yeah, I know, brother. But it can't be helped. The sooner we get this shit settled, the better. Go take your woman into the kitchen and introduce her to the old ladies. They'll take her under their wing and keep an eye on her while we're in church."

I rubbed a hand over my head as I watched her throw back a shot like a pro. Then Taz, who was standing beside her, leaned in to say something in her ear and she tossed her head and laughed loud enough I heard it all the way over here. When Taz moved away, I saw he'd slid another shot over in front of her.

"I better go rescue her before Taz has her so drunk she can't fucking walk."

"Probably a good idea."

Humor laced Scout's voice, and I could see the funny side too. But Zara would be embarrassed tomorrow if she found out I'd let her get so drunk that she made an ass of herself in front of the club the first time she met most of them.

"Taz, did you learn nothing from Eagle? Quit flirting with my fucking woman."

"Aw, come on, mate. I was just helping her relax a little. You know I'm harmless."

I scoffed at that. "Yeah, mate, you're just a harmless sniper the USMC didn't want to let go of."

That got me a wink. "I didn't mean *that* kind of harmless, and you know it."

I gave him a shoulder bump before I wrapped my arm around Zara. "C'mon, bunny. I'll introduce you to the old ladies."

We were a few steps down the hall when she slowed her step. "Um, Mac?"

I stopped and pushed her against the wall. If we were going to stop walking, I might as well make the most of it.

"Yeah, bunny?"

I buried my face against her throat, and started kissing the sensitive skin there.

"Can you not call me bunny in front of the others? It's cute and all, but I don't want to have to tell anyone the reason why you came up with it."

I gave her shoulder a quick nip. "I can try, but not sure I can. I like calling you bunny, and you don't have to tell them why. Basically everyone in the club has a road name, or nickname, and not everyone is open about the reason behind it."

Her body shuddered as I ran my palm up her smooth thigh, lifting her leg over my hip.

"So Mac isn't your real name?"

Her voice had gone husky with her arousal. Slipping my hand under her skirt, I ran my thumb over the damp lace covering her pussy, loving how fast she got hot and wet for me.

"Nope, Mac is short for MacGyver. I earned it in boot camp because I'm fucking great at fixing shit, and even before I joined the USMC, I always carried a Leatherman on me."

"Your nickname has a nickname? Well, aren't you just special? What's your real name?"

I slipped under her thong and thrust two fingers easily into her wet channel. "I love how hot you get for me, bunny."

She tilted her hips back and forth, fucking my fingers with a groan.

"Tell me your name already."

I nipped along her jawline. "You gotta earn it. Once you come, saying my nickname, then I'll tell you my real one."

She shuddered and her fingers dug deeper into my shoulders. "But people will hear."

"Bunny, several of my brothers have already walked past and seen you all flushed and fucking my fingers. You calling out my name ain't gonna change much."

Her face flushed redder as her eyes flew open. She tried to pull away.

"I don't think so." With my fingers deep in her pussy, I ran my thumb over her clit, teasing the hard little nub until her eyes became hooded and she began panting. "There we go. C'mon, babe, come for me."

"Mac..."

She dragged my name out in a stage whisper as her body tightened against me. Tilting my fingers forward, I zeroed in on her g-spot and rubbed until her back bowed, she let out a whine, and her pussy clamped down on my fingers. I wrapped my free hand around her waist and held her to me, not wanting her to fall to the floor with her cataplexy. I feathered kisses over her neck, jaw and up to ear where I took advantage of her inability to respond and whispered to her.

"You're mine, Zara. All of you is fucking mine. I know it's happened fast, but I couldn't help it. I have to have you with me, in my life." Fuck, it was on the tip of my tongue to tell her I loved her. Aside from my mother and sister, I'd never told another woman those words and I found they got caught in my throat now. "Whatever happens, you remember your promise to me. You're not allowed to run from me. Ever."

A few moments passed then her face turned and she nipped my earlobe. Hard. "I never go back on my word, Mac. Now, tell me your fucking name already."

With a laugh, I backed off her a little, smirking as she pulled her skirt back down and smoothed her palms over her shirt.

"Told you that skirt would come in handy."

She glared at me, which looked so fucking adorable. I couldn't help but chuckle again, earning myself a growl.

"Jacob Miller. But no one has called me that in a damn long time."

With a smile, she leaned up and gave my lips a quick peck. "Thank you."

Before I gave into the temptation of shoving her up against the wall again, I wrapped an arm around her shoulders and started walking down the hall toward the kitchen.

"Umm, doesn't that hurt?"

I followed her gaze to the large bulge under the fly of my jeans. "Yeah, bunny. You've got my cock harder than a fucking steel pike, and later I fully expect you to take care of it. But right now, we don't have the time. I'm going to have to leave you for a bit once the Satan's Cowboys get here so I want you settled in with the old ladies before then. I don't want you alone tonight."

Chapter 11

Zara

I gulped and stumbled over my feet.

"Satan's Cowboys?"

Mac held me tighter against his side, not allowing me to fall as I got my feet under me again.

"Yeah. We're hoping they're going to help us with the Iron Hammers. The dead guy you ended up underneath was a Cowboy."

I lifted my hand to chew on my thumbnail. More bikers? My stomach twisted and turned with nerves.

"I don't like it, Mac. Someone is gonna want that money and turn me in. The more people we involve, the more likely that is."

"Bunny, bikers have a code. You're mine, and that makes you Charon MC property. Which means everyone in this club would put their life on the line for you. Satan's Cowboys are the biggest MC in Texas. If they wanted, they could come in and shut down any club they wanted in the state."

Ignoring the property comment, I thought over what else he said and frowned. "So why haven't they? Surely they're not okay with the Iron Hammers killing one of theirs?"

"That's what we're meeting with them about. It's not as simple as you think, but it's club business so I can't tell you. Just know they won't be turning you over to the Hammers and neither will anyone from the Charons. You're family now."

My eyes burned for a moment. After my parents were murdered, I didn't think I'd ever have a family again, and I wasn't quite sure I could trust that all these people were suddenly going to look after me because I'd started having sex with Mac. I wanted to believe, I really did. But my life so far hadn't led me to a place where I could just take something this good at face value.

Thankfully, before Mac could say anything else, we made it to the kitchen, which was bustling with activity.

"Ladies, this is Zara. You may have seen her at Marie's these past few weeks. She's living here with me now and I'd appreciate it if you could all show her around and keep an eye on her. We're gonna have church soon and I don't want her left alone."

A woman around my age with long blonde hair and tattoos covering her whole right arm came up and kissed Mac on the cheek.

"Quit barking orders, Mac. We ain't the Marines." She moved to me, pulling me in for a quick hug. "Hey doll, I'm Silk, Eagle's old lady and Bulldog's niece. Stick with me and I'll make sure you're suitably wrapped in cotton wool for Mac." She gave me a wink that eased some of the tension in my stomach and left me smiling.

"Hi. I don't think I've met Eagle, but I've seen Bulldog in Marie's a time or two."

Another woman came over and pulled first me into a fast hug before she wrapped an arm around Silk. "I'm Rose—this one's aunt, and Bulldog's old lady. The reason no one sees much of Eagle these days is because he knocked this one up and she's been sick as a dog."

"It's getting better. I'm here, aren't I?"

"That you are, baby."

From there I got introduced to several women, who gave me their names and told me who they were attached to. I instantly forgot most of them. There were just too many! I noticed one girl, maybe twenty years old, standing back. She didn't even attempt to come say hi. I frowned as I watched her working silently in a corner. Something about the girl's dark mood had my sixth sense twitching.

Silk moved to block my line of sight to the girl. "Don't pay attention to Em. She's going through her teenage "life sucks" phase. We're all hoping she grows out of real soon."

"She's an old lady?"

"Nah, she's a daughter of the club. That's the title us kids get." She pointed to a patch on her vest—a red heart with barbed wire wrapped around it. "Technically I'm a niece, not a daughter, but since I was raised in the club, I get the title too. It's a patch and title to make it clear to others to not fuck with us even though we're not old ladies. Although, I'm one of them now, too. It also meant Eagle couldn't pursue me while he was a prospect."

I rubbed a hand over the back of my neck. "So many rules."

"Nah, there's not so many. You'll learn it all in no time. Just hang with us old ladies, and you'll be fine."

"Silk's right. You'll have it all nailed in no time. It didn't take me long—"

The woman, who I'd already forgotten the name of, stopped speaking when a young guy poked his head in the room. "Mac? Church."

Mac gave me a fast, hard kiss. "Stick with Silk, okay? I'll be back as soon as I can. Need to show you the fire pit...test out that skirt some more."

With a wink, he strolled from the room. I couldn't help but chuckle, even as I felt the heat in my cheeks.

"And that's how I got knocked up so damn fast. These men are sexy as fuck and completely overloaded on testosterone."

I turned to smile at Silk, who was rubbing a palm over her small baby bump.

"I hear you on that one. So, can I help with anything?"

Determined to keep myself distracted from what was happening nearby, I threw myself into helping prepare salads and other stuff for the barbecue. The old ladies were a great bunch. Most had wicked senses of humor and they teased each other constantly. For the most part I was left in peace. I guessed they were taking it easy on the new girl, or they were too happy to have the help to risk distracting me. The fact I stayed out of the way as much as I could might have had something to do with it too. I'd always preferred the shadows until I knew those around me well enough to play a little. And that damn bounty on my head was really messing with me. I didn't know who I could risk trusting. Ten grand was a lot of money. More than enough to make turning me in worth it to many, I was sure. My eyes burned again as I sent up a silent prayer that somehow the Charons could find a solution that didn't involve me ending up in the Iron Hammers' hands.

"Zara? Can you come with me? I need to check the tables are all set up outside ready to go. The moment church is over, all those men will want food ready to go."

"Sure, Silk."

I followed her out and into the backyard. The fire pit was burning bright, a couple of prospects standing near it chucking on logs to build it up higher. I noticed the various benches to sit on around it, many back in the shadows.

"You can count on Mac getting you back there later. These damn men and their love of short skirts."

Silk's laughter was infectious and I found myself laughing along with her as we adjusted the tables so they were ready for all the food platters we had prepared in the kitchen.

"Oh, shit."

I rushed to Silk as her face paled. "You okay?"

She shook her head. "This morning sickness is gonna kill me."

With that, she clamped a hand over her mouth and bolted inside. My stomach turned. Would I ever get to experience that? Mac seemed all serious and thinking long term now, but what about in a few weeks' time, when I wasn't the shiny new toy?

I slowly made my way back inside, intending on heading back to the kitchen.

"Hey, Zara, is it?"

I looked up to find Em in front of me. "Yeah, what's up?"

"I need to grab some stuff from my mom's car, can you come give me a hand?"

A niggle at the back of my mind told me not to go with her, but I pushed it down. The front yard was guarded by prospects and this girl was part of the club. Mac had told me I'd be safe here. I needed to show the man a little trust. He'd done nothing but help me so far.

"Sure, but before we go I want to check in on Silk. She had to bolt for the bathroom just now so I want to make sure she's okay."

With a shrug, Em turned and I followed her down the hall. When we got the bathroom Em stayed outside while I went in.

"Silk? You doing okay? Want me to get you anything?"

She was in a stall with the door closed. "Nah, I'll be right. Just morning sickness, not much anyone can do. You can head back to the kitchen if you want."

"Em's just asked me to help her get something from her Mom's car so I'll do that, then meet you back there."

I left with a wince as Silk started throwing up some more. *The joys of pregnancy.*

"Okay, Em. Let's go get this stuff."

With a silent nod, she led me out the front door. It wasn't until I stepped off the steps and away from the building that I realized there'd been no prospects guarding the door.

"Em? You know where the prospects are?"

"Probably making the most of church and enjoying the whores while they can. Prospects don't get much time to play while the patched in boys are around."

That didn't sound right to me. Well, the prospects not getting much fun sounded about right from what I'd heard so far... but I'd also heard the prospects took their jobs seriously. If they didn't, they wouldn't get patched in.

"Hey, Em? I'm just gonna run inside and grab one of the—"

"Now, there's no need to go do that."

A meaty hand wrapped around my bicep as I tried to flee. I opened my mouth to scream for help but Em slapped her palm over my mouth.

"Don't even think about it, bitch."

Oh, fuck. I was seriously screwed. I felt a pin-prick in my neck just as my limbs went limp with an attack. Fucking hell. They'd drugged me. Add that to my illnesses and I was going to be lucky to wake up at all. *Bastards.*

Mac

"Where the fuck is she?"

My voice echoed through the clubhouse. Zara was fucking gone. She'd run. She'd promised she wouldn't, but she was gone. The Satan Cowboy's VP, Maverick, had wanted Zara to be brought in to get her side of what happened. And to make sure she had no intention of going to the cops again about what she'd heard in that cafe. I'd come out to get her but she wasn't fucking here.

"What are you roaring about?"

Bulldog, our VP, came charging at me from the meeting room.

"No one's seen Zara in a while. She was last with Silk, who is in the bathroom wrapped around the toilet bowl again."

Bulldog turned and ran to the bathroom. Silk was his niece so naturally he'd be concerned over her being sick, even if we all knew it was just morning sickness. Slowly, my anger began to dissipate and my brain started working and got me wondering if maybe Zara hadn't simply taken off. I needed to talk to Silk. I took long strides toward the bathroom but by the time I got there

Bulldog had already quizzed his niece and was coming back out.

"Em took her outside to get some shit from her mom's car, Silk guesses it was around five to ten minutes ago."

Brushing off the shock that Bulldog had run for my girl's sake, not his niece, I turned and bolted for the front door. "Go get the others. I've got a bad feeling."

By the time I busted through the front door, I had Eagle by my side. He'd always known when shit was going to hit the fan before it hit.

"You're running late, brother."

He winced. "Sorry, Mac. I figured my intuition was flaring because of Silk being sick again."

I shook my head as we hit the parking lot. "Nah, it's not your fault, man. I'm just on edge. We need to spread out and look for her. Em brought her out here and no one's seen either of them since."

Frowning, I scanned the yard. "Where the fuck are the prospects? No one's watching our bikes."

"I was just thinking the same thing. Cowboy's left two of theirs out here to keep guard too. Where the fuck are they?"

I turned to face Scout as he'd spoken. This shit wasn't good. Someone, or several someones had fucking grabbed my girl.

"Over here!"

I jogged over to where Eagle was standing up from kneeling. "Fucking empty syringe here and there's footprints heading that way."

Taz joined us and the three of us each drew a gun as we scanned the area. The rest of the club stayed back, allowing us to do our thing. The whole club knew we'd worked together for over a decade in the Marines and they all knew better than to fuck with a system that worked. When we got close to the shed at the edge of the lot I saw the drag marks in the dirt. *Fuck.* I had a bad feeling we were about to find the prospects. With my gun up, I slipped around the side of the old building and sure enough, came face to face with three bodies. I didn't bother checking for a pulse. Eagle or Taz would do that, my priority was my woman.

I continued to work my way around to the rear of the shed, where a number of the timber slats had been removed, kicked out by the looks of what was left. Glancing over my shoulder to make sure I still had back up, I nodded to Taz before I stepped through the fence.

"Fuck me."

I flicked the safety back on my gun and holstered it. We were too fucking late. With my hands on my hips, I stared at the twin tire marks that had been left in the dirt that led to the road.

"Oh, are you fucking shitting me?"

I turned my head to watch Taz kneel down to Em. The girl was dead. No one's head naturally sat at that angle. A buzzing in my head got louder and louder until I couldn't contain it. I scrubbed my palms over my face before I looked to the sky and let loose a roar loud enough birds left the surrounding trees.

"What the fuck—"

Scout's words cut off as he came through the fence.

"Taz, go get Keys and Donna in my office. This is gonna fucking gut them. All the Charons and Cowboys, including prospects and old ladies in the meeting room. I want all the club whores locked down in the back room. I want to know if anyone saw anything. I'll put Tiny and Arrow on the doors while we sort this shit out. What a fucking cluster fuck."

I couldn't move. I'd promised Zara she'd be safe here and instead she'd been led directly to her enemy. One of our own had sold my fucking woman out. I glared down at Em's lifeless body. Clearly she'd paid a heavy price already, but it didn't stop my rage. Suddenly Eagle was up in my grill.

"Deep breath, Mac. You can do this. Lose your shit, Scout'll lock you down. You want to go get your woman? You gotta keep your shit together. Em's paid for her mistake. Let that part of this go. One of those dead prospects was a Cowboy. That's two of them the Iron

Hammers have taken now, and this boy didn't do shit to deserve it. We will get your girl back. With the Cowboys backing us up, we're gonna wipe the fuckers out for this."

I looked my friend and brother directly in the eye before I spoke. "But will we be in time to save her?"

Eagle's wince wasn't encouraging, but at least he was honest. I forced my legs to move, to take me back inside the clubhouse where I knew plans would already be in the process of being made.

Hold on bunny, I'm coming for you. Just fucking hold on.

Chapter 12

Zara

I tried to swallow but my mouth was too dry. The sounds of moaning and grunts had me not wanting to open my eyes, but I knew full well not looking wasn't going to change anything. At this stage, I figured it was better that I know where I was. Taking a deep breath, I cracked my lids open and scanned the room.

I was on a mattress on the floor, along with several other girls. Naked, or mostly naked girls. A quick glance down had a wave of relief flowing through me when I saw I was still dressed. Fuck, the ones closest to me all looked like teenagers. Babies that should be home with their parents. Most of them were asleep. At least, I hoped they were asleep and not dead. One girl was thrashing her head and moaning, while scratching the holy hell out of her arms. Drugs maybe? I winced when my gaze caught on a man who was pumping into one of the unconscious teens. *Disgusting.* With a loud grunt, he held still a moment before pulling free of her. He stood, leaving the girl as she fell, her legs spread wide to reveal his white cum leaking from her to soak into the mattress. My stomach rolled and I bit my cheek to stop the sound of my gagging from leaving my mouth.

"Need a fix, do ya baby? You know you gotta earn that shit."

He was looming over the thrashing girl now. He hadn't put himself away and I could clearly see his spent dick laying limp out of his open jeans. What did he expect her to do?

"Pleeease. It hurts…"

He stroked her face gently. "Oh, I know it does, sugar. You put that mouth to good use and I'll take care of you."

I turned away and squeezed my eyes shut tight. This was the room Marie had told me about. The Iron Hammers were still doing it. My stomach rolled again. How many girls had this club taken and twisted into drug-addicted whores over the decades? Blocking my sight didn't help prevent my hearing. The sounds of that biker getting his blow job, then him shooting up the girl had me both furious and sick to my stomach.

"Sledge wants the new girl brought to him. She awake yet?"

"Yeah, she woke up a bit ago. Don't think she liked the show I put on for her, though."

The humor in the bastard's voice set my anger off.

"Time to wake up, bitch."

I gasped when I was lifted from the floor with a hand wrapped in my hair. Once I caught my breath, I remembered that class of Mac's I'd taken. Damn, I wish I'd taken more than that one class. I eyed the biker holding me. *Throat.* That was an open soft spot. I swung my arm, aiming high but he easily blocked it with a laugh.

"Aww, the kitten has claws. Sledge'll love that."

Before I could do anything else, he had both my hands in one of his behind me and was guiding me out of the room. He kept his grip on my hair tight enough my eyes watered as he pushed me through hallways and into another room. This one had a raised bed, but not much else. My illnesses were tugging at my mind and body, wanting me to give in, but I fought them. I'd seen these bastards were more than happy to rape an unconscious woman.

With a scream, I thrashed against his hold, not caring about the hair being pulled out or the tension in my arms and shoulders. I had to get free and run. I blindly threw out kicks, smiling whenever I managed to make a connection with flesh. I was released, but before I could work out which way to run, pain shot through my jaw as a fist connected with it. I hit the floor from the force of the blow, then cataplexy took me out the rest of the way.

I was roughly picked up and tossed on the bed as two men cursed me. Guess I landed more than a couple of kicks on them. Go, me! When they started pulling at my clothes, panic had me fighting through the attack. I refused to lie here helpless as I was raped. As my shirt tore and I felt the cool air of the room on my skin, my body finally responded, my fist flying aimlessly in front of me as I opened my eyes.

"Fuckin' hell. Cuff her already."

I knew that voice from the cafe in Galveston. I glanced toward the sound and saw a huge man who had a nasty glint in his eye as he eyed my now-exposed chest. The lacy bra Mac had given me showed more than it covered and I hated that these assholes were seeing me in it.

I growled but couldn't fight free when my wrists were grabbed and held above my head. Metal clinks sounded a moment before cold metal enclosed each wrist. Within seconds, the cuffs cut into my skin painfully as I continued to fight against their hold.

"The club will come for me. They're gonna come in here and destroy you!"

The big man laughed. "Sure they are, sugar. That tiny little pissant club of yours wouldn't dare step foot in my clubhouse. They might be able to keep us out of Bridgewater, but they don't have the fucking numbers to come onto our turf and challenge me directly."

Hands tugged at my skirt and I kicked out as much as I could. It jerked my arms and warm liquid trickled down my arm. Blood. My fucking blood!

"Stop it! You don't need to do this. I ran. I didn't make my statement formal, there's no reason to hurt me!"

Suddenly the big man's face was right in front of mine, his fingers digging painfully into my jaw.

"Bull fucking shit there's no reason. You told that fucking LEO what you heard, got me and my boys a night in lockup. You need to pay for that shit. Since I like how you look, you get to pay on your back. It's especially sweet after what your pops did."

I went silent, stunned at the mention of my father.

Without releasing his hold on my face he glanced around the room, his eyes going hard when he saw something across the room.

"Tic, pass me those bungee cords would ya? Got a better use for this mouth other than talkin'."

My breath caught in my throat as my lungs froze for a moment. What was he planning on doing with those cords? I locked my jaw, clenching it as hard as I could when he took one of the hooked ends and zeroed his gaze in on my mouth with an evil grin.

"Open up, sugar."

He dug his fingers into my cheeks until my eyes watered, and, with a whimper, my jaw unclenched. In one fast movement, he had the hook in my mouth, the cord around the back of my head and the other end hooked into the opposite side of my mouth. The ends of the hooks dug into the insides of my cheeks painfully, and my already-dry lips cracked and pulled with the strain. He grabbed a second one and did the same with that one, putting the two straps in a way that they crossed over behind my head and the hooks pulled my lips wide. My jaw was forced wide open to try to prevent my lips tearing. The pain was almost overwhelming.

"That's better. Now, something to fill that hole with."

He went for his belt and once more, bile rose up my throat. Ignoring the pain, I glared at the asshole as I forced my jaw shut till my teeth met with a snap. Without a word I made it clear what I would do to anything he put in my fucking mouth.

His smile dropped to a frown. "Fucking bitch."

He moved back down to continue to pull at my skirt, scratching my leg in the process, so I started up my kicking again. I managed to land a knee in his face but before I could celebrate, he buried his fist in my stomach, winding me a moment before my stomach called time out and the bile that I'd been fighting since I woke wouldn't be contained. My body convulsed with a groan before I threw up. The hot liquid splashed down my chest and splattered over the bed. My lips being held open really didn't help things.

It wasn't just my food that left me, but all my energy as well. Within moments, I felt waves of lethargy wash over me. I needed to take my meds.

"What the fuck?"

I forced my tired eyes to look up at, who I assumed was Sledge, to see I'd splattered his front, too. Good. I would have grinned at the horrified look on his face if I could have. This big tough, rough biker who'd been ready to rape me a moment ago was grossed out by a bit of puke. I mean, his men were happy to fuck unconscious teenagers so I could only assume he felt the same way. Seemed hilarious that this was a no-go for him. My mind went into a hazy place that meant I was going to be out in a deep sleep soon, but I couldn't muster the energy to care. A chuckle escaped me as I began to float around in my mind.

"You think this is fucking funny, bitch?"

Stars and pain exploded in my head as his fist connected with the opposite side of my face than was hit earlier. Then I was out, my mind detaching completely from my body and various injuries, floating away to someplace else. A place where the pain was gone.

Mac

It seemed to take forever before we got moving. I was about ready to come out of my fucking skin by the time Scout and Maverick gave the go ahead for us all to head south. As I opened the door on the cage, Maverick came to me.

"I know you're pissed we waited, but this is bigger than I think you realize and to ensure the right outcome, we had to wait."

I knew how big this shit was. The Iron Hammers MC was about to be shut down, hard. Doing that and getting out clean was going to be a challenge. Generally speaking, the cops looked the other way when bikers took out bikers, but with the body count we were planning on dropping when we got down there, I doubted it was going to be that easy to clean up after. Not that I gave a fuck at the moment. I planned on getting Zara back at any cost.

"They've had my girl for hours. Fucking hours. I know Scout showed y'all those fucking photos of what they've been doing to women. What the fuck do you think they're doing to my Zara right now? I'm a Marine, I get the need to plan and have back-up sorted out. But when it's my fucking woman's life on the line, my patience is shot to shit."

Maverick gave me a nod. "I can respect that. And that's why, despite your training, you're not in charge here. You're too close. And you're not the only one with military blood, brother. I did my time."

I didn't doubt that for a moment. Maverick was a big, tough bastard and I could easily see him in a uniform. He also had this air of authority around him you couldn't miss. Made me wonder why he was VP, not president. Also made me wonder what kind of man was the damn president, considering the VP. It was equally easy to see why the feds wanted dirt on his club. I doubted Maverick or, assuming their president was of the same breed, their president, were men to be put in anyone's pocket easily.

When I stayed silent, Maverick gave me a grunt and a nod before he left to mount his bike. I hopped in, and after I slammed the door, Keys gunned the engine and we were out the gates. The air around the normally upbeat man was dark with grief.

"I'm sorry about your daughter, brother."

I was a little shocked that both Keys and his old lady, Donna, had insisted on coming.

"Thanks. Not sure exactly what her role in all this shit was yet, but if she led your woman to those bastards, I'm so fucking sorry."

Donna spoke up from the rear of the vehicle. "Em was always a handful, but she'd been even more so these past six months. She'd started doing drugs and staying out all hours. I'd hoped she'd wake up and calm down but it was wishful thinking. Not like I don't see this shit at work every damn day."

Both their voices sounded so fucking weary. I could only imagine what watching your child spiral downward must do to a parent. The fact Donna was a nurse and had seen where Em was heading must have made it so much worse.

"You did all you could, honey."

Rose, Bulldog's old lady had also refused to be left behind. Now the woman wrapped her arm around Donna, pulling her in for a hug. I had to say something, clear the air. I didn't blame either Keys or Donna for Em's choices.

"Whole fucking thing is wrong on so many levels."

"Amen to that, brother. A-fucking-men."

Key's words were the last said for the entire hour-long trip down to Galveston. We pulled up two blocks away from the Iron Hammers' clubhouse in a supermarket parking lot. It was just past two in the morning so the place was empty—well, apart from the dozens of bikes and a few other vehicles that now filled the place. Glancing over all the cuts, I could see there were a few extra Satan's Cowboys that hadn't been at church earlier, along with a few men not wearing cuts but standing tall and proud like they knew where they were and happy to be about to kick some asses. I opened the door and stepped out of the vehicle.

Maverick moved to stand in front of where everyone had gathered. "Everyone, take a good look around. We don't want any one going down to friendly fire. Everyone here is on the same fucking side. Primary goal is to get Mac's old lady, Zara, out of there. Secondary goal is to shut their shit down. That's where these three come into things." He nodded to the men not wearing colors and they stepped forward, the largest of the three in front. "Viper sent these boys in down here a few days before the shooting, they've been doing a little undercover work for us. Once we clean house, they'll be in charge of the Iron Hammers, under Satan's Cowboy's guidance." Annnd there was the "bigger picture". Viper, president of the Satan's Cowboys, apparently wanted a presence down south and the Iron Hammers fucking up had been their in. "Joaquin is a cousin of the president of the Iron Wolves MC up in South Dakota. If you've heard of the club, you know what kind of man he is." He turned his attention to Joaquin. "I thought your cousin was going to be joining us tonight?"

Joaquin moved forward. "He'll be here any moment." He scanned the rest of us. "We used the delivery of a custom ride from the Iron Wolves to their secretary, Trip, as a cover to get in the door so Sledge never suspected we were anything but a couple of men looking for a place to belong. Since coming down here, we've been doing what we can without making it obvious what we're up to. What the club is doing to those girls is some seriously fucked-up shit." He turned to look me in the eye and I had to appreciate the strength behind the stare. "Your woman is in a bad way, but I believe she's been spared from being raped. So far."

One of the men standing behind Joaquin snorted and I growled at the fucker. "You find the idea of a woman being raped funny, boy?"

As I spoke, Joaquin elbowed the man hard in the gut, doubling him over. "Sorry about that. None of us find anything about what those bastards do to girls funny. Your woman fucking puked all over Sledge when he was about to have a go at her. Seeing him covered in that shit was kinda funny. Scott was given the job of cleaning her up—" I stepped forward with fists clenched but didn't get more than two steps before Taz and Eagle had me restrained and Joaquin held his palms up.

"Dammit Jenna, give me some fucking warning before you do that shit."

"Aww, poor Wolfie—"

"Would you two cut the shit, already? You're scaring the natives."

I shook my head and blinked a few times to make sure I was really seeing the two huge men and a tiny woman who seemed to have just appeared out of nowhere. What the fuck?

The men were both over six feet tall and built big. They could be twins, except for their different hair and eye color. The one who'd spoken first was dark as night, with black hair and piercing blue eyes. The other one was blond with intense brown eyes. The aura of power radiating off them had me resting my hand over my sheathed knife. The little pixie-like woman turned her gaze on me and I sucked in a breath. She looked like she was in her twenties, but her unusual turquoise eyes told a different story.

"Oh, no, you don't need to worry, Jacob. Kellen and Xan won't hurt you. Well, if you mess with their mates they might. But since they're not here, but there, you'll be fine."

How the fuck did she know my name? My real one? I licked my lips to question the woman but didn't get a chance to talk before the dark haired man spoke up.

"Right. I'm Kellen, the alpha of the Iron Wolves MC, this is my second, Xan. We're here to help you lot clean out the Iron Hammers, then we'll be on our way."

"Alpha?"

Then the little pixie chick started giggling as she skipped over toward me, where she patted me on the chest before I could duck out of her reach.

"Alpha, president... potato, tomato... it's all the same. No need to worry."

I didn't know what to say. This woman was clearly fucking insane. I couldn't see how she was going be an asset with what we had to do this morning.

"And that is Jenna. Batshit crazy but you learn to love her. She's also tougher than she looks. Don't underestimate her."

The woman's face softened as she turned back to Kellen. "Aww, I knew you loved me."

Maverick stepped in front of Kellen. "You're not planning on cutting out early, are you?"

The lighter-haired one laughed. "Oh, we'll stay till the fun and games are over. Been a while since I got to crack some skulls, but Kellen needs to make sure he gets home before his team arrives."

I was getting a headache trying to follow what the fuck these guys were talking about. Was it some fucked up code their club used?

"Shut the fuck up, Xan. At least I'm not still practicing how to get the fucking job done."

That earned Kellen a nasty glare and growl from Xan.

"Don't frown, Jacob. Or do you prefer Mac?" She shook her head before I could answer. "Kellen's mate is pregnant, with an undetermined number of babies, so he wants to get back to her. Xan's mate isn't knocked up yet, which makes her about the only mated woman up there not pregnant—"

"Jenna, do I need to call your wolpires in to contain you? Quit telling the world shit they shouldn't know."

What the fuck was a wolpire? With a glare, Jenna pointed her dainty finger at the much larger and stronger man. How fucking crazy was she?

"No mentioning those that shall not be named." She dropped her hand down. "They have a nasty habit of showing up when you do that."

Figuring all three of them must be batshit insane, I cleared my throat to stop their shit. "I have no idea what fucking drugs you three are on, and I don't give a fuck. Joaquin, you weren't done telling me about Zara. Make it fast so we can get this show on the fucking road already."

The younger man cut a look to Kellen, like he needed that man's permission. Whatever. So long as we got back on task, I didn't give a shit who held his leash.

"Um, yeah. Sure. Viper had gotten word to me about who she was. So don't get your panties in a twist over it. Be fucking grateful it was one of mine. Scott was a lot more careful with her than any of the others in that place would have been. It also means that when he returned her to the whore room, he didn't shoot her up like he was instructed. The needle got jammed into the mattress, not her arm. She's gonna need medical attention, but not as much as she would have if Sledge and his buddies had finished with her. They told us to clean her up, dump her back in the whore room and drug her up, so she would be ready for them once they got themselves cleaned up. So time is definitely ticking on getting in there to her."

I stepped forward looking between Maverick, Scout and Joaquin. "I want Sledge and whoever else has hurt Zara taken back to the Charons' clubhouse and held. I get to deal with those fuckers personally."

Scout looked to Maverick and shrugged. "We got the cell space."

Maverick nodded at Scout's words. "I'll have to run it past Viper first, but if we can, we will. No promises. There's more important shit going on here than your need for a pound of flesh, we clear?"

I responded with a "Yes, sir" before I realized what I was doing. I'd felt like I was back in the USMC for a moment there.

"Right, then. Let's move out and get this thing done. Just in case it's not Mac that finds Zara, she's to be brought directly to that van. Donna and Rose will tend to her."

I winced as I climbed back in the cage. We all knew in the hours they'd had my girl, they would have done damage to her. Joaquin's words confirming it didn't exactly ease my mind. With a deep breath, I closed my eyes as Keys drove us to the Iron Hammers' compound. *Please be alive, bunny.*

The vehicle we decided to bring down was basically a fucking tank. The club didn't use it much because it wasn't needed, but tonight I was beyond glad we had the thing. The rear interior was kitted out with a basic ambulance-type set-up, perfect for our needs. The bullet-proof glass and armor plating on the exterior were also just what we needed. The huge fucking reinforced grill on the front meant Keys could drive straight through just about anything without having to even slow down. That included the barred gate at the entrance of the Iron Hammers' compound. I had to chuckle at the ease with which the vehicle sent the thing flying. The roar of all the Harleys following us in was deafening. No way did the entire fucking club not hear that we were coming for them.

Slipping my USMC issued k-bar knife free from its sheath, I jumped out of the cage and followed the other men into the building. Just before I stepped through the front door, Jenna grabbed my arm with surprising force. I glared into her strange eyes, pissed off that she'd slowed me down. "Take Joaquin with you. Don't ask questions, just accept the fact that not all humans are, well, human. You've accepted Eagle and his abilities, treat Joaquin in the same way and you'll get to your girl faster. Understand?"

Since Joaquin had spent weeks in this place, it was logical he'd know his fucking way around. I had no fucking clue what she meant about Eagle though, but didn't want to waste time arguing the point with the crazy lady. Not when I was this close to getting Zara back, so I ignored the rest of her comment. "Fine, whatever. I'm going in."

Joaquin pushed in front of me and I frowned at the man when he paused a moment to sniff the fucking air like a damn dog, before he headed off toward a side hall. This day was getting weirder by the moment.

Naturally, fighting had broken out the moment we entered, but I didn't engage. There were enough Charons and Cowboys to keep the Hammers occupied. I caught a glimpse of Kellen and Xan standing together, plowing through men. Fucking hell, those two could fight. I made a mental note to never piss either man off. Even with all my Marine training, I wasn't sure I'd be able to take down either of those two boys.

Turning away from the fighting, I followed Joaquin around the brawling men in the main room. My goal was to find my girl, then I'd worry about fucking up these bastards that dared take her from me. If there were any left, that is.

Moments after we entered the hallway, two bikers, who were still doing up their fucking pants, busted out of a room further up, and with curses, came at us. Joaquin didn't fuck around. He throat punched the first one hard enough I was pretty sure I heard the fucker's spine snap. I slashed my knife across the other man's throat, deep enough to kill the asshole. Only one reason I could think of that he'd be coming out of a room with his pants undone, so I didn't feel one moment of guilt for ending the fucker. Before his body hit the ground I was running for the room he'd come out of. Joaquin stayed a step ahead of me, kicking the door in and moving aside to cover me as I entered first.

"Fuck me."

I'd been told. Seen the old photos, but the sight still knocked the breath out of my lungs. The room was filled with women. No, that wasn't right. They were only fucking girls. Teenagers. Either completely naked or with their clothes torn to shit, they all looked drugged out of their minds. A flash of my sister's broken body filled my vision for a moment as rage flowed through my veins. An animistic growl had me stiffening and glancing toward Joaquin. The man's eyes flashed a bright blue and I could have sworn he had fur for a minute there. What the fuck was he? A familiar feminine groan had me ignoring whatever the fuck was going on with Joaquin and turning to search for my girl.

"Oh, fucking hell. Zara? Baby..."

I carefully and quickly stepped over bodies until I got to her side. She was a fucking mess, but still wore her bra and panties. I hoped like hell that meant Joaquin was right and she hadn't been raped. Her lips were cracked, and the skin around her mouth was a mess. She still smelled like puke, and when I looked closer at her bra, I could see the remnants of it caught in the fabric. With a groan she lifted a hand to me, trying to roll toward me. I hissed at the sight of her flesh cut up around both of her wrists. They'd fucking cuffed her. And they'd been pretty brutal about it.

"Shh, babe. I've got you. You're safe now. I'm gonna lift you up and take you out to Donna. She's a nurse. Rose is out there, too. Then we'll take you home." *Where I'm never letting you outta my sight again.*

As gently as I could, I lifted her up and cradled her against my chest. She shivered and whimpered at the movement, and it broke my damn heart in the process. I looked for Joaquin to ask him to cover me as I took her out, but he was kneeling down beside one of the girls. Checking for a pulse by the looks of it. He wouldn't be any help.

"C'mon, mate. I got your back."

A glance to the door had relief pouring through me. Taz stood at attention, with Eagle by his side. Just like always, my Marine brothers had my back. I strode out of the room and with my brothers surrounding me, I made my way out of the building. I heard a few hisses and curses as we passed through the main room but I didn't stop. In that moment I didn't give a fuck that other men were seeing my girl in her underwear. Her beautiful face was bruised up, her lips torn. Scratch marks ran down her left thigh and a large bruise had formed on the side of her stomach. Not to mention her wrists.

I really hoped they saved at least one of these fuckers for me to take my time destroying. The rage inside me was growing out of control and I knew I was going to need to vent it on something, and soon.

Taz knocked on the rear door of the van before turning to raise his weapon to provide cover. Eagle took the other side in a similar pose as Keys opened the way to allow me to climb in with my precious load.

"It's bad, Donna. She hasn't really woken up since I found her."

Donna's warm hand squeezed my shoulder as I laid Zara out on the stretcher. "That could simply be her narcolepsy. You're too close to do this, Mac. Go with Taz and Eagle and let Rose and me take care of your girl. Keys will stand guard."

"C'mon, brother. Go crack some skulls, vent your anger on them. Then come back and we'll head home."

I knew they were right. I'd just be in the way and make it harder for them to treat her if I stayed.

"Just give me a sec with her, yeah?"

They all backed up as much as the cramped space allowed and I gently stroked fingertips down Zara's cheek before kissing her forehead. She looked like a broken doll lying on the white sheet. With my mouth close to her ear, I whispered to her so no one else would hear me.

"I love you so fucking much, Zara, I can't breathe without you. You hold on and I'll be back by your side before you know it."

With tears stinging my eyes I turned and leapt from the vehicle. Keys followed me out and stood at the rear of the vehicle.

"You armed?"

He frowned at me like I'd insulted him. "Of course. Go on and get in there. I've got this."

With a nod I turned back toward the clubhouse and along with Taz and Eagle went to go see if there were any of the bastards left that needed a beating.

Chapter 13

Mac

The sun still hadn't risen when we pulled into the Charon's compound. I glanced down at Zara again, watching her chest rise and fall with even breaths. Donna had been certain nothing was broken, but that didn't mean Zara wasn't going to be hurting for a while. Her wrists had white bandages around them and her face was shiny from the ointment they'd been continually applying to her jaw and mouth. Donna had also put in a drip to make sure she was fully hydrated, and given her some pain meds to keep her sleeping peacefully for another few hours. When we came to a stop, I carefully untangled my hand from Zara's and moved to open the door. Rolling my shoulders, I stretched out my neck and spine while I watched the bikes and the other vehicles roll in around us.

When Maverick pulled a cuffed Sledge from the rear of another vehicle, I clenched my fists. That fucker was gonna be all mine to deal with.

"What the—"

I glanced to Donna who stood beside me, with her palm cupped over her mouth. Her face had drained of color and she suddenly looked seconds away from passing out. Before I could ask her what was wrong, Sledge started laughing. Crazy bastard.

"Hey, Donna baby, how's that daughter of ours doing? You didn't think I'd ever find out about her, huh?"

Dead fucking silence.

The entire yard seemed to freeze in shock, myself included, before Donna snapped.

"You fucking bastard! It was you who got to her, wasn't it? It was you who took my girl from me!"

"She came to me, darlin'. Not my fault she preferred her real daddy—"

She flew across the yard and delivered a harsh slap across his face. And when the fucker laughed, she followed it up with a kick to his groin before any of us knew what was coming. Whoa. Sledge went down with a groan, Maverick did nothing to stop the bastard from falling in a heap. Nor did he do a thing to stop her from getting a few more kicks in. I couldn't remember ever hearing that woman swear before, let alone drop an F bomb. This violent streak was new, too.

Keys ran to his old lady and pulled her back from Sledge before he scooped her up against him. She wrapped herself around his neck as she started sobbing. No one moved until the door shut behind them.

"Well, I guess that answers the question of who Em's biological father was. Along with why Donna ended up in Bridgewater. I swear we need to start having a fucking sit-down with every fucking woman that enters this damn town to get to the bottom of why the fuck they're here. Way too many fucking secrets." Scout continued to grumble and complain as he strolled toward the front door. "Maverick, bring that piece of shit downstairs, along with the other two. Mac, get your woman settled, then come find me. I'll be in the bar. Need a good strong fucking drink after all this shit."

Scout's rant seemed to break the ice and everyone started talking and moving around the yard. I leaned back in the van to gather Zara in my arms. Rose helped settle a sheet around her so she was covered. Fuck, it felt good to have her warm, soft body against me. Even if she did look like a hot mess.

"I'll carry her drip and get it sorted up in your room, then I'll leave you to it. Are you fine to take it out when the bag's empty?"

"Thanks, Rose. I've got it covered. Listen, I can get her settled on my own, if you want to go help with Donna."

The older woman leaned in and gave me a peck on the cheek. "You're a good man, Mac. Take care of your girl."

With that, Rose set the drip bag on Zara before heading after Donna and Keys. Minutes later, I laid my woman out on my bed, and hung the bag on the edge of the lamp next to the bed. Once I was certain it was all working correctly, I laid down beside Zara and gently ran my hand over her face, avoiding the bruises.

"I'm so fucking sorry, bunny."

Knowing Scout was waiting on me and that Zara wouldn't be waking up for at least another couple of hours, I pressed a kiss to her forehead before I forced myself to get up and leave the room. I found Silk pacing the hallway.

"How is she?"

"Sleeping. She's pretty banged up, but nothing that won't heal. You want to sit with her? I gotta go see Scout before I can call it a night."

When Silk nodded, I unlocked my door to let her in, instantly feeling better that I wasn't leaving Zara alone. I'd hate for her to have woken early and found herself all alone.

"Thanks, Silk."

She winced as she looked Zara over. "I feel so fucking guilty. I should have—"

"Stop, Silk. This isn't on you. You were sick. It's not your fault and we all assumed Zara was safe here in the clubhouse. No way could any of us have known Sledge and gotten to Em somehow."

"Didn't see that one coming."

"Don't think any of us did. Okay, I gotta get moving. I'll be back as soon as I can."

She shooed me out of the room. "Go, do your thing. I've got her covered."

I jogged down to the bar, wanting to get this shit over with fast so I could get back to my woman. Grabbing a beer from the prospect manning the bar, I went to Scout, who was sitting at one of the tables with Bulldog, Maverick and another Cowboy whose name I couldn't remember.

"Where is the fucker?"

Scout raised an eyebrow. "Show some respect, brother. Sledge is down in the basement. He's not going anywhere. Donna got a few good licks in but there's still plenty life left in him for you to beat out of him. Although, I suspect Keys is gonna want a fucking go at him with you. Before either of you kill him, we might want to see what information he can give us about Em."

I scrubbed a palm over my head before I took a seat beside them. "Sorry, no disrespect intended. It's been a helluva long night."

"And as the sun's not yet up, it ain't fucking over."

I nodded at Bulldog's words. "So, what's gonna happen with Iron Hammers now?"

Maverick leaned forward, resting his elbows on the table. "We're going to give Joaquin and his boys a go at running things. If the club folds, another will take its place. Viper would prefer it happen this way, where we've got some control over them. I've seen the Iron Wolves' setup in South Dakota. They run a good, clean club, not dissimilar to you boys here.

"They focus on mechanics and tricking out custom vehicles for their income. Well, that and their bar. I think a similar system would work well down in Galveston, once they get shit sorted with those women. But there'll be none of that kidnapping and drugging shit that Sledge and his boys were pulling."

I took in Maverick for a minute. The Satan's Cowboys were a one-percenter club, so I hadn't been one hundred percent sure they were going to disagree with how the Iron Hammers had dealt with the girls. "So where do the Cowboys draw the line in the sand on this shit? It's not unheard of for one-percenter clubs to trade in skin."

Maverick stiffened and growled at me. "The line is consent and being fucking over the legal age. I got daughters, and I wouldn't stand for that shit happening to them. Sure as hell don't want to see it happen to someone else's baby girl, either."

I lifted my palms. "Don't get pissed off with me, I was just wanting things clear and in the open." I took a swig of my beer as Maverick and the other Cowboy leaned back in the seats, calming down. "Speaking of out in the open—what the fuck is the deal with the Iron Wolves and that chick, Jenna, was it?"

Maverick shook his head. "Don't ask, man. I've got no concrete answers for you. They sure as shit ain't fully human. I've heard stories about Kellen that were enough to have even me watching myself around the man. I'd recommend not pissing him off. The best way to deal with the Wolves is to take a policy of live and let live. And be fucking grateful to have them on your side if you get in a bind. From what I can tell, Joaquin and his boys are of the same breed, so you'd best get used to them being a little different."

I took another long drink of my beer. "They're certainly different that's for sure. What about clean-up down in Galveston? What was the body count in the end?"

"Before Kellen left, he said Jenna would handle the bodies. Not sure on a final number yet, but I'd guess somewhere around twenty. A fair few of them surrendered to us. Bastards seemed relieved when we took down Sledge and dragged his ass out. I'll head back down there later today, after we take the scum downstairs back home, and help Joaquin sort out who's staying and who's going. Nothing the Charons need to get involved in at this point."

Guess the Cowboys were taking the other two Iron Hammers that had been brought in with Sledge. I didn't give a fuck, so long as they left Sledge for me. I gave Maverick a nod before I drained the last of my beer. "Well, if we don't need to go back down south and are going to leave dealing with Sledge until later, do you mind if I get back upstairs?"

Scout chuckled. "Yeah, go take care of your woman. We've got more than just their president downstairs. We'll keep Sledge for you and Keys. But if the boys need something to hit, I'll let them have a go at one of the others, well, at least until Maverick takes them with him that is."

I half wanted to ask how many Iron Hammers had fucking been brought back. But my need to check in with Zara was stronger. I stood, said a quick goodbye and headed upstairs. I knew I wouldn't be inside her any time soon. I didn't deserve the right after I'd not kept her safe. That, and she was too injured. She'd need time to heal. But it didn't matter. If I could just have her in my arms, be close enough to hear her heartbeat, to see her chest rise and fall with her breaths—to fucking know she was alive and safe—that would be enough.

Zara

I frowned at the feel of the soft mattress beneath me. The fact that something was over my naked body keeping me warm had my mind spinning too. Was this another dream? I'd had some fucked-up dreams during the night. Angry men with eyes that flashed a bright blue, Mac coming for me, carrying me away and telling me he loved me. I had no idea what was real and what wasn't.

My thoughts were so jumbled and I was so fucking tired.

I needed to take my meds.

"Wake up, bunny."

I froze and held my breath, praying I was really awake and not dreaming. Callused fingers gently traced over my face.

"C'mon, Zara, open those pretty hazel eyes for me. See for yourself, you're safe."

"Mac?"

Wanting him to be real, I forced my eyes to open. I had to blink a few times before they'd open enough for me to focus on the beautiful face frowning down at me.

"You're real."

I lifted my palm to cup his cheek, and the scratching of his stubble over my palm was another sign this wasn't a dream. He turned to press a kiss against my skin. *So very, definitely, real.* The stark white bandage on my wrist caught my attention and I pulled my hand from his face. Memories of the night before were mixed up with the dreams, but as I ran my gaze over both my wrists the memory of them snapping cuffs on me became crystal clear, making me whimper.

"Your wrists were cut up. Donna cleaned them up and bandaged them. She doesn't think the cuts were deep enough to scar."

I flexed my fingers and rolled my wrists, happy to discover I had full movement. "They didn't like me fighting them, so they cuffed me to the bed." I ran my tongue over my lips, wincing at the sting.

"You want a drink? Your meds?"

I nodded absently as I ran my tongue over the insides of my cheeks. There were small rough patches where the hooks had been. Damn the bastards. Mac helped me sit up, making sure I had enough pillows behind me. He was being painfully gentle with me and I had to wonder if he would still want me like he had before. He was such a strong, powerful man. And his passion was rough. I liked him that way. A lot.

He leaned over me, his scent distracting. Fresh, clean and all man. My favorite smell in the world. I tried to smile, stopping when my lips hurt.

"Here's your meds from your handbag, and some painkillers Donna left for you. She told me these ones wouldn't knock you out, but would just take the edge off."

I quickly took the pills and the glass of water Mac held out, and made fast work of swallowing them. Then I leaned back against the pillows and stared at Mac as he returned everything to the bedside table. He came back with a tube of something in his hand.

"No idea what the fuck they did to your mouth, but your lips are messed up. We've been putting this ointment on every couple hours. It seems to be working. Your mouth is looking a lot better than it was."

I lifted my palm to his face again. He was so sweet, and clearly out of his comfort zone. He was speaking faster, and saying more than he would normally.

"Thank you."

His expression softened as he covered my hand with his, holding it to him for a few seconds before he released me.

"How can you thank me? If it wasn't for me, you wouldn't have been here, wouldn't have been taken."

My heart softened. Seemed my big, tough biker had been busy beating himself up.

"Don't be stupid, Mac. They would have snatched me from wherever I was when they found me. I'm not sure how they knew I was here since I hadn't met Em until last night, but she already knew exactly who I was."

He winced but didn't say another word until he'd carefully applied ointment to my lips and the skin around them.

"What happened when you were taken?"

With a sigh, I stared up at the ceiling. "I was helping Silk set up the tables in the backyard. I guess she pushed it too far and she raced off to the bathroom, looking a little green. I was walking back to the kitchen to join the other women when Em came up to me in the hall and asked if I would help her get something from her mom's car. I stopped at the bathroom quickly to check on Silk, then followed her outside. I knew something was wrong when I realized there were no prospects guarding the door. I tried to come back inside but was grabbed from behind. When I went to scream, Em slapped her hand over my mouth, bitched me out, then a needle was jammed in my neck and I was out."

Hot tears ran down my cheeks as I thought about where I'd woken up. I hoped like hell Mac didn't ask about it. I realized it was a stupid hope. If Mac didn't ask, I knew Scout would. He seemed to want to know all the details about everything.

"What'll happen to Em?"

I had no idea how a MC would deal with such a betrayal. She's the daughter of a brother after all. I probably didn't want to know, especially going by the look on Mac's face, but I needed to know what had happened to the woman who'd handed me over so willingly.

"When we went looking for you, we first found the bodies of the two prospects that had been guarding the front door. You were taken out through a hole in the fence behind the work shed. We found Em with her neck broken, near the fence."

"Oh, fuck. Keys and Donna must be devastated. Wait, you said Donna was the one who patched me up?"

"Yeah, she refused to be left behind. Not sure what she was thinking, but as a trained nurse, we couldn't turn her down."

"Do they know she was the one to hand me over?"

"No, bunny. We didn't know for sure if she handed you over or tried to help save you from being taken. We feared she was behind it, especially after Silk told us she took you out there but we all hoped she wasn't. I'm sure Scout'll want to talk to you when you're feeling up to it." His gaze turned intense. "I hate that you were hurt. That I broke my promise and didn't keep you safe."

Now that my meds had kicked in, I was feeling more myself, with no lethargy, and my thoughts were clearer. I knew I had to cut through Mac's misguided opinion this was his fault. I cupped his face between both my palms.

"Not. Your. Fault. You can't watch me twenty-four/seven. Shit happens to everyone. You came and got me out of there. That's what matters. Stop blaming yourself for shit you didn't do."

His eyes glossed over with moisture, shocking me. "You looked so fucking broken when I found you. I thought—fuck, for a second I thought I was too late. Again."

I frowned as I held his gaze. "Again?"

He pulled from my grip and jumped up from the bed. He paced like a caged lion as my heart thundered in my chest. Something had happened in his past, something big that all this shit with me had triggered his memories of.

"You can tell me anything, Mac. I'll keep your secrets."

He turned to face me, his stare burning with pain. "If I tell you this, bare my soul to you, will you return the gesture? Will you tell me everything those fucking bastards did to you last night? Because I know you don't want me to know, to even ask. But if I do tell you what you're asking of me, you'll have knowledge of me that not even Taz and Eagle have. I've not spoken a word to anyone about it in nearly twenty years."

I had a strong feeling whatever this secret was, it was the reason he'd joined the USMC in the first place. It was something huge, and life-altering, and I knew deep down I needed to know to understand this man fully. As much as I really didn't want to have to rehash last night, I would. For Mac, I would do it. Our relationship was new, but he was already part of my heart and soul. I didn't want to live without this man. So it looked like I was going to have to put my big girl panties on and be brave. Tell him everything I could remember from last night.

"Okay, then. You show me yours, I'll show you mine."

Chapter 14

Mac

Zara had curled her fists tightly into the bedding and her face had paled a little when I'd asked her to share her secrets. I hadn't expected her to actually agree. I'd been sure she was going to back off, but nope. My girl showed how strong she was by squaring her shoulders and daring me with a "You show me yours, I'll show you mine." As though we were in school and comparing test scores or something.

I scrubbed my palms over my face. Was I really going to do this? Tell Zara about my sister? Dropping my hands, I continued with my pacing.

"Bee - Beatrice was only three years younger than me. As a baby she'd been a pretty little thing. That only grew as she got older. She had this thick, black hair, and these big dark brown eyes. Typical Italian I guess, but to me she always reminded me of an angel. And I failed her. Didn't keep her protected. It was my job as her big brother. I knew our parents were too busy working to do it. Fuck."

I had to stop to clear my throat. Talking about Bee like this had memories flashing through my mind. A rustling sound had me turning toward the bed. Zara slipped from the mattress to stand. She was completely naked and I was grateful I'd taken the time to clean her up as best I could while she'd been out with the pain meds. However, even with her skin clean of dirt, her body still bore the marks of what those bastards had done to her and I couldn't hold back the growl that escaped as I saw each and every scratch and bruise. An image of Bee's broken body flickered over Zara's. I closed my eyes and dropped my face, trying to banish the image.

Soft, warm fingers slid over my stomach and around to my back. Lush breasts pressed against my torso a moment before Zara pressed a kiss over my heart. My arms snapped out, one wrapping around her waist, pressing her hard against me, while the other tangled in her hair. I took a deep breath, filling my lungs with Zara's smell. I wanted this over with, then I could bury myself in her body and let it all go. *Hopefully.* If she'd let me.

"Bee was a dreamer. Never saw the bad in people. I guess she was lonely, too. My parents worked hard with the family business. A restaurant. Probably too hard, we didn't get a whole lot of quality time with them growing up. And I was too busy enjoying my final years of high school, distracted with pumping iron, chasing girls and screwing around with my mates to notice Bee was drifting.

"A boy made the most of her loneliness. A fucking gangbanger hooked my sweet, baby sister in when she was just fifteen. Fourteen months later she was dead. The little fucker had been handing her around between his friends, and beating on her. We had no idea until it was too late. Till he took it too fucking far and killed her."

Zara gasped and her arms around me tightened. I pressed my face into her hair, breathing deep against her warmth.

"I was so angry, and I was such a stupid fucking kid. We lived in L.A. and I made a desperate decision to get revenge on the bastard. I went to the fucking mob. Even back then I was tall, and with all the gym work I'd been doing, I was strong. But I didn't have any fucking fighting skills. The mob soon dealt with that. And two months after we buried Bee I got to take that piece of shit out."

I went silent. The only sound in the room was my breathing, which was coming in and out of my lungs in ragged heaves. Fuck, I felt like I'd run a marathon.

"The mob didn't let you leave afterward, did they?"

"No, they didn't. My parents were left empty after Bee was murdered, then when the mob claimed me they couldn't take it. They sold up and moved down to Florida, away from all the memories. I wanted to go with them but the mob wouldn't release me. They knew I'd make a good enforcer and planned to train me as such. But I couldn't do it. Some of the assholes deserved the beat downs they got, but for the most part they were just desperate people who made the wrong choice to ask the mob for help."

"You could relate to them."

"Fuck, yeah. I saw myself in each one. So I enlisted, figuring if anyone wouldn't bend to the mob's pressure it'd be Uncle Sam. Turns out I was right. They left me alone."

"When was the last time you saw your parents, Mac?" Zara voice had gone whisper soft.

"My graduation from MCRD." She looked up at me with confusion in her gaze. "Marine Corp Recruiting Depot, it's the basic training I went through to become a Marine. I saw them in the crowd, but they were gone by the time I went to find them after the ceremony."

Her hot tears landed on my skin, melting my heart. This woman was too good for me. But right now, I didn't care. I wanted to make her mine, keep her always. "When I saw you on that mattress, all torn up, I saw Bee.

Thought I was too late again, that I'd lost you too." I took her face in my palms and tilted it up to mine. Her eyes were glossed over with moisture and her cheeks were wet with the tears she was shedding for me. "I can't lose you, Zara. Especially not like that. I'm gonna be over-protective and a pain in your ass, but I can't let you go."

Her lips kicked up a little. "Guess it's a good thing I like you all growly and caveman-like then, huh?"

"Growly? I'll show you growly, woman."

I lowered my face to hers, intending on taking her mouth hard but pulled back at the last moment. I'd nearly forgotten about her ripped up lips. Dammit. I'd nearly hurt her. I feathered light kisses over her healing skin. Her body went liquid against mine, all her weight leaning against me as she sighed. I ran my hands down her back until I could cup her delectable ass. I lifted her easily and she wrapped her legs around my waist as I stepped over to the bed. I moved over the mattress so I sat against the headboard, keeping her in my lap before I spoke again.

"Your turn, bunny."

Zara

Those three words had me stiffening. I was still reeling from his story, the trauma that had led him to the Marines and obviously onto the MC afterward. And his sister—I shuddered. No wonder he was the way he was about women. I pressed another kiss to his chest, right over his rapidly beating heart. I was straddling his lap, buck-ass naked, while he wore only a pair of gym shorts. But sex wouldn't be happening any time soon. Not until he got all the gory details, then who knew where things would go. I shifted so I sat sideways, his arms coming around me so I could comfortably snuggle up against his chest. I ran my fingertips through his chest hair, loving how he didn't wax or shave it like so many men did these days. Taking a deep breath, I rushed the story out, wanting to get it over with as fast as possible.

"I told you how I was taken already. I woke up lying on a filthy mattress to see a man screwing an unconscious girl near me. I tried to stay quiet, hoping he hadn't noticed I'd woken up. He finished with the first girl and moved to another, one that was begging him for drugs. Another man came in and said Sledge was asking for me to be brought to him. So they dragged me out of the room. I tried to remember what you'd taught me in that class, I tried to fight them off, but I couldn't." A sob tore free, forcing me to stop speaking.

"Oh, baby. Even with a heap of training, not many can fight off two men who are so much bigger than them, on their own. Especially when coming off whatever drug they gave you."

He pressed a kiss to the top of my head as I took a couple of deep breaths. I really wanted to get this over with. I knew Mac was going to get really pissed off over what happened next. I just hoped he wouldn't get up to start pacing again. Being curled up in his lap had me feeling safe and protected. I wasn't sure I'd be able to keep speaking if he didn't have me in his arms like this.

"They took me to Sledge in another room. When I kept lashing out at them, one of them punched me in the face. After that my mind went a little fuzzy. I still can't remember everything. I know I managed to hit Sledge in the face, and that was when they cuffed my hands to the headboard. I guess I must have run my mouth too much and pissed Sledge off enough he wanted to shut me up." I paused to gently touch my lips. They were a lot better after having all the ointment rubbed in, but they were still rough to touch, and ached. "He used a couple of bungee cords to hold my mouth open. He wanted to fuck my mouth but knew I'd fucking bite him if I could. Even with those damn things cutting into my cheeks and stretching my lips I still managed to clench my teeth shut. I think that's why my lips are so torn up, because I fought against them. He got the message I'd bite his dick off if he put it anywhere near my mouth."

I stopped speaking when I realized how still Mac was beneath me. I slowly shifted to glance up at his face and recoiled. His jaw was clenched tight, the muscles all rigid. His eyes were burning with fury as he stared at something over my head. His arms, which had been cradling me so carefully, had gone tight and now held me firmly against his body. The only part of him that was moving was his chest. His breaths were sawing in and out of his lungs as though he were running. Maybe I shouldn't have shared so many details?

"Mac? Babe?"

With a wince, he closed his eyes. When they opened again his gaze was filled with pain as he focused on my face. Lifting a hand he lightly ran his thumb over my mouth.

"Tell me the rest. Get it all out. Then I can go take my fury out on Sledge."

I jerked in his grip, eyes wide. "Sledge is here? In this building?"

Panic ran through me, and I tried to wriggle off Mac's lap. I had to leave, get away…

"Stop. You don't need to run. He's down in the basement, fully restrained and waiting for me to go deliver his punishment. You're safe. What happened after they fucked up your mouth, bunny?"

"He started pulling at my skirt and I kicked out at him. I caught Sledge in the face with my knee, so he punched me in the stomach. It made me throw up. I guess that saved me. I remember seeing I'd splattered him with it. They left me then. But throwing up sucked all my energy. I was so tired and I could feel the cataplexy attack coming. I had no energy left to fight it. Things got really hazy after that. I think a different couple of men came in. I'm not sure what I dreamt and what was real. I mean the man with the eyes that flashed to blue can't be real, right?" I shook my head. "Somehow I ended up back in that room on the disgusting mattress and then you came..."

I didn't mention the words I thought he whispered to me, just in case they hadn't been real.

"The man with the freaky eyes was real. I'm not sure what the fuck they are but there are three of them and they've now taken over the Iron Hammers. Maverick, you remember him? The vice president of the Satan's Cowboys? He vouched for them. But I've never seen anything like it, babe. The way they fought, and I saw the flashing eye thing too."

I continued to twirl my fingers through his chest hair, nerves building in my stomach.

"Mac?"

"Hmmm?"

"Love me?"

He went still again and I winced. Had I pushed too hard, or too soon? Did he not want me anymore? Now the others had touched me, did he see me as dirty? I tried again to scoot off his lap and when he let me, my heart cracked wide open. I wiped a tear from my face as I rose to my feet.

"You don't have to do that, Zara. I don't want to pressure you into something you're not ready for. I refuse to be the cause of more of your pain."

He didn't think this rejection was hurting me? Fury raced through my veins, wiping out the sadness.

"Too late for that one, you already did. I'm going to go have a shower and you better be gone when I get out." I walked over to the bathroom, mumbling as I went. "Guess I was dreaming when I heard you say you loved me. Clearly, you don't."

By the time I stood at the bathroom sink, tugging off the bandages on my wrists, I felt like someone had taken an axe to my heart. In a blur, I turned on the shower and held my hand under the cold spray, waiting for the heat to come. Numbness filled me from the inside out.

"You didn't dream that."

I yelped as I jumped. Mac was standing directly behind me and had spoken right next to my ear.

"Don't sneak up on me like that!"

I pressed a hand over my heart while I tried to get my heart rate to slow down. Mac's large palms cupped my hips and brought me back against his body. His hot, hard, very naked body. I opened my mouth to get enough air in my lungs as steam from the now-hot shower curled around us. His lips pressed kisses across my shoulder and I tilted my head so he could continue up my neck. He stopped near my ear.

"I'd just carried your battered body out of that place, after I thought I'd lost you. Before I'd let Donna and Rose treat you, I demanded a moment. I used that time to whisper to you. I had no idea if you heard me or not, until just now. It wasn't a dream, bunny. I do love you, so fucking much that I can't breathe without you. Don't *ever* doubt that."

He reached into the stall and adjusted the temperature, then guided me under the spray. As I stood there in silent shock, he soaped up his hands, then set about cleaning every inch of my skin. He left me breathless. I didn't know what to say. He was washing away more than simply the dirt from my skin.

"I took your bra and panties off earlier and cleaned you up the best I could. I wanted you to be comfortable while you slept and not have to wake to the smell of puke. But I couldn't wash you properly. Not like I can now. I'll always want my hands on you, Zara. No matter what happens. I. Will. Always. Want. You. I didn't mean to hurt you just now. You threw me for a minute because I didn't think you'd want me to touch you after what happened. I thought you were trying to give me what you thought I wanted. But that wasn't it, was it?"

I shook my head as he turned me around to face him. I pressed my soapy front up against him, rising up on my toes to get closer to his face.

"Kiss me. Like you did yesterday."

"I don't want to hurt you, babe."

"I'm not made of spun glass, Mac. I'm not gonna break. I need to feel alive, need to know you still want me like you did yesterday."

He took my face between his palms, holding me still as his gaze drilled into mine. "You are the most precious thing in my world, Zara. And I don't want you the same as I did yesterday. I want you more. Each day my need for you grows."

With that, he slammed his mouth down over mine and I whimpered. The arousal that shot through my system like lightning wiped out any discomfort from my injured mouth. This is what I needed. For him to fill me with his passion, to wipe away last night with his love.

Chapter 15

Mac

Mac

I silently cursed when she whimpered as I took her mouth, but she wouldn't let me pull back. Her hands wrapped around my head to hold me to her. I ran my tongue over her lower lip and when she opened, I thrust it into her mouth, fucking it like I wanted to do to her pussy.

When she lifted a leg up over my hip, I lost my damn mind. Releasing her from the kiss, I gripped her ass and lifted her up as I spun to press her against the wall. She wrapped her lean legs around my waist as I thrust forward, driving my cock deep inside her slick heat.

"Fuck, you feel so good."

I took her mouth again as I set a brutal pace. All the emotions that had been running wild inside me over the past twelve hours came to the surface and mixed into a storm that needed to be released. Dropping my head down, I nuzzled against the side of her face as I reached a hand around her hip to tease her clit. She clenched around my cock and had me groaning as I thrust in deep again.

"Mac! Stop. Fuck. Condom."

Despite the fact that the last thing I wanted to do was stop, I stilled my movements, shocked at myself. I'd never taken a woman bare before, no wonder she felt so fucking good.

"I'm clean. I've never not used a condom."

"Yeah, well, I'm not on birth control and I'm not ready to be a mother so you need to wrap it up."

With a growl, I lifted her off me and set her on her feet. I flicked the taps off before I scooped her up and strode out of the bathroom. She laughed when I tossed her on the mattress but I didn't see the funny side. I wanted back inside my woman. Pretty sure I set some kind of record with how fast I gloved up.

"Roll over, bunny. Want you on all fours, right here."

Cheeky minx took her time, rolling her hips as she crawled over to me. She was dripping water all over the bed but I didn't give a fuck. When she got close enough for me to grab, I did just that, shifting her into position so I could slide in deep.

Groaning, I leaned forward, covering her back with my chest as I slid in and out of her tight pussy. I sucked on her shoulder, hard enough to leave another mark for the world to see. Unable to keep up the slow pace for long, I straightened up, and, gripping her hips, began to pound into her, needing to brand her mine in as many ways as I could.

Slipping one hand around her front, I lifted her back so she was kneeling in front of me. She wrapped her hands behind my neck as she threw her head back against my shoulder with a moan. The position had her tits pressed up and out, and unable to resist, I twisted the tight peaks until her pussy clamped down on me as she whimpered. Her body moved with mine, pushing back as I thrust deep inside her. I didn't want it to end but knew it had to. Dropping one hand from her breast down to tease her clit, I sped up my pace until she shuddered and screamed my name as she came. The rippling of her pussy over my cock took me with her and I wrapped my arms around her waist, holding her tight against me so she wouldn't fall as my cock jerked my release inside her heat.

Once I was able, I laid us both down on the bed. Pulling free of her body, I quickly dealt with the condom and tossed it in the trash can near the bed. Then I moved so I lay on my side next to her. She was on her back, watching me with a small little smile that let me know she was one satisfied, well-loved woman. It was a nice fucking boost to a man's ego, a smile like that.

"You wanna rest some more?"

She shook her head. "I've taken my meds, so I'm going to be awake for hours now."

I ran my palms over her body, loving how her silky skin felt under my hands. Her nipples puckered up as I stroked over her tits. I leaned down and took one in my mouth, suckling it deep until, with a gasp, she arched up off the mattress.

A pounding on the door had me jerking off her and leaping from the bed, ready to kill whoever was on the other side.

"Whoa. For such a big man, you sure are fast."

"Don't move." Tugging on my gym shorts, I went to the door, opening it a crack. "What the fuck happened now?"

Scout was standing in the hallway with a thunderous look on his face. "Sledge is gone. You know anything about that?"

I frowned. "Why? Wait, you think I'd go set the bastard loose so I could go after him, or something? Scout, I don't work like that. I've been with Zara all morning. Check the damn cameras if you don't believe me."

Scout adjusted his bandana. "I don't need to check the fucking cameras. I believe you. But I had to ask. Get your shit together and meet me downstairs."

"What about Zara? I'm not leaving her alone again."

Scout didn't look happy with my statement, but I was serious. After last night, I was not letting her be alone today. Especially if Sledge was back on the loose.

"Oh, for fuck's sake! Bring her downstairs. We'll have all the women locked down in the main room with all the prospects watching them. She can't come in with you, brother. You know she can't, so don't ask."

Knowing that was as good as I was going to get, I told him we'd be down in five minutes. Closing the door, I silently cursed. *So much for a leisurely morning enjoying my woman.*

"Sledge got free?"

The fear in her voice had me wincing. "Yeah, looks like it. Don't worry, bunny, we'll catch him. He's got nothing fucking left down in Galveston. No support system. He won't last long before we find him. Now, we need to get downstairs. I got church."

"You're wrong. He has to have some support, how else did he break free? Someone here had to have helped him. Think about it. And last night, there is no way Em could have killed those prospects, come got me, then what? Broke her own neck? And she was just a damn kid.

No way was she behind the plan to take me. She had help. Someone else here betrayed me, and the club."

I stopped dead in my tracks. Zara was right. And I felt so fucking stupid for not seeing it earlier.

"Quickly, get dressed. I need you to tell that to Scout before we start. You can't be in church with us and Scout wants the prospects guarding you. But it might be one of them fucking us over."

She stood and pulled on a pair of jeans as she continued to speak. "Think about it, Mac. It's only been, what? A few hours since we got back, Sledge couldn't have been gone long. Whoever helped him will most likely still be with him. I highly doubt they're here. Are Donna and Rose still here? I could hang with them while you do your church thing."

I could see she was nervous, and I didn't think she fully believed what she was saying. I suspected she was trying to put me at ease, more than anything else. I shook my head as I rested my hands on my hips. "One day, you need to tell me how you came to be stuck working as a waitress. Why didn't you go to college? You've clearly got the smarts to do whatever you wanted."

Pain flared in her expression before she turned away. I winced as she headed into the bathroom. Fuck, I hadn't meant to hurt her.

"Zara? Bunny, that was meant to be a compliment. I'm sorry if it brought up shit for you. That wasn't my intention."

I followed her and found her brushing her hair with way more force than was fucking necessary.

"Don't worry about it. You didn't know."

"I still don't know!" Taking the brush from her hands, I put it on the bench before wrapping my arms around her waist. "I want to know everything about you, Zara. Your past is what made you who you are today. That makes it important. I intend to keep you in my life for a very, very long time. I also intend to learn all your secrets, babe."

"Mac, we don't have time for me to tell you my entire life history. I thought Scout wanted you down there yesterday?"

"He does. But I've got five fucking minutes for my woman. Especially since I've got a feeling it's relevant. Give me the basics, and we'll discuss it more, later."

She actually growled at me. It was completely fucking adorable. I kissed the top of her head as she continued to glare at me in the mirror.

"Fine! In my final year of school my mom got diagnosed with cancer. Instead of going off to college, I stayed home to help care for her while my dad worked himself to the bone to pay for all the treatments. She went into remission, but I still stayed. By then I had a waitressing job and had all but forgotten about my childhood career dreams. Then, three years ago I came home from the movies one night to discover both my parents murdered in our family room. The reason *that* is relevant, is because it was a fucking Iron Hammer prospect who killed them."

My blood ran cold. That was more than relevant. "Why? What did your parents do to bring the club's wrath down on them?"

She blinked up at me blankly. *Fuck.* She didn't know. Maybe hadn't even considered it.

Zara

"It was a robbery gone wrong. That's what the police said."

My mind was suddenly in overdrive. Was there more to it than that?

"I get you don't know much about how MCs work, but you know some. Think about it, Zara. You said you had to stay home while your dad worked his ass off. That tells me your family wasn't rich."

I shook my head. "We never had much and after Mom got sick, we had even less. We got by, always had food on the table but there wasn't any fancy jewelry or expensive technology lying around the house. I figured that was why they got shot, because they didn't have anything to give."

And I'd known nothing about motorcycle clubs back then, but Mac was right. I knew a little now, enough to know they were all about dealing out retribution.

"I doubt they even looked at your parents' belongings, babe. We need to tell Scout. It might be why the club had such a hard-on for you after the cafe shooting. Because that shit about you talking to the cops shouldn't have caused them to put a fucking ten grand bounty on your head. Not when you didn't follow up with it."

My body trembled as everything about my parents' deaths came back to me. I tried to look for things I'd missed, but I couldn't focus enough to think clearly. When I would have crumbled, Mac swung me up against his chest. *Fucking cataplexy!*

"It'll be okay, bunny. I've got you and the club has my back. We'll keep you safe. And when we get our hands on Sledge, we'll fucking make that bastard tell us what really went on with your folks. If that's what you want."

Did I want that? It would give me some closure. Now I knew it wasn't as simple as I'd always believed, I found myself wanting to know. Of course, until this attack passed, I couldn't verbalize anything so I simply enjoyed being pressed against Mac's warm chest as he carried me down the stairs and into the lower level of the Charon's clubhouse. I idly wondered what those who I could hear murmuring around us thought of Mac carrying what looked like an unconscious woman. I probably should get Scout to make a public announcement, or something, about my conditions to everyone. It would save on time and me having to explain shit over and over.

With a sharp intake of breath, I flexed my fingers against Mac's cut as I regained control of my muscles. Blinking my eyes open, I found myself lowering with Mac as he sat, keeping me on his lap even though he had to know I was now awake. Several men were sitting around us, all watching me with intense stares.

"Mac, you know the rules. No bitches in church."

I winced at being called a bitch, and apparently Mac didn't like it any more than I did if his growl and the way his body tensed beneath me were any indication.

"She ain't a bitch and she has information you all need to hear."

I didn't want to cause trouble for Mac, nor did I want to rehash my parents' murders again. "Mac can tell you. I can go wait out in the main room for ya'll to finish."

"I'd prefer to hear what you have to say first-hand, Zara. But then I am going to need you to head out to the main room."

At Scout's clear order, I sighed as I banged my head lightly against Mac's shoulder. "Fine. Mac seems to think that my parents' murders three years ago might be connected to why the Iron Hammers want me so badly now…"

I went on to explain about how they'd died and who'd done it.

"Yeah, no way was it that fucking simple, and I'll put money on the fact that the prospect that went down for it didn't pull the fucking trigger."

Scout glared at the man who'd spoken and he shut up fast.

"Okay, we've heard enough. Thanks, Zara. Can you go wait out in the bar? Do not, for any reason, leave the building. Understand?"

"Trust me, after last night, I'm not going anywhere."

Mac rose with me and escorted me out, giving the poor prospects out in the bar area death threats before he delivered a hard, fast kiss to my lips, then disappeared back into the meeting room. Not feeling like socializing, I made my way to a table against the rear wall and threw myself against the booth seat. With my back against the wall, I could see the whole room and anyone that came to or went from the space. That seemed like a good thing after the last twenty-four hours. I stiffened when a young guy approached me.

"Can I get you something to drink?"

"Um, a bottle of water would be great." Because it would be sealed and I'd know it wasn't fucking drugged. Gah, I hated not being able to trust anyone.

"No offense, but you kinda look like you could use something stronger. No one here will hurt you. Mac was serious about skinning us alive if something happened to you."

Relived that Mac had made it safe here for me, I smiled. "Guess you can take a man out of the Marines, but you can't take the Marine out of the man, huh?"

"Something like that, and that man of yours does love his knives."

"It's a little early in the morning for me to be tossing back hard liquor, but if there's coffee available, I'd love one."

"Sure thing. How do you take it?"

"White with one, thanks."

With a smile, the young guy swaggered off toward the hallway that led to the kitchen. Seemed like a nice enough kid. Gah, was I really that old that I was referring to twenty-year-old men as kids? I shook my head and began chewing on my thumbnail as more important thoughts ran through my mind. If my folks had somehow gotten mixed up with the Iron Hammers, surely I would have noticed something. Wouldn't I? I frowned as I thought back to before the attack. Dad had kept working long hours right up until his death. Why hadn't I questioned that? And if he continued to work all those years, why didn't they have more money? Surely Mom's medical bills hadn't been that much.

My imagination took off with the possibilities of what my dad had been doing all those nights and when the prospect approached me with a coffee I was grateful for the distraction.

"Thank you so much. What's your name?"

I felt guilty for not already knowing it.

"It's Jake, ma'am. I don't have a road name yet."

I gave him a smile when he blushed. "So how does that work? The road name thing. Do you pick your own?"

His face lit up and all traces of his blush vanished. "Oh, no. It's given to you, you can't choose your own."

"I thought only the military did that."

"Well, considering motorcycle clubs were originally created by vets returning from war, it makes sense there are some similarities between the two. Especially considering how many current brothers are either active duty or retired."

That had me eying him from head to foot. He didn't have the look of a man who'd served, but really, what did I know? "How about you?"

"Oh, no. I haven't served. My pops did though. He was a Charon right up until he passed away a few years ago. He served with Scout, actually."

A gasp slipped out before I could catch it. "You lost him young."

"Um. Yeah, he didn't fare as well as Scout and came back with some health issues that never healed up. Eventually he lost his battle. Sucks, but hey—that's life, right? Shit happens."

My gut told me it was mental illness that had taken Jake's father and clearly the young man was still affected by the loss. It left me wanting to make him feel better.

"I lost both my parents three years ago. Murdered in our home. So I know all about what grief can do to a person."

Jake frowned down at the floor for a minute, looking tense.

"Just ask me whatever it is, Jake. I'm pretty open." *And really, after telling the boy about my parents, what the hell could he be nervous about asking me?*

"When Mac brought you down, you looked like you were out for the count. He didn't hurt you did he?"

I smiled up at him. Such a sweet boy, he'd make some girl very happy in the future.

"Mac has never hurt me, Jake. When I found my parents, it triggered a couple of things in my head. I now suffer from narcolepsy and cataplexy." He gave me such a blank look, I chuckled. "Narcolepsy means I'm always tired, and if I don't take my meds, it's hard to do anything but sleep all the time. Cataplexy affects my muscles and leaves me paralyzed for short periods of time. When it happens I can still hear and feel, I just can't move and my eyes normally close so I look like I'm asleep."

His posture relaxed and he smiled at me. "That doesn't sound like much fun."

Lifting my coffee for a drink, I looked Jake in the eye. "You have no idea how much 'not fun' it can be."

Chapter 16

Mac

The second Scout ended church, I was out of my seat and through the door. I didn't give a fuck that the entire club was laughing at me and calling me whipped. Their woman hadn't been taken out from under their noses the night before. I strode out to the main room and found her smiling and chatting with one of the younger prospects. I couldn't think of his name, but so long as Zara's look had no kind of sexual heat in it, I was happy.

"Hey, bunny."

The prospect raised a brow at Zara.

"Like you said, Jake, nicknames are given, not chosen. And I definitely didn't pick that one."

I grinned as I sat down beside her. The lad's cheeks had reddened with a blush.

"Keep that shit up and you'll get pinned with Bashful or something, kid."

Unfortunately for Jake, Bulldog came up behind him at that moment. "I like it. Bash works. We'll all know it's really Bashful, but you can hold your head up with a name like Bash."

Jake stiffened and his eyes went wide as Bulldog slapped him on the back. I couldn't help but chuckle, even as I apologized.

"Sorry, buddy. Didn't see Bulldog behind you."

"No problem. Bash isn't a bad road name. I'm just not gonna tell anyone how I earned it." The kid gave me a smirk and the way his eyes lit up at all the attention he was suddenly getting had me relaxing that I hadn't pissed him off.

"Hey, Scout! Prospect's earned himself his road name!"

"Yeah?" Scout strolled over, along with several other brothers. Poor kid looked like he was about to pass out. "What'd you land the poor boy with?"

"Bash. Because he's so bashful with the way he's fucking blushing and stammering over words all the damn time."

Scout rolled his eyes with a laugh. "Yeah, he'll get over doing all that shit in a couple of months and be left with the name to explain for the rest of his days. I like it. We'll have a few drinks later to celebrate, but for now, all you lazy bastards have jobs to do, so go get to them."

Zara stiffened beside me. "Oh, shit. What's the time? I need to get changed and to Marie's!"

I pulled her against my side and kissed her temple. "Babe, it's Sunday. You don't have anywhere you need to be. Relax and finish your coffee. We called Marie last night to tell her not to come over, and to let her know you were missing—"

Scout cut me off. "So naturally the woman was on my phone at the fucking ass-crack of dawn this morning asking about you. She's going to be here any minute to see you for herself. Since, apparently, my word don't mean shit." Zara smiled sweetly up at Scout, which made the man frown. "Just ask me already, darlin'."

"You intending on letting me work tomorrow?"

"Well, considering Marie threatened to stop serving all Charons if we cost her her best worker…"

That had my girl laughing. "I can totally see her going through with that one."

Scout shook his head at my woman. "So can I. Hence, you get to go to work tomorrow, when I'd much rather you stay on lockdown here. Mac'll be your bodyguard while you work. There'll still be prospects outside the cafe keeping watch, but Mac'll be inside with you and Marie all day. I'm not taking any chances until we've got our hands on Sledge."

Zara sighed, but thankfully didn't argue. There was nothing she could do or say that would change the president's mind. I was actually a little surprised Scout was agreeing for her to leave the clubhouse at all before we had Sledge dealt with. Guess Marie had more of a hold over him that I first thought. Zara finished her coffee, then moved to stand.

"Well, in that case. I'm going to go freshen up before Marie gets here."

She sauntered across the room and Jake, sorry, Bash's gaze followed her like a puppy whose master just left him behind. Kid had it bad. Good thing I didn't pick up any kind of lust or sexual vibes coming off either him or Zara.

"Stop eyeing my woman, boy."

Still, I needed to let the kid know I wouldn't stand for him trying anything, just in case I missed something.

The poor kid mumbled something before he took off toward the bar, where he scooted behind it and started wiping down shit that didn't need to be cleaned.

Scout laughed as he adjusted his bandana. "Quit messing with the poor kid. Like every motherfucker here, he's well aware of who Zara belongs to. I'm outta here. Got phone calls to make. Don't you let that woman of yours leave the damn building all day today, okay?"

"That's the plan, Prez. Let me know what you and Keys find."

I'd explained in church Zara's theory about how, whoever had helped Sledge would most likely still be with him, and therefore missing. It was a great theory, except for the fact all our guys were accounted for. Maverick and his crew had taken the other two Iron Hammers we were holding, Trip and Chuck, with them earlier this morning. Maverick had agreed that I had the right to finish Sledge off, while they'd take care of the others for all the shit the Iron Hammers had done to their club. They'd left before Sledge went missing, so Scout was going to call Maverick to see if they were missing anyone. Because Maverick's crew had brought a couple prospects with them—prospects that should have been out the front last night guarding bikes when Zara had been taken, yet they hadn't been there. If they had been, they would have ended up dead like our own prospects.

Keys was going over the video footage from last night through to this morning to see if the cameras had caught anything. Apparently, Keys had put hidden cameras in places no one knew about. And because he wanted to keep it that way, he'd put layers of security on the access to the feeds. It was going to take him a little time to get into the right files to download them. Not to mention the time it was going to take to scan each camera's feed. Paranoid fucker was paying for his issues today.

After Scout left and the others headed out, I decided to head up and see how Zara was doing. Finding her freshly showered and dressed in only a lacy bra and panties had all my blood rushing to my cock.

"Fuck me, bunny. You are so beautiful."

Even with all the bruises on her, she was still sexy as fuck. Tossing my cut and shirt on the end of the bed I came up behind her as she stood in front of a chair that she'd set her now-open suitcase on. Pressing my chest against her back I reached around her to slip my palms inside her bra. I grinned when her nipples instantly formed hard little points. With a shuddering sigh she leaned back against me, her head on my shoulder. I looked down her front, lifting her tits out of her bra so I could see as I tugged on her nipples. With a groan she started wriggling her ass against my rock-hard cock.

"Mac."

Her breathy whisper pushed me over the edge. I had to take her, be inside her.

"Lean forward and grip the back of the chair."

Like the good girl she was, she leaned over and wrapped her fingers over the top of the chair. I ran my palms down her spine, unclipping her bra on my way down. I wanted her to feel the sway of her tits with each of my thrusts. Taking a step back, I leaned down to take a bite of her lush ass.

She squealed and pushed up onto her tip-toes, making me chuckle. She really was sexy as fuck. Hooking a thumb into each side of her panties, I pulled them down and loved how she automatically lifted each foot to free herself from the scrap of lace.

Slipping my own foot between hers, I tapped her legs wider apart.

"You wet for me, bunny?"

"Uh huh."

With a grin, I undid my belt and jeans, pulling a condom from the pocket before I shoved the material down to my knees. I was too keyed up to be fucked stripping them all the way off. I gloved up and, gripping her hips so she couldn't move, I slid my cock in deep on one thrust. *Fuck.* Every single time was like heaven with Zara. I kept my gaze on where we were joined, loving how her body sucked me back in on each thrust. After a minute, I couldn't stand the burn any longer and sped up, pounding into her. With a groan, she slapped one hand against the wall to keep herself steady.

I reached around and wrapped a palm over each of her tits, giving them a squeeze before moving to tug on her nipples. A tremor ran through her body, letting me know how much she liked what I was doing, so I pinched her nipples again and gave them another tug, which earned me a groan and her pussy clenching down on my cock like a vise. *Nice.* I kept up the tit torture until I felt my balls tighten up, ready to blow. Releasing her nipples, I set one hand back on her hip, and the other found her clit and started working that hard little nub as I pounded harder and faster into her.

She came crying out my name as her body convulsed beneath me. The ripples of her channel against my cock had me going cross-eyed as I came inside her. Somehow, I managed to pull her back up against me before she crumpled to the floor. In the aftermath of coming so hard, I felt raw. Like she'd stripped me bare. As my mouth ran off before my brain could filter my words, I was grateful she wouldn't be able to respond.

"Fuck me, Zara. You fry my brain, woman. Fucking love you, babe. I want you to be my old lady, to wear my property patch. I know you're not ready yet, but one day soon, you will be and the moment you are. I'm claiming you. For good. You hear me? You're fucking mine, Zara. All fucking mine."

Zara

Damn the man! He was using my weakness against me. Whispering the sweetest words while he knew I couldn't respond. Then when I could, he made sure he had me on the move, not allowing me a chance to respond. I swore that one of these days, I'd tie him up and maybe even gag him so I could say a few things to him while he couldn't respond. See how he liked it.

Of course, I couldn't be too mad, considering he did confess to loving me, along with basically proposing to me. Sort of. At least, that's what I understood an old lady to be—a biker's wife.

"C'mon, Zara. Get that pretty ass of yours moving. Don't want Marie mad—she'll take it out on Scout, who'll take it out on all of us."

With a chuckle, I finished putting my hair up. I twisted to see each side of my bruised jaw. I thought about putting on some makeup but decided against it. Everyone here had already seen it and Marie would be able to see through any attempt I made to cover up anyhow. Easier to just let her see all my battle wounds now.

"What's the deal between Scout and Marie?"

"No idea, babe. You'll have to ask Marie, because Scout sure as shit won't be telling us anything." He paused for a second. "If you do find out anything, you'll tell me won't you?"

That made me laugh.

"Sure, babe. I'll totally share any juicy gossip I hear with you."

When I came out of the bathroom he was waiting for me. "Woman, are you laughing at your man?"

I went up to him, and pushing up on my toes, I pressed a soft kiss to the corner of his mouth. "Maybe."

With a growl, he wrapped his hands in my hair and moved me so he could cover my lips with his. A shiver ran over me as I melted into my man. His kisses were lethal. *So good.* I closed my eyes and let all my thoughts float away as he deepened the kiss, his tongue dancing with mine.

When the kiss ended, I snuggled in against his soft t-shirt. With a contented sigh, I burrowed under his cut to get to his warmth. I could stay here forever, with his arms wrapped around me, holding me close against him. Keeping me safe.

"You know, you could try saying what you did earlier when I can actually respond to it. I mean, it's a bit rude to ask questions when a person can't answer."

Mac's arms tightened and his heart rate picked up speed beneath my ear.

"I don't want to rush you, bunny. I can be patient."

I ran my palms up and down his strong back beneath his cut, loving how his muscles moved under my touch, even as I wanted to shake him for being such an idiot.

"I don't need a long time to know what's in my heart, Mac. I've never felt like this before, never experienced the instant connection we have. I love you, and I can't imagine anything that would change how I feel about you."

He was silent for a moment, and I tried to pull away, afraid I'd pushed him too hard and ruined my chance at a future with him. Tears pricked my eyes as I struggled to get free from his embrace.

"Zara, stop it. Stop fighting me."

A small sob slipped free as I stilled. He was so much stronger than me. I wasn't going anywhere until he set me free. His arms released me but before I could get away from him, his hands ran up my arms until he had my face between his palms. He, thankfully, kept the contact light enough it didn't hurt the bruising as I stubbornly refused to meet his gaze. Instead, I focused on the patches on his cut, while willing my stinging eyes to not let the tears fall.

"Zara, look at me."

"I am."

Yeah, even I knew I sounded like a grumpy toddler and wasn't surprised when a growl rumbled from his chest.

"I need your eyes on mine." He waited a heartbeat. "Now, bunny."

With a sigh, and wince, I forced my gaze to lift to his, dreading what I'd see in his ice-blue irises.

When our gazes did meet, a lump formed in my throat. His eyes blazed with intensity.

"Just because I need a second to process something you say, doesn't mean I'm rejecting you, sweetheart." He paused and scrutinized my face as he swiped his thumbs gently under my eyes. Guess I hadn't been very successful at stopping my tears from escaping.

He leaned down and pressed the most gentle, reverent kiss I'd ever received against my temple. "Zara, will you be mine? Wear my property patch and be my old lady?"

With a grin, I smoothed my palms up his chest until I could wrap my arms around his neck. "I'm already yours, Mac. Always will be. So, yeah, I'll wear your patch." I frowned as I thought of something. "Um, does this mean I get to wear a cut too? Or is the patch a tattoo?"

He barked out a laugh loud enough it echoed for a second. "If you want to get ink for me, you're welcome to go for it. You've seen the cuts Silk and the other old ladies wear? On the back it has 'Property of' on the top rocker, then the name of their old man on the bottom one. They have another smaller patch on the front that says the same thing. I'll have to order yours, and I'm not sure how long it'll take. But I'll see Scout about it this morning. I want my mark on you as soon as I can."

I rolled my eyes. "Babe, I'm pretty sure your caveman antics have already made it perfectly clear to everyone in the club that I'm yours. Only yours."

He grunted. "I'd like to make sure they all know."

With a chuckle I nuzzled back in against his chest. His strong arms wrapped around me again and I took a deep breath and smiled at how good this felt.

Mac had claimed me.

I was his, he was mine.

Chapter 17

Zara

The next morning I came out of the bathroom all ready to head into Marie's.

"Okay, I'm ready to head out. What are you going to do all day? Won't you get bored just sitting around, watching me work?"

He pulled me against him and pressed a kiss to my temple that never failed to melt my insides.

"I can think of a lot of worse ways to spend my day than staring at your sexy ass working."

I rolled my eyes. "Sure, right. I'm serious, Mac. What are you going to do all day?"

Because if he planned to simply sit there staring at me all day, I'd lose my damn mind before lunch.

"I'll probably spend at least half the damn day on my phone sorting various things out. And I've got paperwork for the gym to do, lesson plans to write. But my main mission today is to make sure you stay safe, so mostly I'll be staying in the shadows, making sure no one tries anything with you. Or Marie."

I gave him a nod as I broke out of his hold to grab my handbag. That sounded like one hell of a boring day for the poor man, but who was I to argue? I made my way downstairs, and taking my hand, Mac took the lead as we headed outside. He brought me to his bike and I winced when he handed me my helmet.

"What's that look for? Didn't you like the ride the other night?"

"Oh, I liked it. Way too much to be doing it on the way to work." I mumbled the last part, but he still heard me if the very satisfied male-sounding chuckle was any indication.

"You'll be fine, bunny."

Minutes later we were roaring down the road toward Marie's with me trying really hard to not focus on either feeling the very pleasant vibrations coming from beneath me, or the very fine man I was sitting pressed up against. Not sure how successful I was at either task, as by the time I got off his bike, my legs were feeling a little weak at the arousal that coursed through me. *Damn man.*

Without saying a word, I took my helmet off and handed it to Mac to deal with. Then, when he gave me a smirk and a shake of his head, I stormed off toward Marie's front door. I headed straight for the back room, where I dumped my bag and did a hair check in the mirror. While I did a quick re-do of my pony-tail Marie poked her head in.

"You okay, sugar? You had this thunderous expression when you came in."

I gave her a grin. "Oh, that was just because Mac was being a tease. I'm fine. Thanks for coming over yesterday, it was nice to just sit down and chat."

She smiled. "It was nice." Her gaze narrowed on me as she ran it over me. "Would have preferred to be meeting up to shoot the breeze with you, rather than checking how wounded you are."

I winced. "You and me both."

Marie had released her hold on my face as I spoke and now she pulled me in for a tight hug. "Still think you should be in bed resting up, but I need the help so I'll just shut up and make sure you don't push yourself too hard today."

"I promise I'll let you know if I start feeling ill, or super tired."

She nodded. "Good. Now, c'mon, sugar. We got work to do."

With a smile, I followed her out to the cafe, to start my work day. It was about two hours later when Scout came barreling into the place like his ass had caught fire and we had the only water in town. His fierce gaze quickly found both Marie and me before he strode over to where Mac was leaning against a wall near the back of the place. Scout leaned in close to Mac's ear and said something that had my man frowning deep enough I could clearly see the expression from across the room.

"Sugar, how about you take these coffees over to the boys and have a break? See if you can find out what's got their panties in a twist this time."

With a nod, I absently took the tray from Marie and headed over to them. I set the drinks on the table nearest them before I said anything.

"Mac? Scout? Why don't you sit down and have a drink?"

I frowned when Scout grabbed Mac's arm, halting him when he went to move toward me. He growled something about "club business". Mac responded with something about learning from past mistakes. I stayed silent as they glared at each other for a while, then just when I was about to go back to Marie, Scout released his hold with a sigh and they both came over. Mac held a chair out for me to sit in, then both men seated themselves and reached for their coffees.

"For the record, I don't like this shit."

Mac raised an eyebrow at Scout. "You want a repeat of what happened with Silk because of old traditions about who gets to know club business?"

Scout shocked a gasp out of me when he actually growled at Mac. "It keeps the women safe if they don't know shit. They can't rat us out if they don't fucking know anything."

"I'm not saying we start airing every damn thing. But stuff that's relevant, that affects someone's safety—no matter if they're a prospect, old lady or daughter of the club—they should be told about it."

I sat sipping my coffee, wondering if I should leave them to their argument. "Would you like me to give you two a few minutes?"

While still staring at Scout, Mac reached over and wrapped his large palm around my forearm. Okay, guess I wasn't going anywhere then. This scary silence was worse than the arguing. With a sigh, I spoke up again.

"Any word on Sledge? I'd certainly feel better knowing he wasn't roaming the streets."

With a huff, Scout readjusted his bandana and scanned the cafe. No one was anywhere near us. "Sorry, darlin' he's still on the loose. However, we did work out how he got free."

I carefully put my coffee down before I turned my full attention to the Charon president. "And how was that?"

"Seems we have a rat problem. Well, us and the Satan's Cowboys both."

"Rats?" I frowned as my gaze flicked between the two men. I needed to find a book or something that would teach me this biker code they seemed to speak all the damn time.

Mac's palm stroked up and down my arm before he spoke. "A rat, as in someone who was one of us but was betraying us to someone else."

"Ah. Okay. Was I right? Was it whoever was missing?"

Scout shook his head with a low curse. Mac grinned proudly as he spoke. "Told you she had it figured out."

The president turned a serious expression on me. "We went over the video feeds from cameras hidden around the clubhouse. No one but me and Keys know where the fuckers are. Actually, it wouldn't surprise me if Keys added some even I don't know about. The paranoid bastard put so much security on accessing the feeds, it took a while to get to it. Then some more time to go over it all but we've now managed to piece together most of what went down both Saturday night and Sunday morning."

I stiffened until Mac moved to lace his fingers in with mine, giving me a squeeze.

"We know Em sold you out. But I don't think she realized what the fuck she was getting involved with. It was the Satan's Cowboy's prospects that killed our boys, and we assume Em. No cameras outside the fence line. Although, I'm sure Keys has that covered now. It was also one of those prospects that fucking busted Sledge out this morning."

I frowned, again, as my mind reeled with the details. "How'd he manage that on his own?"

"He had help. Two of the club whores were with him."

At Scout's words, Mac flinched and suddenly he couldn't look me in the eye. He tried to pull his hand away but I tightened my grip, not letting him. "What does that have to do with you?"

Scout answered my question when Mac stayed silent, grinding his jaw.

"Because the two whores are ones known for liking Mac's cock."

The crude language had me wincing but before I could react to the information, Mac cursed and rose up from the table, jerking free from my hold on him, before he stormed off outside. What the fuck?

"I'm not sure I understand what just happened."

I didn't think Mac had cheated on me with one of them. He wasn't that sort of man. But our relationship was so new, and we'd gotten together under pretty extreme circumstances. So, I could be wrong.

"The stupid bitches were jealous of you and wanted you gone so Mac would go back to using them. Mac seems to think that makes this shit his fault."

I rubbed my chest. That hurt. I knew Mac hadn't been celibate before meeting me but still, listening to Scout talk about him screwing whores hurt. "Why are you telling me all this again?"

"Because we kept information from Eagle and Silk and it nearly got her killed. More than once. Mac seems to think if you know who's gunning for you, you'll be safer."

Clearly Scout didn't agree. At least not fully. With a small nod, I rose from the table. This was all too much to process.

"I gotta get back to work."

Without looking back, I went behind the counter and started giving the coffee machine a cleaning. One, it, no doubt, didn't need. I couldn't believe the mess my life had become. And I knew it was only going to get worse. Especially, since I apparently wasn't safe at the clubhouse like everyone had promised me.

Mac

I stormed around to the cafe's parking lot, where I started pacing. I'd brought Zara to the clubhouse to be safe. Instead it had put her in more danger. *Because of me and my fucking cock.* Fucking whores. They knew the score. At least, they were supposed to know the score. And that was, that they were there to ease the brothers' needs. Not get fucking attached to any one of us. *Dammit!* And I'd stormed out before Scout could tell me what had happened to the bitches. I needed to be sure they were gone from the clubhouse before I took Zara back there.

I scrubbed my hands over my head. It really was past time I bought a house. I wasn't a prospect anymore, and didn't have to live at the clubhouse. Maybe something near Eagle and Silk? The club could work on buying all the houses on that little dead-end street they lived on, and create a mini gated community for club brothers and their old ladies. It would be easier to keep everyone safe that way.

My phone ringing ended that line of thought, especially when I saw it was from a private number. There were few possibilities of who would be calling me from an unlisted number, none of them someone I wanted to speak with.

"What?"

"Jacob Miller, you are a hard man to get hold of."

Mr. Smith. Our FBI contact was at the top of the list of who I'd guessed would be calling. And the reason I answered the damn call. I'd heard stories of how the feds would come arrest their undercovers if they went silent on them. That was the last fucking thing I needed right now.

"I can't talk right now."

"Oh, I think you can. You are, after all, all on your own, pacing around a parking lot. Is there a reason you haven't been keeping me updated with the club's activities?"

My hand tightened on my phone as I pondered how to answer without just telling him to fuck off. I was pretty sure that wouldn't go over well. When I heard a crack, I eased up the pressure. Breaking my phone wasn't going to help any.

"Any reason why you're spying on me?"

"I needed to talk to you, so I simply watched you until you were alone. You, Mr. Miller, are not alone much these days. Now, I've answered your question, how about you answer mine?"

I moved to lean against the back wall of the cafe, where I could keep an eye on anyone approaching. I did not want this conversation overheard.

"What activity in particular are you wanting to know about?"

"Don't play dumb with me. You won't like how that ends. I'm talking about the little trip the Charon MC made down south in the early hours of Saturday morning. And how you have one Ms. Claire Flynn in your custody, yet didn't inform me about it. You need to turn that girl over to us. We'll take very good care of her, I assure you."

I counted to ten, trying to stay fucking calm, when what I really wanted to do, was to figure out where he was watching me from, go there and pound him into the ground.

"Not sure I trust the FBI with an actual person, Mr. Smith. Considering how fast the L.A. mob knew about the information we gave you, I wonder how long it would be before the Iron Hammers knew about you having Claire? And how long until someone got to her and took her out? She's safe where she is."

"We could simply come into that cafe and arrest her, you know."

That was a good point. "Then why haven't you?"

"Because we don't want to lose you boys as assets."

I scoffed at the idiot. "Should have thought about that before you leaked that info to the mob, then. It left a bad taste in our mouths."

"Yes, that was unfortunate. The FBI is not unlike any other organization. We have our disloyal members. I believe you're familiar with that?"

It took all my willpower to not growl out loud. "Sounds like you know everything without my help. Not sure why you're even talking to me. Cut the shit and tell me what you really want, since you know I won't hand over my woman to you."

"Ah, so she is warming your bed. Good. I need you to tell me everything she's told you about the Iron Hammers. And about the work her father was doing."

I froze at that reference. "What has her father got to do with anything? He was murdered by the Iron Hammers three years ago, along with her mother."

Sure, after Zara told me about the murders I'd started to wonder about the possibility that her father may have been up to something involving the club, but it wasn't a priority to work that shit out. He was dead and buried. Finding and eliminating Sledge was my number one priority right now. Well, that was my number two. My first priority was keeping Zara safe.

"You are not that naive, Jacob. Or that stupid. I need you to use Claire to dig into her father's dealings. There's a link there between him and the club."

"Why don't you question the prospect that went away for his murder?"

"We did. He didn't know anything about the crime. He was a scapegoat the club used, nothing more."

I got the impression Mr. Smith knew more than he was telling me. But I also knew he wasn't going to tell me whatever it was, so I didn't bother trying to get him to.

"I can try, but Claire doesn't know anything. She still believes that it was a robbery gone wrong that got her parents killed."

"I very much doubt that. A robbery where nothing at all was taken? Not even jewelry? And where the getaway vehicle is a bike? She can't be that stupid."

"Trauma and grief will allow the brain to believe all sorts of things, Mr. Smith."

He sighed into the phone. "Get me something, or we'll be forced to pick her up and get the information ourselves. Understand?"

At that I did growl, unable to hold back my anger. "Don't you ever threaten my woman."

"Mr. Miller, I am not threatening anyone. Just giving you some facts. Goodbye."

I hung up the phone and nearly threw it across the parking lot. Fuck! Forcing myself to pocket the phone before I gave in to the temptation to smash the thing, I started looking around for something I could fucking hit.

I needed to vent in a bad fucking way, but there was nothing for me to channel it at.

"How about you head up to the gym and I'll take Zara home?"

I spun to see Scout coming toward me with Zara walking beside him. My gaze landed on her and refused to leave. She was so fucking gorgeous. And innocent. So fucking innocent in all of this. And she looked a little shell-shocked, making me wonder if maybe Scout had been right and we shouldn't have told her so much about what was going on. But, dammit, she needed to know that the whores at the clubhouse weren't loyal, that we had some rats that we needed to clean out. I winced. Technically Eagle, Taz and I were rats. Really fucking bad ones because we hadn't told the feds one single thing about the Charons yet.

I ran my gaze over her face and noticed her skin was more pale than normal. She loved her parents. What would it do to her if we found out her father was a piece of scum like Sledge? *It would fucking destroy her.* How the fuck was I going to do this without actually involving her?

"I'm not leaving her side, Scout. We got anyone downstairs I can work out with?"

With a chuckle, Scout shook his head. "Sorry, brother. Cowboys took the others with them."

Zara cleared her throat, cutting Scout off. "I can go to the gym with you. Work out for a bit, while you do your thing."

I nodded. "That'll work. Let's go grab our gear and head over there. What happened to the women?"

I needed to know they wouldn't be waiting at the clubhouse when we returned later. "They haven't been stupid enough to show their faces yet. The prospects on the door know what to do with them if they do show up."

I gave Scout a nod. "Good. C'mon, babe."

I held out my hand and she came straight to me, no hesitation.

"I'll leave you to it then. I'll catch you both later."

Scout went to his ride and headed off as I tucked Zara under my arm and led her over to my bike.

"You know, how I said I couldn't remember everything that happened while the Iron Hammers had me? Well, I just remembered something."

I paused in the process of getting out her helmet to look over at her. "What'd you remember?"

"When I was cuffed to the bed, I told Sledge that I hadn't made my report to the police official. That I wasn't going to, so there was no reason for him to hurt me. He responded that I'd caused enough trouble already and I was going to pay for it on my back. But he also said something about my dad. He said *it's especially sweet after what your pops did.* Then earlier you were talking about their murders, now I'm wondering if there isn't something more to it."

I forced myself to move, to hand her a helmet before I spoke. This was the perfect opportunity. "It's probably worth looking into."

With a huff, she put the helmet on and buckled it. "I have no idea where to start. Would be easier if we could just beat it out of Sledge, huh?"

She gave me a smirk as she tried to joke but I couldn't muster even a smile at the moment. She slid up against me, rubbing her soft body against mine as she leaned up to cup my face in her palms. "What's wrong, babe?"

"I'm worried about you, about how you'll handle whatever dirt we dig up on your father." I leaned down and kissed her before she could say a word, not wanting her to respond.

"C'mon, bunny. Let's get moving."

Zara

By the time we got back to the clubhouse after spending time at the gym it was well past dark. I snuggled into Mac's side as he wrapped his arm around my shoulder when we came into the main room. Though there were people all over the place, it wasn't as loud or noisy as last night. But it was clearly party time. Jake, or I guess it was Bash now, was sitting in one of the booths with a woman on each side of him. He was kissing the hell out of one, while the other was working to get his jeans undone. Heat raced over my cheeks when she pulled his dick out and lowered her mouth to suck on it. Guess this was his party for his new road name, so he didn't have to do any prospect work tonight.

"You don't need to be looking at another man's cock, bunny."

"Trust me, it wasn't intentional. Looks like he's not so bashful anymore."

That got a chuckle out of him as he guided me over to the bar. We'd both had showers back at the gym, but I'd only had my work clothes to change into. "Mac?"

"Yeah, babe?"

"I'm just gonna run up and change out of my work stuff, 'k?"

He pulled me around and kissed me, hot and heavy like always. He pulled back with a grin as I stayed where I was, trying to get my brain to re-engage.

"Hurry back."

He gave my ass a tap when I turned to go. I rolled my eyes at him over my shoulder, before I jogged up the stairs. When I got to the room, I didn't get changed right away. I went and sat on the edge of the bed, before flopping back to stare up at the ceiling. Mac hadn't spoken another word about my dad, the Iron Hammers, or the traitors within this club since we left Marie's parking lot. Didn't change the fact it's pretty much all I'd thought about since then. Well, except for when Mac was sparing with Taz. No red-blooded woman was going to be able to ignore those two hot, inked-up men shirtless, sweaty and knocking each other around the ring.

But I didn't have the luxury of focusing on that right now. I needed to work out a way to find out what my father had been doing before his death, and hopefully that would lead us to wherever Sledge was hiding out. I also needed to figure out where I stood with the cops. Because to sort out anything to do with my dad, I was going to have to visit my place in Galveston and go through the boxes from my dad's office that I really should have gone through before now, but had always found a reason to put off. I'd even been too much of a coward to box it all up. I'd gotten a moving company to pack up the whole house and all the boxes were cluttering up my small place.

I had gone through a lot of the boxes over the past three years. I'd barely been able to move around my apartment with them all in there to start with, so it was kind of a necessity. But I hadn't touched any of the ones from their bedroom or his office. Looked like I was going to have to suck it up and go through them now.

The last thing I needed when I did go down to get them was to be picked up by the police and put in lock-up. I wasn't sure exactly what happened the morning I was rescued, whether the Iron Hammers got wiped out completely or if there were still enough of them left that wanted to come after me. Because Mac had been right earlier—clearly Sledge was after me for a more personal reason than what I'd said after the shooting, and now I remembered him mentioning my dad, it seemed that was a good place to start looking.

A soft knock on the door had me pulling myself up from the bed and going over to it.

"Who is it?"

I called out before I opened it. Saturday night was too fresh in my mind for me to blindly trust the unknown person on the other side of Mac's door.

"It's Silk. On my own. Let me in?"

I flicked the lock and opened up the door. "Hey."

Silk came at me, forcing me back into the room as she wrapped me in a hug.

"I am so fucking sorry, Zara!"

Feeling totally out of my element, I patted the woman on the back. "It wasn't your fault, Silk. Any more than it was Mac's."

She pulled back, and holding my shoulders, ran her gaze over me from head to foot. Between working out and showering at the gym, my make-up was non-existent, so Silk could see all the bruising on my face. And since she hadn't been around yesterday, this was the first time she was seeing it.

"Damn, they did a number on you, huh? How are you feeling, really?"

I pulled free of her grip and headed to my suitcase. "I'll be fine. I was only knocked around a little. It looks worse than it feels. You here for the party?"

"I'm here because I had to work all day yesterday so I couldn't make it over to check on you, and I'm worried about you. I did not come here to watch Jake—sorry, Bash—getting groped by whores all night long."

I grinned at that.

"Gotta see the funny side to it, though. They name the guy Bash because he's bashful, and he celebrates by screwing whores all night. Not real bashful behavior."

Silk barked out a laugh. "I did wonder how they came up with Bash. Eagle wouldn't tell me. Bastard."

"I doubt Jake will want people to know the why. It's kind of Mac's fault. He was teasing the kid when

Bulldog came in and overheard. It all snowballed from there."

I started pawing through my clothes. Where the hell were my jeans?

"That'd be right. Sounds like my uncle. What are you looking for?"

"Something to wear downstairs. Preferably jeans."

I finally located them and tossed them onto the bed as Silk laughed. "Make the most of wearing them. If Mac's anything like Eagle, he'll keep at you until all you wear is short skirts."

With a raised brow, I looked over at Silk, who was wearing jeans and didn't look like a short skirt kinda girl.

"Oh, while I'm pregnant I'm wearing jeans. That man doesn't get to throw me up against walls to fuck me when I puke with any sudden movement. And he's learned already not to argue with a pregnant woman. This gig does have a few perks."

"I'm struggling to see you in a skirt at all, to be honest. You don't seem like that kinda woman."

She smirked at me. "Yeah, I wasn't. And I don't wear girly-girl looking shit. My skirts are all leather or dark denim. The only flowers on me are my tatts, thank you very much. Speaking of which, you don't have any ink?"

"Ah, no. I don't. Why?"

"I'm a tattooist. I own Silky Ink here in town. You should come in some time, let me color you up a bit."

I spun to look at her, as my jaw dropped open a little. I wasn't really sure how to respond. I'd never even considered getting a tattoo before. Never had the spare cash for one, either.

"Don't look so shocked, doll. Think it over. I'll take real good care of you. If you decide you don't want any, that's cool. I'm not going to force you, or anything. Just wanted to put the offer out there." She smirked as she came over to my side. "That, and I love doing people's first tattoos. Nothing quite like watching someone get their first taste of ink." She reached past me and grabbed a shirt out of my bag. "Here, wear this one with your jeans, then we'll head down."

I took the shirt and went to grab my jeans. "Not sure I want to go down there if there's gonna be an orgy going on in the main room."

Silk laughed again. "Bash'll be in the back room by now. We'll sit at the bar and take bets on whether Eagle or Mac will be the first one to kick Taz's ass for flirting with us. It'll be fun."

With a smile I headed to the bathroom. "That man is a shameless tease."

"That, he is. Can't wait for him to meet a woman strong enough to wrangle him into line. Gonna be a hell of a good show."

I changed quickly, unable to imagine Taz settling down with just one woman. Too much of a flirt. And manwhore, if what I'd heard from the others was to be believed.

We were half way down the stairs when Silk stopped with a gasp.

"Are you okay? What's wrong?"

I was nearly panicking that something was wrong with her baby when I saw the wide grin spread over her face. "A Playboy bunny."

I frowned at her as I tried to figure out what the fuck she was on about. "What?"

"For your tattoo, you should totally get a sexy little Playboy bunny. Oh, you totally should get it on your ass, or maybe just inside of your hip bone. That would look sexy as fuck."

I shook my head and kept moving. "That's not why Mac calls me bunny, and no way am I getting a slutty little rabbit inked on me. Dream on, Silk."

"Girl, you're no fun. Mac would totally dig it, even if it isn't the reason behind you being his bunny."

I gritted my teeth as we entered the main room. I was going to throttle Mac over that damn name. "Do all the old ladies really think that's why he calls me bunny?"

Silk was laughing when we got to the bar. "Probably. I mean you're a knockout. Clearly the man likes what he sees, so why wouldn't he call you his pinup girl?"

"Pinup girl sounds so much better than fucking Playboy bunny."

The prospect behind the bar was obviously trying really hard to not laugh as he handed Silk a bottle of water and set a soda down for me. Taz didn't bother trying to hide his amusement. Damn man came to stand between us and wrapped an arm around us both as he chuckled.

"Ladies, after that comment, I really want to know what you two are talking about."

A second later Taz was gone and Mac was wrapping an arm around me. A glance over to the side showed Eagle had done the same to Silk.

"Taz, you have got to fucking quit messing with our old ladies."

The man didn't seem to be affected by Mac's dark tone as he laughed and moved away.

"You know he only does it because it sets you both off so easily, right?"

I had to agree with Silk. But the way both our men growled, I didn't think it a good idea to vocalize the opinion.

Chapter 18

Mac

The closer we got to Galveston, the more anxious Zara became. I had her in the van with me, while Arrow, Nitro and Taz rode alongside us, as we headed to her place.

"You okay, bunny?"

She gave me a small smile before I turned my attention back to the road.

"Yeah, just nervous. I've got no idea what we'll find. I hope the Iron Hammers haven't destroyed it."

"I doubt it. More likely they'd have someone watching for your return. They were after you, not anything you owned."

At least, I hoped that was the case. She was looking pale at the mere suggestion her things might be gone.

"I wonder if Gemma will be home. Although, even if she is, she probably won't come out with all you bikers around."

"She's your neighbor, right?"

"Yeah, the one who told me to come to Bridgewater."

I grinned at her. "Well, I'll have to make sure to thank her for sending you my way."

She chuckled quietly at my comment but soon grew serious again when we pulled up into her driveway. I hopped out and went around to help her down from the high seat.

"Where's your key? I want you to stay here, while I go check the interior."

With a shaky nod she handed her keys over and, unable to resist, I leaned down to give her a quick kiss. It had been four days since she'd been taken and all the bruises were still fading. She'd done her best to cover up the ones on her jaw with makeup, and had been pretty successful. But I knew what was underneath, and it made my gut roil with anger.

When I turned from her, I saw that Nitro had taken his place at the end of her driveway, while Arrow was standing about two feet from us and Taz was already at the front door waiting for me. I forced myself to leave Zara to go check her house. Arrow would keep her safe from anything that came at her while we searched the interior.

I slid the key into the lock and stood to the side of the door, with a gun in my free hand, as I pushed it open. When nothing jumped out at us, or shot at us, I entered with Taz on my six. We both had our weapons raised, and using our Marine training, went through the entire place to check for anyone hiding. It didn't take long as the place was small. Only two bedrooms, one bathroom and an open plan living area that included the kitchen.

"All clear. Let's get Zara inside."

I didn't like her standing out there in the open, even if we did have two men on her. I strode outside and motioned for them to come in. Arrow came in with Zara, while Nitro stayed on guard duty outside. The man was our sergeant in arms and bloody good at his job. I knew he would catch anything that might happen out there, while we sorted out what Zara wanted to take from inside.

Zara blew out a breath when she stepped into her living area. "Everything looks the same."

The relief on her face was enough to make me smile. Also made me grateful the fuckers hadn't broken in and messed up her place.

"The faster we load up and move out, the better. What did you want to take?"

She stopped looking around the space and focused on me as I'd spoken.

"The boxes from my parents' house are all in the second bedroom. I guess any box that has office written on it needs to come. If you guys don't mind, I might go pack a bag or two of stuff from my bedroom."

I pulled her against me for a hug, like we'd refuse her that?

"Go pack up your bedroom, babe. We'll start loading up the boxes."

Unable to resist, I took her mouth for a minute or two, not pulling back until Taz started snickering.

"Thought you wanted to hurry, Mac? Or would you like Arrow and me to go outside while you get busy with your bunny?"

Zara's cheeks pinkened, and with a muttered curse she bolted for her bedroom, shutting the door behind her. Hard.

Taz and Arrow were both laughing openly now and when I growled at them to shut the fuck up, they just laughed louder. Bastards. I turned away from them so they couldn't see my grin as I led them to the other bedroom.

"C'mon, you two clowns. Let's get these loaded up."

The boxes were clearly marked, as you'd expect, since a professional moving company packed the things.

"Whoa. That's a lot of boxes."

"Yeah, after her folks were killed she had all their stuff boxed up. Understandably, she couldn't bring herself to face it all. Let's start with the office boxes, then if we have room, we'll take the others too. Save us from coming back down if she doesn't find anything in the office ones."

Arrow nodded as he grabbed the first box. "Fair enough. Who's going to help her go through it all now? Because if she does this shit on her own, it's gonna take her fucking months."

"Silk offered, as did Marie. But with their work hours, it'll come down mostly to me and Zara, I guess. She's hesitant to trust any of the other women. Which, after Em, I can fucking understand."

I was incredibly grateful Chip was happy running the gym on his own, and Taz had stepped in to do the classes for me. That was one of the great things about the Charon MC, we all had each other's backs.

"That was a clusterfuck none of us saw coming. Not sure how long it'll be before Donna comes back to the clubhouse. Keys said she's refusing. Now they know for certain that Em led your girl out of there to be taken, she's feeling guilty over it."

I shook my head as I followed him out with a box. "That's a load of shit. Em was an adult and she made her own choices. Not Donna's fault."

Nitro opened the back of the van and Arrow put his box in before turning to me. "Seems to me half the damn club is taking blame for what went down Saturday night, when it wasn't the fault of any of you."

I winced as I put my own box down. "Yeah, well, it's hard to not feel at least a little guilty when your woman gets fucking snatched from the very place you promised her was safe."

Arrow shook his head at me as Taz put his box into the van. "Let it go, brother. Nothing good will come from you beating yourself up over it."

I headed back inside. "Yeah, I know. Now, quit nagging me and let's get moving."

I really didn't want to have Arrow bitching in my ear all day over shit I didn't want to think about.

With the three of us working, we had the van all loaded up in no time. I went in search of Zara as the others waited out the front.

"Zara?"

I pushed the door open and found her standing next to the bed, staring at a full suitcase. I walked up behind her and wrapped my arms around her middle, pulling her back against me as I pressed a kiss to the top of her head.

"You ready to head out? We've got all the boxes loaded up."

"Ah, yeah, sure. Sorry I took so long. I should have been helping you guys."

I turned her so I could see her face, frowning at the tears in her eyes. "Bunny, you have four strong men here with you, there is no reason you should have to lift anything. What's wrong?"

She shrugged. "I don't know. Just feeling a little adrift I guess. This place, isn't home for me anymore. But your room at the clubhouse doesn't feel like home either."

Before she could go any further, I silenced her with a gentle kiss.

"I was thinking yesterday that I really should look into buying a house. I was only living at the clubhouse because it was convenient. Generally speaking, only prospects actually live there. We all sleep there on occasion, but most don't live there full-time." I cleared my throat. "There's a house for sale two doors down from Eagle and Silk's place. We could go check it out if you want?"

She tilted her head at me, frowning a moment before a small, beautiful smile lit up her face. "Are you asking me to move in with you, Jacob Miller?"

I chuckled at that. "Bunny, you agreed to be my old lady already, so this shouldn't be a big deal. That and you kinda already *are* living with me. So I'm just asking if you'd like to share a bigger space with me. I don't think it would be a good idea to move until after we sort out this shit with Sledge, but it'll take some time to sort out the paperwork on buying a place anyway."

With her arms wrapped around my neck, she pushed up on her toes. I took the hint and lowered my mouth to kiss her again. And again. I loved her mouth, her taste, the way she filled the emptiness that had been inside me since my sister's murder. With a groan, she pulled back.

"I've fallen head over heels in love with you, my sweet gentleman-biker."

I grinned like a fool as my heart damn near exploded out of my chest. "Not so sure about that sweet gentleman-biker comment, but I like the sound of the rest of that statement. Because, Zara, I meant what I said yesterday, and the day before. I love you so fucking much."

I took her mouth again, cupping her face to hold her to me. She opened her lips and I delved in, my tongue dancing with hers. She wriggled her body against mine, her tummy rubbing over my rock-hard cock.

"Oh for fuck's sake. And you call me sex crazed. C'mon, you two. We got places to be. You can screw all you like once we get back to the clubhouse."

With a growl, I pulled away from Zara. "Shut the fuck up, Taz. We're coming."

He chuckled. "Well, if I hadn't interrupted you, you would have been coming, I'm sure."

I turned around and gave him a hard shove. "Go outside already, we'll be there in a sec."

Still laughing it up, Taz headed out. I turned to see Zara zipping up the suitcase with a smile on her face. I grabbed the bag that sat on the floor as she lifted the one off the bed and we headed out.

Zara

With my hands on my hips, I turned in a circle. The men had unloaded all the boxes into one of the unused bedrooms upstairs after we got back last night. There were so many. At least I didn't have to go through all of them. Mac had decided to bring all the boxes back, since he was certain I'd be moving everything up here soon anyway. And as Arrow pointed out, my father may have kept something in the bedroom that related to whatever he did. It was easier to bring it all up now, than to find the time to go down there again to collect it later.

The question was, where the fuck did I start?

A tap on the door sounded before Silk came in. She wasn't working this afternoon, so was going to help me out. Mac was down with the other men in church so we had a chance to get started without male interruptions.

"I grabbed a roll of garbage bags, just in case."

"Good idea. Might as well cull this stuff while we're at it."

I pulled Mac's Leatherman from my pocket and flicked open the knife. "Right. Pick a box, any box!"

I pulled the closest one over and sliced the tape holding it closed.

"I can't believe Mac gave you his knife. He's never without that thing."

I grinned at her. "He told me he still has his k-bar knife on him, so he'll survive without this one for a few hours."

Silk laughed as she kneeled down on the opposite side of the box I was opening. "Men."

"Thanks for helping me with this."

She smiled gently over at me. "I know how it feels to find shit out about your father you never had any clue about. Hopefully you'll find better news than I did."

I tilted my head at her as I opened the top of the box. "What did you find out?"

"That my dad was basically an information broker, and a thief. Well, he wasn't really a broker. As far as we can tell, he collected a fuck-load of information on several organizations, but it appears that he didn't do anything with it. My parents died in the 9/11 attacks.

They were on the plane that crashed into the south tower. That's how I came to live with Uncle Clint—Bulldog."

Holy shit, that was a hell of a secret to find out. I hoped like hell I wasn't going to find something similar.

"Wow. When did you find out about him?"

"Only a month or so ago. I think I'm still in shock about it all."

I started pulling out photo frames, trying really hard to not look at the images they contained. "I bet you are. I've got no idea what I'm gonna find in all this shit, but my hopes of it being good aren't high. Not with the way things have been going lately."

Silk gave my arm a squeeze. "We'll deal with it, whatever you find. Hopefully, we'll discover something we can use to either figure out where Sledge is hiding or to flush him out into the open."

Hope bubbled up inside me. "I hope so. I know the club wants to be the ones to deal with him, but I really don't give a fuck if it's the club or the cops that pick him up. Just so long as he's not out there roaming around waiting to grab me."

"I hear you. Although, in your shoes, I'd want the club to get to him first. It'll be a more permanent solution. You'll learn MCs prefer to deal with this kinda shit themselves."

I chose to not continue that line of thinking. I didn't want to think about how they'd make it permanent. I wasn't ready to even think about that side of biker life at the moment.

We settled into a quiet routine as we went through each box. It was about an hour later when we finally found something. This sixth box was half-filled with folders from a filing cabinet. Silk and I were both skim reading each file, looking for anything that might clue us in.

"Fucking hell, Zara. This is massive."

I put down the useless file I was looking over and moved to sit next to Silk. "What is it?"

"It looks like your dad was part of a team. These are just notes on the when and where, but Zara, this proves your dad wasn't helping the Iron Hammers. It actually looks like he was sabotaging them."

Excitement had me reaching for the file that was underneath the one Silk was currently reading. Opening it up, I found a notebook and started looking over its pages, hardly able to believe what I was reading.

After about ten minutes, Silk interrupted me. "Did you find more information?"

"You could say that. Holy shit, Silk."

Of course that was the moment the door opened and Mac, Eagle and Scout all walked in.

"What did you find, babe?"

I blinked up at Mac, too shocked to speak. He came over and sat behind me on the floor before he pulled me into his lap.

Silk snorted a laugh. "I think Zara's in shock. To be honest, I'm a little awestruck too. Looks like Zara's father was part of a team that was sabotaging runs the Iron Hammers were making. I haven't found what the runs were for though. Or know whether this makes him a good or bad guy."

I'd found that information. Shaking my head I licked my lips, then cleared my throat. "I know." I held up the notebook. "I guess my dad figured the club might catch him, so he wrote this. I'm not sure what to call it. It's addressed to me like a letter, but after this first page, it reads more like a diary. Do any of you guys know when Sledge became the president of the Iron Hammers?"

Scout spoke from where he was leaning against the door frame. "I don't know the date off the top of my head, but it was about ten years ago. Why's that?"

I flicked back to the first page to see the date. "Okay, so I haven't read all his notes, only the first few pages. But from what Dad wrote, I've found the link between him and the Iron Hammers. It was in 2002 that my Mom was diagnosed with cancer and he took the second job as a taxi driver. He wrote this first page in 2007, six months after he started working with the others to save girls."

"Save girls?"

At the sound of Bulldog's voice, I looked up to see he and Nitro had joined Scout near the door.

"Yeah. He says here that late one night in August 2006, he found a girl struggling to run down the road. She'd obviously been physically beaten, and he later found out she'd been raped multiple times too. He took her to the hospital, and on the way, she admitted she'd gone out to a party at the Iron Hammer's clubhouse. He made his statement to the police at the hospital after he dropped her off, and figuring she was safe there, he left her." My eyes began to burn. "She was found dead in her hospital bed a few hours later. She'd been smothered with a pillow."

Mac held me tighter and pressed a kiss against the top of my head as Scout spoke up.

"Their inside man with the cops would have stepped in to clean up the mess. I bet your dad's statement went missing, too."

I nodded. "Makes the most sense. Anyway, Dad goes on to explain how he ended up forming a team with a couple of the cops that weren't on Iron Hammer's payroll, a doctor and a few nurses, along with another taxi driver. Between them, they gathered information and would snatch girls when they could." I paused to look around at everyone in the room. "The Iron Hammers were selling girls across the border."

My gut rolled and bile rose up my throat. With a cough I swallowed it down as the men all let out curses. Silk burst into tears, causing me to jerk against Mac in shock. Eagle had her up in his arms within moments. I frowned at her for a minute. She'd gone real pale and seemed to be shaking. It could be morning sickness again, but something told me that wasn't the case.

"Take her out of here, Eagle."

With a nod, the man followed Scout's gruffly issued order. Once they left, Bulldog let out a groan before he spoke.

"Silk found out last month that her mother had been one of Iron Hammer's captive women. That her father got her out when she was pregnant with her."

That had me frowning. Again. "But that doesn't add up. From what I've just read, this all only started about ten years ago."

Nitro spoke up from the doorway. "At a guess? They've been snatching women for a good, long time, but only a few. Just enough for themselves. Sledge obviously saw a way to profit from the process, so upped the snatch rate. We've been hearing stories of women escaping from their clubhouse for decades. Although, this is the first time I've heard of anyone trying to go against the club to stop them. Your dad must have really been something. You should be proud, Zara."

I was. But the pride was mixed with grief and pain. I thought about Marie and what she'd said about her and her friend. At a guess that had happened before Sledge became president, proving Nitro's point.

Scout cleared his throat. "Sledge could have been selling girls before he became president. Most likely it was only a few here and there. He's selfish enough to have wanted the profits all to himself." He paused and adjusted his bandana. "Fucking hell, how many girls is he responsible for selling into hell?"

The room went silent after that.

Wrapping my arms around Mac's neck, I buried my face against his throat. I didn't want to do the math on that score.

Chapter 19

Mac

After what Zara discovered yesterday, I figured she could use a break from it all today. And I had a surprise for her.

I stayed out of the way as my girl helped Marie close up the cafe. Then, Zara came over to me as she'd done each day this week. When she got to me, instead of taking her hand and heading out, like we normally do, I handed her the backpack I'd brought in with me this morning.

"Could you get changed before we go? I wanna take you someplace that's a bit of a ride away, and you'll be more comfortable in jeans than your work pants."

"Okaaaay."

She drew the word out as she frowned up at me, which made me smile. "Don't over think it, babe. Just go get changed so we can go for a ride."

"What about safety? I thought I wasn't supposed to go anywhere but here, the gym or the clubhouse?"

I glared at her. "What the fuck, Zara? You think I can't keep you safe?"

A moment later, she was wrapped around me, pressing a kiss to the corner of my mouth. "I didn't mean it like that. Of course I trust you to keep me safe. I was just checking if we had Scout's permission. Isn't that how the club works? You need Scout's okay to do stuff?"

I scoffed as I wrapped my arm around her waist. "On some things. When it comes to taking my old lady out, he gets no fucking say at all. Now, go on, hurry up and get changed."

What I didn't tell her was that I had told Scout exactly where we were going, and he'd agreed with me that it was far enough away that it was unlikely Sledge would be anywhere near us. And if the bastard did show up? Well, I am a fucking Marine, after all. No way will that fucker get anywhere near Zara so long as I'm breathing.

While Zara was in the back, Marie got busy moving around behind the counter. I wasn't sure what the woman was doing since the place was now all closed up for the day. When Zara came out, as she passed Marie, the older woman grabbed her. I grinned as she gave my woman a hug then handed her another pack. Marie was a real gem. She'd obviously made some food for our little adventure.

With a smile, Zara came over to me and I took the bags from her hands as I called out over her shoulder. "Thanks Marie!"

"No worries, sugar. Take care of our girl and I'll see you both tomorrow."

I followed Zara out and we headed around to the parking lot. I handed Zara her helmet and while she was occupied putting the thing on, I stowed the bags, being careful to not let her see the surprise that was waiting for her in my saddle bag.

"You going to tell me where we're going?"

I pulled her to me, kissing her until she relaxed against me with a sigh. "You'll see soon enough."

Slipping my leg over my bike, I sat, then helped her on behind me. The way she instantly wrapped her arms around my middle, sneaking her fingers up under my shirt had me chuckling even though the action had my cock punching against my zipper. *Riding was gonna hurt like a mother until that bastard went down.*

I took it slow until I was out of the parking lot, then gunned it down the street as I headed out of town. I saw a few of my brothers on the way, giving them a nod as I passed. They were all on the lookout for anyone trying to follow us. Once on the open road, with still no sign of anyone trying to tail us, I relaxed and focused on enjoying the feel of having the wind in my face, my ride beneath me and my girl behind me.

Life was good.

About an hour and a half, and two stops, later, I pulled off the road. Carefully, I parked my bike on a patch of grass, making sure it was well clear of the softer sand not far away. Last thing I wanted was to drop my Harley, especially on fucking sand. I'd driven up the coast of Texas until I found a road that ran close to the edge of the beach. That way, my ride was close by if we needed to leave in a hurry, but we were basically on the beach, so we'd get a great view of the sunset over the water a bit later.

"Off you get, bunny."

I followed suit and once I was standing, I stretched out my back and shoulders as I took a deep breath of the salty, sea air. With a wide grin, Zara snuggled against me, running her hands under my cut and down over my ribs.

"It's beautiful here."

"Wait until the sun sets. Nothing's quite like a Texas sunset over the water."

I turned away from her, back to my bike and opening up the saddlebag. I took the pack from Marie out, and quickly snatched up my surprise for Zara, keeping it hidden. Probably should have wrapped it up in something, but I hadn't thought of that earlier.

"Come sit with me, we'll see what Marie made us."

The sun was low in the sky, the first splashes of the color from the coming sunset slashing across the clouds. I sat a little in front of my bike, keeping the gift behind my back as I did. As Zara started to lower herself down, I tugged on her arm, pulling her over me so she was straddling my thighs, facing me. I ran my hands up her arms, then neck, before I delved my fingers into her hair as I drew her mouth to mine for a quick kiss. I loved how she smelled: Jasmine and sunshine, and mine.

"Got something for you, bunny."

She pushed her palms against my chest so she sat up straighter. "Yeah?"

"Close your eyes for a sec."

She stilled and raised an eyebrow, but did as instructed. I pulled out the cut Scout had given me last night. He'd apparently known I was going to claim Zara so had ordered it for me already by the time I asked him about it. Making sure her eyes were still closed, I gently set the leather over her shoulders. With a gasp her eyes flew open, and she looked down. The squeal she let out left me wincing, even as I grinned. She shrugged it off and held it between us, running her fingers softly over the embroidery.

"It feels wrong that I'm this excited to have you putting a *property patch* on me. It's not very new-age thinking.

I chuckled as I picked it up again and helped her to put it on properly.

"It's not wrong. It's so fucking right. Damn, you look good with my name on you, bunny."

It wasn't a lie. My dick was throbbing against my jeans as I focused on how good she looked with *Property of Mac* written on her. I needed her. Right now. I glanced up and down the beach, making sure we were still alone out here. Winter in Texas didn't involve snow and ice, thank fuck, and today had actually been fairly warm. But because it was winter, not too many people came down to the beach. If someone did happen to drive past us, all they'd see was my bike as it sat between us and the road. I'd just have to pull her flush against me, and no one would see any of her sexy skin.

When Zara had gotten changed back at Marie's, she'd only changed her pants so she still wore her buttoned up work shirt. With a growl, I attacked the buttons until I could push it apart. Her bra had a front clasp and I flicked it open in less than a heartbeat, shoving all the material under the leather. Her nipples pebbled in the cool evening air and a shiver passed over her, making the leather shift to cover them.

"Now *that* is sexy as fuck."

Her chest heaved with each breath she took. Unable to resist, I leaned in and, starting just below her ear, kissing and nipping my way down her neck, over her collarbone then down to suckle her hard little nipples.

"Mac!"

Her fingers slid over my head as she started grinding her pelvis against me. With a groan I released her nipple. Letting my hands take over tormenting her tits, I whispered against her lips.

"See now, bunny. If you were wearing a cute little skirt, I could flip it up and fuck you right now."

Her eyes slid shut as she moaned. "Seriously, babe?"

Interesting. I'd expected her to laugh off my comment, but instead her cheeks pinkened and the pulse at the base of her neck sped up. She liked the idea, did she?

Before she knew what I was going to do, I had her flipped around on my lap so she was facing out with her back against my chest. I had my legs straight in front of me, and her sexy thighs were spread so she straddled me. I lowered my mouth to her neck as my hands went back to her tits.

"Watch the sunset, bunny. I'll keep you warm."

With her head on my shoulder, she wrapped her arm up around my neck as she arched her back, pushing her tits harder against my palms.

"I'm sure you will."

As the sky turned orange in front of us, I slid one hand down her body until I got to her jeans. After flicking open her button fly, I slipped my hand inside, under her panties, to palm her pussy. I grinned like a motherfucker when damp heat greeted me.

"Hmm, so you like the idea of me fucking you out here in the open, do you?"

I didn't really give her a chance to respond as I took that moment to thrust two fingers deep inside her. My cock was throbbing painfully against the zipper of my own jeans. I was starting to worry I'd end up with a permanent zipper indentation if I didn't unzip soon. But Zara's little whimpers, along with the way she was tilting her hips, fucking my fingers, was too good to stop. When I looked over her shoulder, down her body, the sight nearly had me coming in my pants. My patch sat right next to her exposed rock-hard little nipple. *Mine.* She was all mine, and now I had her marked and claimed.

Her next little whimper set me over the edge.

"Grip my neck and lift up your ass, baby."

She did as instructed, without any hesitation and after I tore open my own jeans, releasing my granite-hard cock, I shoved her jeans and panties down to the middle of her thighs. I didn't want her to get too cold, but I had to be inside her right fucking now. With a hand wrapped around each hip, I moved her over me, and my eyes crossed when she reached a hand between her thighs to guide me inside her. With her pants stopping her from spreading her legs too wide, it was a fucking tight fit. I thrust in deep.

"Fuck, bunny. I love how tight you are like this. Fucking love you, Zara."

She hummed happily as she swiveled her hips on me. "Love you too, babe."

"Now you're officially mine, you gonna let me fill you up?"

She shuddered and arched her back again. "I sure as fuck don't want you to stop and pull out now." She paused to moan as I hit her g-spot. "And I kinda like the idea of having your baby."

That left me growling as I gripped her hips harder to slam her down on me with more force. Images of her with her belly swollen with my baby, of her nursing a sweet, dark haired baby to her breast had tingles running down my spine and tightening up my balls. I slammed her down over me hard and held her to me as I started to come inside her. I shifted my hand to rub her clit until she tightened around me and screamed for me.

I'd never get enough of this woman, no matter how many times I took her. I knew, I'd always want more.

Zara

It had been a full week since I was taken, six days since Sledge went missing and two days since I first let Mac fuck me without a condom. A smile curved my lips as I thought back to that evening. Watching the sky change colors as the sun set while Mac loved me. I clenched my thighs together at the memory.

"Girl, get your head out of the clouds and go deliver this to table six."

Heat flashed over my cheeks as I winced at Marie. "Sorry."

She shook her head with a chuckle. "I was young once, so I understand, sugar. And if I had a man like yours, I'd be behaving worse than you are."

I rolled my eyes and took the tray to deliver table six's order. When I got back to the counter I moved up close to Marie so no one else would overhear me.

"You're not too old to be having some fun with a man. And I've seen how you watch Scout."

She stiffened and a flash of hurt passed over her eyes. "I don't know what you're talking about. Would you mind taking this out to the dumpster?"

There was definitely a story behind that look, but it was clearly one Marie didn't want to discuss. I tied off the garbage bag before I lifted it up and headed to the front door, calling out to Bash as I went. Mac had to work at the gym today and it felt strange to not have him here in the cafe with me. He was still going to be here to take me home when we closed, but the daytime guard duty had fallen to Bash. I knew Mac would have preferred have a patched in brother on me, but that hadn't been an option today. And after nearly a week of no one even seeing Sledge around town, I'd tried to tell the club we didn't need anyone sitting in the cafe all day. Surely, they all had more important things to do with their day? Not that they'd even listened to that suggestion.

"You want me to run that out?"

I smiled over at him. "Nah, just come with me so Mac doesn't lose his shit that I went outside on my own."

I could use the fresh air, and Marie looked like she could use a minute without me in her face. I guess I shouldn't have brought up Scout during work hours. Ah well. Live and learn.

Happily lost in my little bubble of happiness, I made my way to the parking lot with Bash by my side. He lifted the dumpster's lid for me, and I tossed the bag in. I winced a little when the lid came down with a crash.

"Sorry."

"No worries. Damn, it's cold out here today, isn't it?"

I looked up at the clouds wondering if it was going to get stormy later.

Bash made a noise I think was meant to indicate he agreed with me. Then he stiffened. Curious, I followed his gaze to see one of the women from the clubhouse. *Great.* I hoped Bash wasn't going to accept a blowjob from her or something, because I'd already seen more of the man's junk than I ever wanted, or needed to.

"Hey, Jake baby, how you doing? Sorry I missed your party the other night."

With my intuition twitching, I tilted my head as I frowned over at her. She'd called him Jake. Did that mean she didn't know about his name change? Or had she just forgotten it? And why would she have missed the party? The club whores—my skin crawled a little every time I heard that term—seemed to be at the clubhouse every night of the week, like they didn't have anything else to do. I wasn't sure if the club paid them, but assumed they must, since they seemed to spend so much damn time there.

As I was trying to puzzle out why she had the hair on my arms standing up, she'd moved in and now had her palms on Bash's chest as she purred at him. Seriously, the woman was actually purring. Meanwhile, Bash looked like a fucking statue. Clearly, the poor boy had no idea how to deal with such a pushy woman.

"I'm going to head back inside."

My voice seemed to snap Bash out of his stupor and he started to shove the woman off him. Before he could say a word, the loud noise of a car's engine filled the air. I turned in time to see a black SUV gunning straight for us.

"Ah, fuck."

Bash grabbed my arm and pulled me back behind him as he reversed up next to the dumpster. I ended up next to the damn whore who was glaring at me with a look of hatred that had my memory coughing up what I was trying to think of earlier. Scout had said two of the club whores had helped Sledge escape. I narrowed my eyes at her. Was this one of them? Why else wouldn't she have been at the party Monday night?

"You were one of the ones that freed Sledge, weren't you?"

Bash stiffened with a curse, but before he could do anything, the SUV squealed to a stop about five feet away from us. Within seconds the back door opened and the front passenger window rolled down. The muzzle of a gun flashed within the vehicle. I screamed as the sound echoed around us. Bash jerked, and with a curse, reached under his cut. Before I could see what he was grabbing, the whore put her whole body into shoving me out from behind him and toward the car. I hadn't been expecting it, and as I stumbled to get my feet under me, I was grabbed and thrown head first into the rear of the vehicle before I knew what was going on. I twisted to look out the open door in time to see Bash bring down the butt of his gun on the bitch's head, knocking her out before he lined up a shot at the car. *Please let him be a good shot.*

I heard two tink noises as his bullets hit the metal of the car. At the same time the driver took another shot, Bash fired again and a grunt of pain sounded next to me. Snapping out of my shock, I scrambled over the seat, reaching for the opposite door. I pulled the handle but it refused to open. I tried to find the locking mechanism but the man who'd tossed me in grabbed my shoulder, pulling me away from the door, he'd spun me around and I was face to face with a man I didn't recognize.

"If you don't let me go, the Charons are gonna kill you."

His eyes narrowed for a moment, then without uttering a word, his fist came up to connect with my jaw. I was already struggling to fight off my cataplexy, and the blow made it impossible to not fall limply against the seat.

"She out?"

"Yeah. Hurry the fuck up and get us to the meet site. Then Sledge can fucking deal with her. Bastard put a bullet in my thigh. Hurts like a motherfucker."

"How bad you hit?"

"Bad. And the bullet's still fucking in there."

"I nailed his shoulder a good one, I'm sure he's in worse shape than you. Drug the bitch. If you pass out from blood loss or some shit, I do not want her to be waking up and trying something fucking stupid that'll get us all killed."

No, no, no. I didn't want to be drugged again! At least with the cataplexy, I could hear them and knew what was going on. Someone yanked my arm out and I felt a needle dig into the crook of my elbow moments before fire raced up my arm and I floated away.

Chapter 20

Mac

Fury radiated from me as I paced around Marie's. The first fucking day I'm not by her side all day and she's snatched. *Again.* I glanced over at the prospect who was currently being laid out over two tables that had been pushed together as Taz pawed through a first aid kit beside him. I wanted to be mad at the kid, but he didn't deserve my anger. He'd honestly done his best. After taking a bullet to his shoulder, he still managed to knock out the piece of shit whore who'd helped them take my woman, and got three shots off into their vehicle. Pity he hadn't hit a tire or two. He better have not hit Zara. Then I'd be more than angry with him.

With a growl, I turned my focus back to Keys, who'd set up on the opposite side of the cafe with his laptop.

"Hurry the fuck up, man. It's been over an hour already."

Keys flipped me the bird before he went back to taping away. "Fuck you, Mac. I'm going as fast as I can here."

Marie had closed the place down, shutting the blinds and locking the door, so I couldn't see anything out the windows. Which was infuriating, as I had nothing to focus on outside the people in this room, none of whom deserved my fury.

I needed to be moving, searching for my girl. With a snarl I threw a punch at the wall, feeling the sting as the skin on my knuckles split while the sheetrock gave out.

"Calm your shit down, Mac. You need to be calm and with a clear head, or I'll lock your ass down while we go out and get your woman. Understand?"

My vision turned red for a few moments. "No way in hell will you, or anyone, stop me from finding her. Just try it and see how that shit goes for you."

Scout let out a string of curses before he got up in my grill. "As president it's my fucking job to keep all of you safe. Which includes stopping a brother, who's being a stupid bastard, from getting himself killed. Zara's your old lady. That makes her one of us. Which means the whole fucking club will be behind you to get her back. But I won't let you join them if you're running purely on emotion. Because that means you're not using your fucking head, which will get you—and possibly Zara—killed."

I clenched my jaw and stayed silent as I seethed. I knew he was right. I needed to get my emotions in check. Dropping my head down, with my eyes closed, I took a few deep breaths and tried to gain control.

When I looked back up, Scout had moved away from me and over toward Marie, who was looking like she was having some kind of meltdown. She wasn't saying anything, but she had that special, wild look in her eyes that indicated she was battling some kind of internal war. Scout was slow in approaching her, speaking in a low voice that I couldn't quite hear well enough to make out the words. Not that it mattered, she wasn't hearing him. I frowned when Scout crowded in close against her, cupping her face in his large palms. Yeah, there was definitely something going on between those two. Although, I had no idea if they'd once been a couple and it had ended, or if they'd just danced around each other for years.

Marie shuddered, then slid her arms around the man's waist, as she leaned her head against his shoulder. The way Scout returned the embrace, holding the woman like she was made of glass, left me thinking we'd be seeing a lot more of Marie around at the clubhouse in the future.

"Right. Got her. Mac? Give me your phone."

I rushed to hand over the device to Keys as I looked at the laptop screen. While Keys screwed around with my phone, I leaned in and moved the map around to work out where the flashing dot was located.

"They didn't go very far."

How stupid were they? In their shoes, I'd be running as far and fast as possible. But these fuckers appeared to have stopped just north of Angleton.

"They might not be there. I'm tracking her phone, not her. But it's the only lead we have." He handed my phone back. "I've got it set to follow that signal, just in case it moves again."

"Great. I'm going after her. Who's coming?"

Scout moved toward me. "I'm going with you. Keys? You and Nitro gather the rest of the brothers and ride out to join us as soon as you can. Leave three brothers at the clubhouse and get all the women locked down there, including Marie." He eyed off the still-unconscious woman on the floor. "Take that bitch down to a cell. We'll deal with her later."

Taz peeled off the gloves he'd worn to work on Bash. "I'm good to leave now. Bash'll be fine. The bullet missed everything important and he's all sewn up."

I relaxed a little, knowing Taz and Scout were with me all the way. And damn, but it was fucking nice to know I had an entire club at my back. I glanced over to see one of the prospects that had been on guard duty out in front of Marie's help Bash sit up.

"Thanks."

My voice cracked a little and I headed for the door before anyone could say another fucking word. I made it all the way to my bike before Taz grabbed my arm.

"Whoa, Mac. Hold up. You armed?"

"Of course. Got my knife and my piece." I patted my palm over the gun concealed under my cut. I'd been wearing my under-arm harness all week, just in case that fucker turned up.

"Perfect."

With that, Taz jogged over to his ride. I clipped my helmet on and started mine up in record time.

Hold on, Zara. I'm coming for you.

And this time I'd make sure to eliminate all threats to her, even if I had to chase that fucker Sledge all the way to Mexico. I would see him dead by the end of the day.

Zara

As I slowly surfaced through the drug-induced haze, it took me a few minutes to get my mind to clear. What the fuck did they give me? An ear-piercing scream made me jerk awake, my eyes opening to see I was in a dim, dirty barn. Charming. I'd been propped against the wall with my arms bound above my head. I tugged on them a few times, but they didn't budge at all. *Just fucking great.* At least my legs were free.

"Fucking hell. Hold him down already."

I looked over toward the gruff voice to see Sledge and the driver leaning over the man who'd been with me in the rear of the SUV. I recalled hearing him say he'd been shot. Sledge was digging something into his thigh while the driver did his best to pin the man to the table. I couldn't help but wince when the man let out another scream of agony.

The sound cut off when the man went limp.

"Thank fuck. About fucking time."

Sledge kept mumbling under his breath as he worked on the man. But I stopped paying attention when the driver looked up and caught my gaze. Pain and fury blazed strong enough I shuddered in response.

"She's awake."

"Good. Go vent your anger on her and give me some fucking peace to deal with this shit."

The driver shook his head. "No way. I'm staying with him."

"Whip, he's fucking unconscious. And it's her damn fault your boy got shot in the first place. Go vent your frustrations on her rather than hovering over me like some kinda fucked-up mother hen."

What the fuck? It was my fault Sledge decided to risk everything to capture me. Again. I tried to swallow past the lump in my throat when the big man stepped toward where I sat on the floor. I was sure the evil glint in his dark eyes didn't bode well for me.

"He's wrong, it wasn't my fault. I didn't pull that trigger."

He lunged for me and backhanded me hard enough I went a little dizzy.

"Shut up, bitch."

While my head was still foggy, he undid my hands and dragged me up off the floor. I stumbled as I tried to get my feet under me, my movements slow and clumsy. Obviously, whatever drug they gave me was still in my system. Before I could muster the energy to fight, he took my hands and used a thick metal chain to bind them together in front of me.

When he shoved them up, my gaze followed and my blood ran cold. A hook was slipped between my bound wrists before he went to wind a lever that raised the hook, and my wrists. The chain twisted against the still-healing skin of my wrists as it went higher. I rose up on my toes to try to relieve the pressure but the bastard just chuckled and cranked the lever again. Then I crashed, cataplexy leaving me hanging from that damn hook.

"Fucking weak bitch."

I wanted to sigh in relief when I was lowered enough my feet were flat on the floor. I was just starting to get control of my muscles when a crack filled the air. I tensed as Sledge's laugh floated over from where he was still working on the other man.

"Little girl's about to find out why we call you Whip."

Whip growled. "Don't you worry about what I'm doing. You need to focus on what's in front of you."

"Don't forget who I am, boy. I could end you both in a heartbeat. Take her fucking shirt off before you start, give me something pretty to look at while I try to save your boy here."

A shudder ran through me, strong enough to make my teeth rattle. Desperation fueling me, I started to tug on my arms while Whip dropped his nasty looking whip on a chair before coming to stand in front of me. My hands were going numb, my wrists screaming in pain as I continued to tug and twist them. When he reached for my shirt, I pulled my leg back and thrust it up with all my strength. The bastard turned to the side so I caught his thigh, not his groin like I was aiming for. *Bastard.*

"Fucking bitch. You'll pay for that."

In a flash he gripped each side of my shirt and ripped it open, sending the buttons flying. I tried to back up when he pulled a knife from a sheath on his belt. Standing to my side, so I couldn't reach to kick him, he cut my shirt off, then my bra. But he didn't touch me. With a frown, I ran my gaze over him. It wasn't like I wanted to be raped, but his actions were not what I expected. Surely he'd at least cop a feel? Not like I could do shit about it.

"Such pretty tits, nice and lush. I want my turn with them later, Whip. So work over her back. I want her front intact for me to destroy."

With a grunt, Whip snatched up his bullwhip before disappearing behind me. I licked my dry lips and tried to think of something I could do to get out of this. I could turn around, but that would just get me lashed on my front. I'd never been whipped before, but I could only guess it would hurt less on my back than my front. I sure as fuck regretted putting my hair in a bun this morning. That might have given my skin a little cushioning.

I jerked and yelped when fire licked across my upper back. As I panted through the pain, another lash landed just below the first. Once again, I went limp as I lost control over my body, but the pain kept coming. In what felt like a crisscross pattern, the fucker worked his way down my back and then over my ass before heading up again. The thin material of my work pants quickly gave way to the whip, offering me no protection. I'd never felt agony like that and when I started to fade in and out of awareness I knew it wasn't my illnesses causing it.

A wet hand gripped my jaw, forcing my face up as a coppery smell filled my nose.

"Wake the fuck up, bitch. We ain't done with you yet."

I wasn't sure how long I'd been out, but as I raised my gaze it caught on the scene behind Sledge. Whip was hunched over the table, his shoulders bunched tight. One of his hands was wrapped in the hair of the man who lay still on the table.

"Yeah, he died. Because of you he's now lost his lover."

That explained the lack of interest Whip had in my body. There was a note to Sledge's voice that made me think he didn't think much of the fact that the two men had been lovers. My focus shifted back to Sledge and I recoiled. His grip slipped off my face as his hands were slippery. Oh fuck. I gagged. His hands were covered in blood. A dead man's blood was now smeared all over my face. Suddenly my head was ripped back, extending my throat in a way that forced me to swallow down the bile or choke on it.

"Oh, no you fucking don't. You ain't puking on me again, bitch."

He kept his grip on my hair tight as his other hand went for the front of my pants. He pulled and tugged at them, each movement causing what was left of the material on my ass to slide over the raw wounds. Tears burned, then fell down my cheeks as the pain fired up again.

With a curse he released my hair and pulling his own knife, he cut through my pants, slicing them away from me until I was naked. My body shook and sobs tore from my throat.

"Please, don't do this."

He laughed at my begging before wrapping his fist in my hair once again.

"I can, and will, do whatever the fuck I want with you. Your daddy and his buddies cost me a fucking fortune before we took them out. Now, thanks to you, I've lost my fucking club. You have one hell of a fucking debt to repay, bitch. And when you're done paying, I'm gonna sell you to my friends over the border. They'll have fun with such a pretty thing down there. Of course, you might not be so pretty by the time I'm through with you but they won't give a fuck. They'll just give you to the sadistic ones. Those fuckers don't care if you're scarred because they'll want to add their own to your collection."

My heart was racing, and my lungs burned with the effort to breathe through the nightmare playing through my mind. The picture Sledge painted was graphic and horrific and more than I could take. My brain started to spin and Sledge's words became distorted, cutting in and out. I vaguely heard the sound of a heavy belt buckle chunking open before Sledge was standing up close to me. He ran his hand over my hip and reached back to grip my ass. Pain flared from the open whip wounds he was pulling at, but it didn't hurt like before. My body was becoming numb, sensations muted, as my thoughts floated in the murky fog that now filled my mind.

Chapter 21

Mac

I'd never ridden so fucking fast in my life. I didn't care that it had started to rain, or that lightning was streaking across the sky above me. The sense of urgency I felt grew, the closer I got to the property north of Angleton where Zara's phone was located. I fucking hoped I wasn't too late. I didn't want to think about life without Zara in it. Or the hell I'd bring down on every fucker I could find that had anything to do with whatever had been done to her.

With Scout and Taz at my back, I roared my bike up the driveway to the farm and on instinct, headed to the large barn. I didn't give a fuck that the noise we were making would alert them to our presence. Hopefully they'd think it was more thunder. Either way, I wasn't going to take the time to park and walk in. They'd had my girl for too fucking long already. When I saw the side door had been left open, I gunned straight for it. It was a people door, not a vehicle one, but my bike passed through with no problem.

As I burst into the interior, I skidded to a stop and was off my bike in a flash. Not caring if the machine fell.

"You motherfucker!"

The second I spoke, Sledge froze as he looked over his shoulder. Zara was hanging, naked and bloody from a fucking hook, and that fucker was standing between her thighs. His jeans hung loose on his hips as though they were open, and he had my girl's leg hitched up in one of his hands.

"You're too fucking late to save her. She's mine now. Might as well just leave her with me at this point."

Like fucking hell I would just leave her. I'd draw my gun to shoot the bastard, but he was too fucking close to risk a shot, and I knew I was too fucking far away to stop him from thrusting into her if his pants were, in fact, open. But I wasn't going to let it stop me from trying. With a roar, I lunged forward as I pulled my knife free. Before I made it more than a handful of steps, two gunshots rang out from behind me, echoing around the space. Knowing they were from Taz and Scout, I didn't stop. Just kept moving forward until I knocked into Sledge, shoving him away from Zara. He hit the floor with a thud as I saw the hole in the side of his temple.

Had to have been Taz. He was the only man I knew who could have pulled off that shot with a fucking handgun.

Ignoring the dead man, I scrambled to get back to my feet, to get to Zara. I got to her at the same time as Taz.

"What did those fuckers do to her?"

Taz's accent had deepened, a sure sign the Aussie was furious. I reached up to lift her wrists off the hook as Taz moved around behind her. He winced and let loose another string of curses. "They died too fucking fast. They didn't suffer nearly enough."

I slowly lowered her arms, Taz slipping his hands under her armpits to keep her from falling to the floor. I frowned when she continued to stare off over my shoulder in complete silence. She had to have felt a rush of pain when her blood flowed back into her arms just now. She had blood smeared over her face, but I couldn't see any open wounds. I went to wrap my arm around her waist, to pull her against me, but Taz yelled out and shifted her so I couldn't touch her.

"Don't touch her back, it's a fucking mess."

That had me freezing for a moment before fury blasted through me.

"What the fuck did they do, Taz?"

"She's been whipped raw. Shoulders to ass. It's a bloody mess."

Rage had my vision turning red for a minute. Scout came up beside me and hissed out a curse. I gave my head a shake to clear my vision. Zara needed me. I'd get angry later, after she was safe and had medical care. With Taz holding her steady on her feet, I focused on getting the fucking chains off her wrists. I tensed when Scout gently gripped her jaw and tilted her face so he could look into her eyes.

"Looks like she's in shock, unless this is part of one of her conditions."

"Her eyes are open, and she's standing up, sort of. This isn't an episode."

I got her wrists free and lifted them up to inspect the wounds. They hadn't fully healed from the last time Sledge hurt her, now they were a real mess. Clearly she'd fought to get free.

"Scout, how far out are the others? We need the truck to get her to hospital."

"Messaging them now."

Squeezing my eyes shut against the tears burning them, I leaned in and pressed a kiss to her temple, praying we hadn't been too late. That she'd snap out of this weird zombie thing she had going on and come back to me.

"Taz, I need to hold her."

I watched as he ran his gaze down her back. "I'm not sure how you're gonna do that without hurting her and making this mess worse." He was silent for a bit. "Maybe if you sit down, and we lay her on her side over your lap, with her face against your shoulder. You'll need to make sure you don't touch her below her neck. And if you wrap your other arm around her legs, keeping them folded up, but don't let them touch her ass, she shouldn't be too uncomfortable. Hopefully it won't make any of her wounds worse."

That sounded doable, and I needed to touch her, to have her pressed against me, more than I needed my next breath. "Help me."

I sat on the lone chair that was nearby, and with Scout and Taz both helping, I soon had my woman bundled against me. Tilting her body towards me, I could finally see her back and hissed out a string of curses of my own. Why would anyone do something like that? Especially to someone as innocent as Zara. Taz lifted her arm and rested her palm against my chest, over my heart. A moment later her fingers twitched and I held my breath as I focused on her face.

"Zara? C'mon, bunny. Wake up for me."

Her fingers flexed against me again but her pupils were still dilated and she showed no other sign of coming back to me. Taking a deep breath, I looked away from her and around the barn, for the first time seeing the dead man on the table and another in a heap on the floor in front of it. Guess that was the second gunshot, Scout shooting that bastard. Scout glanced up to me from where he was standing over the guy on the table.

"Looks like Bash scored a hit on this one. Guess neither Sledge or that other fucker were too good at being medics."

Scout's phone pinged and a moment later I could hear the sound of engines getting closer. At least, I hoped it was engines and not more fucking thunder.

"Truck's here. Taz, help me open the door for them."

I sat nursing my woman, counting her shallow breaths as Taz and Scout got the big doors open. The same armored vehicle we used to treat Zara last time backed through the opening. The second it stopped, the rear doors opened and Donna jumped out. She made it two steps before her gaze landed on me and Zara and she stumbled with a curse. Seconds later, her expression cleared as she obviously switched into nurse mode.

"Keys? Help me get the gurney out. Mac, stay where you are. We need to limit moving her as much as possible."

I turned to press another kiss to Zara's temple when they came toward us with the stretcher. When they stopped in front of us, I slowly stood and placed her on the mattress on her side.

"Hold her in that position." With a palm on her shoulder and thigh, I kept her from moving as Donna put two pillows in front of Zara. "Okay, roll her onto her front. Great."

I watched, feeling useless as Donna did her thing, getting a drip into Zara's inner elbow—because her wrists and hands were too fucked up to find a vein—before carefully strapping her down and into the back of the truck.

"You coming with us, Mac?"

"Yeah, I'll follow you on my bike."

Scout growled behind me. "Like hell you will. Get in the damn truck with your woman, brother. We'll see your bike gets home."

With a nod, I climbed in, and as I turned to shut the door, I saw Scout ordering around the rest of the Charons that had ridden out to help save my woman. The last thing I heard before we took off out of the barn was Scout ordering that the place be burned to the ground.

Zara

My head felt like it had been stuffed with cotton wool, and my throat was parched. Voices filtered through to me, making me frown. Who were they? My eyelids were heavy, but after taking a deep breath and catching the smell of antiseptic, I forced them open to take in my surroundings. White. It was all I could see. Maybe my eyes were still shut? Or was I blind now? Closing my lids again, I focused on my other senses. I was lying halfway between being on my side and front, something firm but soft keeping my body at this angle, and my face resting on a smooth pillow. Testing my body, I attempted to roll onto my back. And promptly gasped when pain shot up my spine as though I'd been struck by lightning.

"Mac, she's awake." I knew that voice! That was Marie. She was my new boss. "Don't move, Zara. You have to stay off your back while it heals, sugar."

With a frown, I had another go at opening my eyes, this time blinking until the white fog cleared and I could see Marie sitting in a chair beside me.

"Hey."

She smiled gently at me and gave my hand a light pat. "Hey there, sugar." Tears filled her eyes and she stopped speaking. Her gaze shifted away from me for a moment, then she stood. "I'm going to go find the doctor to let him know you're awake."

The moment she moved, Mac took her place. My man crumbled into the small seat. He looked terrible. I frowned again as I took in his red rimmed eyes, and the stubble on his skull. Even his skin looked paler than normal.

"What's wrong? What happened?"

He shook his head and smirked for a moment. "Nothing's wrong now you're awake, bunny." He softly ran his knuckles down my cheek before tucking my hair behind my ear. "Don't you remember what happened? That you were snatched from the parking lot behind Marie's?"

As though that one sentence triggered the door in my mind, all the memories came flooding back and I trembled as I struggled to breathe through the remembered agony.

"Shhh. It's all over now. There's no one left to come after you."

"I don't remember getting free. You came for me? How?"

He kept stroking my face and neck, then down my arm, as though he had to touch me. Not that I was complaining, I loved the feel of his hands on me, and his touch was currently helping me stay focused on the here and now.

"The prospects guarding the front of the cafe heard the shots and alerted us. Then Keys hacked into your phone to give us your location. I took off the moment he had it." He winced. "I'm so fucking sorry it took so long, bunny."

"You came. That's all that matters."

My last memory was Sledge cutting my pants off my body. I closed my eyes as I tried to catch the full memory. Had he raped me? I didn't feel sore between my thighs. A knock on the door stopped my spiraling thoughts.

"Ah, so our patient is finally awake. Hello, Zara, my name is Dr. Tod Johnson and I've been in charge of you since you came in yesterday."

My breath caught and I twisted my neck so I could stare at the doctor. "A whole day? I've been out that long?"

"Yes, we've kept you sedated to give your body a chance to physically heal. Now, you're awake, I'll get the hospital's psychiatrist to come visit you."

I cut him off with a frown. "Why would I need to talk to a shrink?"

The doctor came over to stand near Mac, which I was grateful for. It meant I didn't have to twist my neck anymore.

"It's standard practice in cases like yours. You've suffered not only physically, but mentally. Nightmares are common, and sometimes the victim struggles to adjust back to normal life. It's not a sign of weakness to seek out help, Zara, but strength. That you want to get well and move forward with your life, not let those that hurt you continue to do so."

I took a deep breath. "Okay. I, ah, I can't remember if he—" I couldn't get the words to form. "My last memory is of him cutting my pants off. I don't know if he—" Tears burned my eyes but I still couldn't say the word, as though saying it would make it real somehow.

The doctor smiled gently at me. "No, you were not sexually assaulted." He started to move toward the end of the bed. "Let me check how your back is looking."

A shudder ran through me while a whimper escaped my throat as I remembered the pain of each of the strikes Whip had landed against me.

"Shhh, sweetheart."

Mac leaned in and pressed kisses against my temple, cheek, then mouth, his soft lips caressing my skin bringing me back to now. I held his gaze with mine as the doctor lifted the blanket, then peeled something else off my skin.

"Now, several of these lacerations were deep enough to require stitches. They're looking good. Let me just put a new dressing over them."

I stayed silent, staring into Mac's ice-blue irises as the doctor did his thing. He was my anchor, my protector, my guardian. Tears blurred my vision as emotion overwhelmed me.

"He's nearly finished. Does it hurt? Do you need something for the pain?"

With a watery smile, I shook my head a little. I was in pain, but not enough to complain about. "Love you."

His expression softened and the tension in his body seemed to drain away. He wiped his fingertips under my eye, wiping the moisture away. "Love you too, bunny. But loving me shouldn't make you cry, sweetheart."

I wasn't entirely sure why I was crying, so I didn't know how to explain to him why I was.

"Kiss me."

He leaned in and gently kissed my mouth. It wasn't the usual heat-filled mating of mouths that we normally shared. But this sweet brush of his lips over mine cracked my heart wide open and shook me all the way to my soul. When the doctor cleared his throat, Mac pulled back. I chuckled when I noticed the color in his cheeks. Big, tough Marine biker, Mac was blushing.

The doctor came over and did something with the tube that was connected to my inner elbow before he spoke again. "Okay, so, like I said, those lacerations on your back are healing well so far. I'm not sure how severe the scaring will be at this stage. We had our plastic surgeon sew you up, so hopefully the scars won't be more than thin lines that'll barely be noticeable in time."

I gave him a nod. Scars had never bothered me. They told a person's story that made them who they are. However, I was glad they were on my back so I wouldn't have to see them every time I looked at myself in the mirror.

"When can I go home?"

"We had to give you a transfusion due to how much blood you'd lost. We've also given you intravenous antibiotics to eliminate the risk of infection. You're still on morphine for the pain. I'd like to keep you in for at least another day, to make sure everything is still on track and healing as it should. However, if you're desperate to get out of here, we can arrange that for you. It would mean less potent pain killers, oral antibiotics, and you'll need someone to change your dressings regularly."

I gave him a nod, suddenly feeling really tired and more than a little fuzzy. Guess he'd given me a shot of morphine when he was mucking around with my drip.

"As much as I know Mac would deal with everything if I went home, I think I'd like to stay here for a while longer."

The pain was already nearly gone. This morphine was good stuff.

"Excellent. Well, I'll leave you to get some rest for now. I'll be back later to check on you again."

With that, the doctor left and before I could say a word, Mac softly kissed my lips again.

"Go to sleep, bunny. I'll be here when you wake up."

Mac

It was well past dark when I returned to the hospital. Silk and Eagle had come to see Zara, and after taking one look at me, Silk had demanded I go get cleaned up and find something to eat. These last thirty-six hours had been some of the longest of my life. I knew she was safe and would heal from her wounds. But seeing my woman looking so pale, lying on a hospital bed was seriously screwing with my head. The doctor confirming she hadn't been raped had been some of the sweetest words I'd ever heard. I swear, if that fucker had forced himself on her, I would have dug up his body and killed him all over again.

I was nearly at the elevator when I was approached by a familiar–and unwanted—man.

"Come with me."

With a sigh, I glanced around to make sure no one club-related was around before following Mr. Smith. I should have guessed he'd show up at some point. He led me to a small exam room and locked the door.

"You didn't call."

"Sorry, I've had my hands full. Haven't found the time."

His gaze hardened. "You should have called me when Claire went missing. Both times."

I scoffed at that. I hadn't even considered calling in the feds to find Zara. "Her name is Zara, not Claire. And she would have been raped, possibly murdered by the time your bunch finished with all your paperwork and protocols to go look for her. The club has its own resources, and by using them I got to my girl in time. I'm not apologizing for that."

He sighed heavily, like I was a stubborn toddler or some shit. "Do you have information about her father for me? Or do I need to go talk to her? I can, quite easily, you know? Now she's here in the hospital, after being attacked, it's standard protocol to have a police officer interview her."

The threat was bullshit. I knew Scout had contacted Donald, the local cop who was friendly with the club, and explained the situation. Zara wasn't going to be interviewed by the local guys. However, that didn't mean Mr. Smith couldn't pull strings and cause trouble.

"Zara spent last week going through boxes from her father's office. She found a diary he left her. It told her how he'd found a beaten girl one night down in Galveston. She'd been at the Iron Hammer's clubhouse for a party. They'd raped and beaten her but she'd somehow managed to escape. He took her to the hospital, and by morning she was dead. Inside job. After that, he joined a team. Couple of cops that weren't on the Hammer's books, a doctor, nurses and another taxi driver all joined up and started going after the girls the Iron Hammers were snatching to sell across the border.

"So the guy was a fucking saint, saved who knows how many girls from a lifetime of sexual slavery. And for his efforts? He got himself and his wife murdered. It's also why Sledge had such a hard-on for Zara. He wanted her to pay for what her daddy had cost him. But none of that matters now. The Iron Hammers have been cleaned out and that shit will never happen again with the new leadership in charge."

Mr. Smith just nodded as he rubbed his jaw, which had my anger building. I hadn't set my eyes on Zara for over an hour. I was done wasting time with this bastard.

"Can I go now?"

"Yeah, you can. Thank you for the information. You may like to know, Claire's parents weren't the only ones murdered that day. Over half a dozen seemingly unrelated deaths occurred within hours of each other."

That had me blowing out a breath. "The whole team. Sledge found out who was sabotaging his runs."

"However, there wasn't a second taxi driver in the mix. That diary didn't mention names, did it?"

I shook my head as I reached for the door. "Nope, no names. You'll have to find some other way of identifying the rat. I'm done helping."

Before he could respond, I pushed out and hurried down the hallway. Skipping the elevator, I hit the stairs. Taking two at a time, I got up to the third floor quickly. By the time I hit the door to Zara's room I was breathing heavily.

"What the fuck?"

Eagle cursed as he and Silk jerked in their seats.

"Mac, I suggested you go get cleaned up. Not rush around so you're sweatier than before you left. What the hell did you do?"

Eagle's gaze narrowed on me and when he raised an eyebrow I shrugged, not wanting him to worry.

"Sorry, Silk. I was in a rush to get back to Zara."

Zara smiled as I went to her. She tilted her face up in silent invitation so I leaned down and gave her what we both needed. With a palm cupping her cheek, I took her mouth, pouring all my love for her into the kiss.

Silk sighed loudly and with a chuckle I pulled back. "Shut it, Silk. I've had to watch you and Eagle do worse."

Epilogue

Three months later…

Zara

With a deep breath, I headed out our back door and smiled. Our backyard was full of people and activity. I walked over to where Silk was sitting. At five months pregnant, she was well and truly showing now. I handed her a glass of lemonade before I sat beside her and sipped my own drink.

"You know, they're having way too much fun with this."

I nodded. "Boys will be boys."

We sat in silence for a few minutes, watching the men as they pulled down the side fence—with way too much force and enthusiasm.

"You know, I'm surprised they haven't decided to blow it up."

I groaned at Silk's suggestion. "Please don't say that too loud. You know they will."

That had us both laughing hard enough our men heard and glared over at us for a moment before they went back to smashing out sections of the fence. I couldn't wait for them to get done with it.

Just as Mac had said, the house two doors up from Silk and Eagle's place had been for sale, and he'd bought it for us. We'd moved in two months ago, just after Christmas. Then last week, Taz had settled on the house between us. Now the three men, along with several other Charons, were tearing down the fences that separated the three houses. I rubbed a palm over my tummy as I imagined how, in several years' time, when we all had kids, how they would be constantly going between the houses. I couldn't wait for that to happen.

"Um, Zara? You got something to tell me?"

Heat raced over my face when I realized Silk was staring at my tummy. I wasn't going to say anything until later. We had a big barbecue planned for dinner and Mac was going to tell the club then. Guess I sort of let the cat out of the bag early. Oops. I looked over and when I caught Mac's gaze, he grinned widely before coming over, shaking his head.

"Knew you wouldn't last until tonight. Go on bunny, tell them all the news."

Eagle, Taz and the other men all had come over with Mac.

"We're pregnant. Ah, due in mid-September."

I'd just started to get worried about the silence when the men began hooting and slapping Mac's back with words of congratulations. Silk rose and pulled me in for a hug.

"Congratulations, doll! This is so cool. Our kids will grow up together!"

Eagle was snickering when he spoke up over the other men. "Don't need to ask how you two celebrated the new house then, huh?"

My cheeks flashed hot again. We'd already worked out that I'd gotten pregnant that first week after we moved in.

"I'm just gonna run in and check everything's ready to go for the barbecue."

I scurried away like a coward before the men could start making any more jokes about our sex life. They were horrible teases, the lot of them. But they were family. My chosen family that I knew would do anything for me. I also knew, without a doubt, that our child would have a life filled with love from lots of uncles and aunties. They'd also be protected at all times. I winced at the thought of a daughter. Poor girl would probably be a virgin into her thirties.

"Nah, she'd find a way. I did."

Shit. I hadn't meant to say any of that out loud. Nor was Silk supposed to have followed me inside.

"I can just imagine how much she will moan and complain about her father and uncles ruining her life, if we have a daughter."

Silk laughed. "Yeah, she'll complain, trust me. But it's not a bad thing, it means that only boys who are real serious about her will come sniffing. And we'll make sure the men don't pull shit like they did with Eagle. That was ridiculous."

"What did they do?"

She waved me off. "Oh, they made up some bullshit reason to give him a beat down. I actually walked away from the club when I found out what they'd done."

I looked out the window into the yard at Eagle. "He doesn't look like a man easily taken down."

"Oh no, the stupid jerk agreed to it. Idiot males, the lot of them. It was him who came and got me and brought me back to the club after he healed up."

"Yeah, they definitely have their moments."

The men had finished taking down the fence. The timber had been stacked for a bonfire, which Mac was currently lighting. The rest of them all stood around with beers in their hands as they teased and carried on with each other. I couldn't hold in the grin.

"They might behave like little boys half the time, but they are awesome, aren't they?"

Silk scoffed. "Oh, yeah. MC men are a breed apart. All growly alpha male, until you get them alone. Then they're nothing but big ol' teddy bears."

I gave Silk a raised eyebrow. Mac was pretty damn growly alpha man in the bedroom. "Not sure I agree with the teddy bear part. Mac likes to be in control all the time. Likes to tell me what to do all the damn time, too."

Not that I was complaining. I loved every single thing that man did, in and out of the bedroom. The only time he'd been all soft and gentle was the first week or so after I got out of the hospital, and it drove me nuts. I knew he'd been holding back. After the doctor confirmed everything had healed up well at my appointment ten days after the attack, we'd come back to the clubhouse and I'd jumped on him. He struggled for a few minutes as he tried to stay gentle and soft with me, until I snarled at him that I wasn't made of glass. After that, he got the message about what I wanted and I got my *growly alpha male* back.

"Hey bunny, ready for me to start grilling the meat?"

Mac's strong arms came around me from behind, his palms resting over my still-flat tummy. I tilted my head to the side and his lips were kissing up my neck within moments.

"You already put a bun in that oven, Mac. Here, take this out and try not to burn any of it."

Silk was trying to be stern, but I could hear the humor in her voice and when I glanced up at her, she winked at me. Mac nipped my ear before he released me to grab the tray of meat from Silk. I watched him walk back out, each flex of muscle as he strode out with powerful steps making me clench my thighs. A sigh escaped me and Silk snickered again.

"Oh, shut up. Like you don't ogle your man."

"And you laugh at me when I do it, too."

I grinned at my friend before I turned back to preparing the salads. After my parents died and I'd gotten sick, I'd given up ever having a man or family of my own. But here I was, with not just a wonderful man I could call my own, but pregnant with his baby. To top it off, I also had this huge bunch of crazy friends.

Life was good. Really good. And for the first time in a damn long time, I couldn't wait to see where my future was going to take me.

Other Charon MC Books:

Book 1:
Inking Eagle

The sins of her father will be her undoing… unless a hero rides to her rescue.

As the 15th anniversary of the 9/11 attacks nears, Silk struggles to avoid all reminders of the day she was orphaned. She's working hard in her tattoo shop, Silky Ink, and working even harder to keep her eyes and her hands off her bodyguard, Eagle. She'd love to forget her sorrows in his strong arms.

But Eagle is a prospect in the Charon MC, and her uncle is the VP. As a Daughter of the Club, she's off limits to the former Marine. But not for long. As soon as he patches in, he intends to claim Silk for his old lady. He'll wear her ink, and she'll wear his patch.

Too late, they learn that Silk's father had dark secrets, ones that have lived beyond his grave. When demons from the past come for Silk, Eagle will need all the skills he learned in the Marines to get his woman back safe, and keep her that way.

Book 3:
Chasing Taz

He lived his life one conquest at a time. She calculated her every move… until she met him.

Former Marine Donovan 'Taz' Lee might appear to be a carefree Aussie bloke living it up as a member of the Texan motorcycle club, Charon MC, but the truth is so much more complicated. With blood and tears haunting his past and threatening to destroy his future, Taz is completely unprepared for the woman of his dreams, when she comes in and knocks him on his ass. Literally.

Felicity "Flick" Vaughn joined the FBI to get answers behind her brother's dishonorable discharge and abandonment of his family. Knowing Taz was a part of her brother's final mission, she agrees to partner with him to go after a bigger club, The Satan's Cowboys MC.

However, nothing in life is ever simple and Flick is totally unprepared to have genuine feelings for the sexy Aussie. When secrets are revealed and their worlds are busted wide open, will they be strong enough to still be standing when the dust settles?

CPSIA information can be obtained
at www.ICGtesting.com
Printed in the USA
LVHW030716080622
720770LV00017B/1779